Donald Pfarrer's astonishing new novel is about the existentialist act of deciding what kind of human being we will be — even in the face of death. It is spellbinding. It is painful to keep reading. But go on we must.

Sure, *Temple and Shipman* could be described as a crime novel, just as Homer's *Odyssey* could be called a seafaring yarn. In the end, though, we read a literary book like this in order to learn more about humanity while we get our kicks. In *Temple and Shipman* Donald Pfarrer has brilliantly succeeded at both tasks.

The novel bursts with power and passion. From the opening police chase to the ending manhunt, Pfarrer is in tune with rage — the murderous fury of his working-class White policemen and the weary hatred of his self-educated Black protagonist. In a socio-literary tour de force, the novel descends into the chasm between the races. In the authentic voices of all his characters, Pfarrer scrutinizes the anguished, pre-racial needs of our nation's Caucasians and African-Americans. Can we all get along? The answer may very well be "hell no."

The book starts with a bang and ends with a shudder. I could not put it down, and I was sorry when it was over. Donald Pfarrer has written a great and important novel.

— Roberto Mighty
Filmmaker; director, "Chinese Lessons"

The picture is too familiar. In a small Midwestern city a black man's son is dead. The father believes a white police officer is the killer. Trapped by circumstance and upbringing, these two strong and virtuous men are plunged by a single violent act into a drama of tragic inevitability.

In *Temple and Shipman* Donald Pfarrer asks timeless ethical questions with brutal immediacy. Pfarrer's spare prose never releases his protagonists or the reader from the bitter necessities of moral judgement. Guilt, innocence, accountability, forgiveness, compassion, and revenge are his themes. A gritty modern urban setting is his stage.

This is a book for our time. It is a hard book. You will feel pain in this book. You will feel pity in this book. And you will feel them for all of us.

— John A. Pope Jr.
former chief editor, Reader's Digest General Books

This is a story about aspiration, race, rage and real life, for urban police officers and black families who deal with them. ... Pfarrer's storytelling reflects a kind of thoroughness that comes from his background as a reporter. He has learned to see details others miss. Though this is fiction, not journalism, one does not reach his level of understanding by sitting and thinking. Even great thinkers need material for thought.

To prepare for this book Pfarrer rode with both black and white police officers for 51 nights in the mostly black precinct of a Midwestern city. The effort shows in language and description, but mostly in a depth of understanding.

— David B. Offer
Newport [RI] *Daily News*

Temple and Shipman is that rarity of narrative entertainment — a fast-paced action story enriched by complex and engaging characters. At the heart of the novel are considerations of ideas, faith and race upon which the future of our nation may very well depend. — A stunning achievement of the novelist's craft.

— Sidney Offit
author, *Memoir of the Bookie's Son*
president, Authors' Guild Foundation

I shall from time to time continue this journal.
It is true that I may not find an opportunity of
transmitting it to the world, but I will not fail
to make the endeavor. At the last moment I
will enclose the MS in a bottle, and cast it
within the sea.

Edgar Allan Poe
"MS Found in a Bottle", 1831

**MS IN A
BOTTLE**

18 Brown Street
Cambridge, Mass 02138

Toll free number:
1-877-MS BOTTLE
1-877-672-6885

TEMPLE

AND
SHIPMAN

DONALD PFARRER

Cover paintings by Bill Brauer
Used by generous permission of the artist

Artist representation:
Chase Gallery
129 Newbury Street
Boston, Mass. 02116

Design and production by Susan Gately

MS IN A
BOTTLE

Chapter 1
Temple in the Alley

Jeffrey Temple leaned forward from the back seat and almost shouted: "Where are we going?"

"Yeah," said Ruthenbeck, "what are we doing seventy in this traffic for, you lunatic."

Banes slowed down.

Ruthenbeck shouted: "Stop the car! Stop the car!"

Banes whopped the car against the curb and looked at Ruthenbeck with wild adrenaline eyes.

All three had the rank of patrolman but Ruthenbeck was senior man. Said he: "Too many morons get a tone and wow! a tone! and zoom! siren-and-lights to the scene. But I ask you, Banes, who's the one guy who ain't at the scene?"

"Uh — Mr. Raper," said Banes groping his way to sanity.

"And what's the one place in the city where the guy ain't going to be if we go there?"

"Uh — the scene," said Banes.

"Listen to the fuckers scream," Ruthenbeck said. "Hear that, Banes? That's the whole Relief going siren-and-lights you know where. Lady in distress! I say let's stay clear of the traffic jam."

"And do what," said Banes.

"I don't know."

"And just sit here," said Banes bitterly.

"We can watch this route," Temple said.

"Oh Jesus," cried Banes. "Now he's a big-time lawyer and all, he says sit on our ass and watch the route."

"No more a lawyer than you are, Banes."

"So 'watch this route.' For what? We don't have any fuckin idea —"

"Listen!" said Ruthenbeck.

The radio on the dash said: "All Six crews. Description on the rape and agg battery in alley behind Majestic, between Middle Lane and Roselawn."

Temple tried to visualize Majestic Avenue with its great ruinous mansions set back from the sidewalk, divided now into five, six, or a dozen apartments each. He realized the lights were blinding him when he might be needing his night vision; he closed his eyes and listened.

"Black male, mid-twenties, five feet ten, weight one fifty, medium Afro, light skin, blue jeans, dark windbreaker, tennis shoes, no gloves, no hat."

"Must be one cold nigger," Banes offered. Now his tone madness was down he spoke in a small squeaky voice. "We should get closer," he insisted. "What if he's got a car?"

"If he's got a car he's gone," Ruthenbeck said. "We're going to sit here for thirty seconds and figure somethin out and fuckin do it, and it'll make sense for a change. Now we know what the spliv looks like."

Temple said: "The actor."

"What do you mean *actor*?" Banes interjected.

"What actor?" asked Ruthenbeck twisting to face Temple.

"The guy swinging his arms. The guy making a speech."

"Christ you're right."

"He was on Majestic."

"He was at the fuckin Irish Video."

A few minutes ago the Tactical Squad — Ruthenbeck, Banes and Temple, riding in an unmarked car and free to roam the District at will — when gliding past the Irish Video had seen a young black man doing a wild monologue. He gesticulated in the zone of light as on the stage of a darkened theater, apparently making some kind of speech. Temple saw an image of the young man raising his arms as he spoke, as if pleading for understanding. Seeing an audience of three white cops suddenly at his side the "actor" jerked into an indifferent attitude and hustled along Majestic Avenue, thrusting his hands into the pockets of his jacket.

But this was a sport jacket tailored like a suitcoat. It was not a windbreaker. Temple said so.

"So what," said Ruthenbeck.

"Let's nail the crazy black shit," said Banes. "He's our guy and if he ain't we should f. i. the fucker for being a mental."

Temple said: "Drop me at the plasma center. I'll do the alley, you do Majestic."

"Drive!" said Ruthenbeck.

Banes peeled away and butted into traffic. The cruiser was a wallowing sedan that took curves like a full bath tub but Banes rammed in almost to the tail-pipe of a car ahead and flashed his lights till the driver looked in his mirror and then slowed down in defiance.

"Hit it," Ruthenbeck ordered, and Banes touched the wail siren. You could see the driver jump in his seat.

The cruiser made a long insane dive down the funnel of First Street, and for a second all three men went tone mad again together, as if the tone had just been sounded by the dispatcher.

The cruiser swung into the empty lot of the plasma center and slowed. Temple opened the rear door and leaped out. Ruthenbeck said, leaning out the passenger window: "First Street. Five minutes."

The cruiser swayed into a skid turn and left the parking lot, and Jeffrey Temple watched the red lights slide into Majestic and disappear to the left, toward the Irish Video. Temple stood alone in the dark. The asphalt spread black before him and all the lights had been stoned out. The alley entrance lay on the other side of the dark.

His heart jolted inside him as if he'd run a mile. An envelope of silver frost chilled the torso inside his flak jacket. Sweat colder than mercury streamed down his sides.

He reached up to his shoulder and turned down the volume on his radio and began to walk. He couldn't see them or hear their voices murmuring out ahead but he knew they were there and what they were saying.

Temple as always had left his stick in the car. Carrying a stick made him feel gloomy. He touched his gun and radio and skipped a few steps testing the knee that had brought his football career to an early end.

He walked toward the men and soon he could see them in their corner. Of course they were watching and of course they were silent, and by this silence and by the steady gazes that he could almost see they declared all that was necessary. Temple said not a word but examined them closely in the beam of his Maglite, torching each exhausted and wrecked face from a distance of three feet, looking into the eyes of each one. When the beam hit their eyes some looked straight into it.

He pulled away as if reluctantly and plunged into the alley. This ran between Perkins Place, a public housing project, and Majestic Avenue. There was an aura of amber window light and nothing brighter in the alley.

He looked quickly down the row of cement stoops, each with a cement-block trash cage in front of it, which he could barely see, and strode as fast as he dared to the first cage. He shone his light in and scared a rat and himself. He let slip an audible curse and moved to the next cage.

This was exactly what he had expected when he joined the police — to walk in the alley of the shadow of death. He knew he'd walk alone at night in the darkest alley of the blackest project, and he knew Sandra would leave him.

"This is insane," Sandra cried. "You are insane, Jeffrey. A policeman? You're going to be a policeman?"

The black men he had scrutinized seemed to follow him. He could see his own eyes as bloodshot as theirs. This and another strange idea displaced the "actor." If Temple was alone that man was alone too. Or that boy. If Temple was pursued he was pursued too.

Thus without realizing it Temple thought of the actor as a man or boy, not a rapist. He looked behind him and there was nobody there.

The first time Temple had entered this alley was on a summer afternoon two years ago, on his first day as a rook in the Sixth District. He was riding in a marked cruiser with Ruthenbeck as his training officer. They turned slowly into the alley, all the windows rolled up and the air conditioner pulling on max.

Stretching out ahead was the line of cement stoops, like rocks in a river of heat, each one surmounted by three, four or five black people of both sexes and all ages, dressed in as little as possible, escaping from the heat inside their apartments, their "units," to the heat of the alley.

Ruthenbeck said, "The negroes be hot." This voice which mocked the blacks while acknowledging they had a better way of talking was Ruthenbeck's trademark. He sometimes even talked like that in the locker room and the black cops would raise a fist as if to kill him but Ruthenbeck would stick out his hands, make his knees shake, and say, "Brotherhood, man, brotherhood!"

Temple's radio emitted a whispering sound but he squelched it and kept walking. One by one the cement stoops and trash cages passed on his left, while on the right a row of garage doors, each one fastened and padlocked, formed an uneven but solid wall. There was nobody in the alley and no place to hide except in the trash. Temple shone his light into each cage, looking ahead in case anybody should enter the alley from the Meredith Street end. Letting his eyes sweep over the trash and garbage he felt almost as if the stuff swept over him. It was dark, it was cold, and deserted, and it was squalid even in the darkness. He was searching for some black mental.

"Yes Sandra I'm going to be a cop." And here he was in this alley looking for a — "But I've got a letter!" It was in his jacket hanging in his locker —

He came out onto Meredith Street and strode along silently till he came to Majestic. One block to the left the Irish Video illumined the night and Temple realized that the actor had passed this spot five to seven minutes before. He turned from the Video.

Holding his gun tight against his hip and steadying his microphone on his shoulder Temple began to run toward First Street.

A siren waved out through the black sky. Temple saw another ambulance speed across the intersection of First and Majestic with its red lights strobing out in big wheeling cycles. He stopped and turned up his speaker, then ran toward First.

The radio began to squawk. It was some cop telling the world where he was.

Temple came into First Street as onto a beach, against a kinetic barrier of traffic and a new boundary of brighter light. Entering into the light he turned to his left and saw the Tactical Squad's car half on the sidewalk and half in the street, with the front doors flopped open. Just beyond it the red and white "Shipman's Barbecue" sign glowed and blinked inside its circling snake of white. The headlights shone against the plate glass of a deserted store. He could not see Banes or Ruthenbeck. He drew his gun and ran right through the traffic, and he never saw and could not afterwards remember how he got through unscathed. He was racing up the sidewalk towards the car. The curious thing was he felt good running. He wasn't really worried about his partners.

Unconscious of the weight he was carrying, of the radio, leather belt, handcuffs, ammo and body armor, he ran like an athlete with two good knees, and all he actually knew at that moment was power — no stress at all, only speed and power.

Chapter 2
The Actor

"*The History of Race in America* by John Shipman Jr., professor of history at the university of someplace and guest lecturer in American civilization, if that's what it is, at Oxford University, Oxford, England.

"Shipman *Junior*. Will I still be Junior when Pop dies? John Shipman Junior, Martin Luther King *Junior*. So the book comes out twenty or twenty-five years from now, in 2000 or 2010. Will Pop be alive in 2000?

"Son I always knew you'd do something big. Hell you did, Pop. Son we're so damn proud of this book. *Then read it!* I already started. Hmm! Nine hundred pages, shit, he won't read ten. He be a man of business, ribs, booze and dice! That's business. Ribs! Booze! Dice!"

Hawk let out a snort. He was walking fast along Majestic with a cold wind biting him from behind. Blacks lived on Majestic like an immigrant race settled amid the ruins of a past civilization. That the builders should have abandoned these solid homes and imposing mansions with their leaded-glass cabinets, sun porches and heavy sliding doors was inexplicable, except that race explained it. The mansions were cut up into apartments, the doubles were now quads and the single-family houses sheltered more lives under their eaves than ever before. Hawk lived here by choice, because there was something here he couldn't find in a better neighborhood, much less at home.

Being black wasn't enough, he was an alien here and not much safer on the street at midnight than a white man. To those who didn't know him he was nobody; to those who did, he was the son of one of the richest black men in the city, living where he didn't belong.

"Pop won't be alive — Pop'll be gone, he'll never see it." His hands were freezing in his pockets and his ears were stinging. "Damn hat, damn gloves! So Pop'll never see it," he repeated. "Pop'll never know." See the book that was going to vindicate him; never. Pop'd be gone. He hastened along. "Trouble with Pop, he puts black too far behind. Black has to be front, first, forever." The street was empty of souls, full of shadows and darkness. Those streetlights that hadn't been stoned out had simply gone out, and the city was slow to repair them. "Hell, I don't blame the city," he thought. He pondered this problem of the streetlights and added: "A writer of history pursues the truth. Faces the truth on matters great and small. The truth alone makes him free. A scholar first, then after years working hard, a black scholar; then a black historian; then at the turn of the century a *historian of the black people.*

"So-and-so's an intellectual means he's a deadbeat, got no job is what it means. A black intellectual means: *got a mission,* got a life!"

"They'd just pop out the new lights, sure, I know that," he said a minute later, with his breath puffing clouds of smoke in front, "but the city doesn't clean the alleys either. Can't blame that on the kids. Truth the first: the bureaucrat downtown in his folded, spindled and mutilated mind says 'Hell, we put in new lights, the little niggers bust em. So let'm live in the dark, right?' Truth the second: Clean the alleys, you honky fart!" On a sudden impulse he turned right and went a half-block along Middle Lane, which was utterly dark, and then left into the alley that ran behind the mansions of Majestic. He tripped on some scattered trash, slipped on a frozen puddle, and saw what must have been a heap of tumbled old mattresses half blocking the way. The cars had made a path around these, whose course took Hawk against a chainlink fence. The curve lay before him almost visible in the gloom. Wearing leather-soled shoes on this ice was ridiculous. He slipped again and one arm flew up instinctively. "Truth Number Three: truth has more than one dimension. What if it has six or ten or twenty? How do you decide?" He concluded triumphantly, "That's why you keep black in front. When confused, consult your blackness!"

He turned left when the alley hit Meredith, and gained Majestic. He was now approaching the Irish Video, the oasis of light in the shadow zone between his apartment and the traffic-and-light stream of First. A criminal lawyer named Murphy, who was completely white, had restored one of the old mansions and surrounded it with floodlights. Within this glitter-compound Murphy possessed more mahogany, filigree and sculpture than any of his peers at the bar, yet nobody worth half as much as Murphy dared visit him, not even in daylight. It was said on Majestic that Murphy was a fool but evidently not a bigot. The kids did not break his lights. On winter nights, both before Christmas and after, the Irish Video sent a trembling bright emanation of electric colors into the cold and dark.

"When truths conflict," Hawk continued, "I will pull up and say, *You are black*, remember? I will never say as Pop does, *What do you expect me to do about it?* Other paw, I will never suppress the truth, distort, lie or propagandize for any cause, not even the black cause, but neither will I put blackness behind me — for one reason, it can't be done!"

Here he stopped and fell into a whispered drama.

"Speak to win respect, to be somebody, project character. Not just a rich college boy. Speak, act to burn your character into their memory, then when they see I uphold the truth —

"They could not make him flinch or deviate, neither white bigots nor black militants, and he always scorned popularity and vulgar praise. He was nobody's puppy. Within the swirl and chaos of history he sought the standard of truth from the experience and perspective of blackness. Only a historian so equipped could have written the history that he wrote. — Uh, let's see —

With a prose style as vivid in its way as Francis Parkman's, as sonorous and powerful as Frederick Douglass's . . . Only a man born black and living black, yet self-disciplined in the sternest rigorous traditions of objective scholarship — mastering the domain of knowledge — uh, let's see —"

Hawk felt uneasy, and quickly looking left he saw that a car had slowed behind him, as he stood exposed in the light of the Irish Video. He resumed his quick pace, not wanting to go into the darkness ahead but even more unwilling to stand irresolute. As the car drew abreast he recognized it as a patrol car of the Tactical Squad. It bore no police markings but the three white men inside were uniformed cops. "Unmarked car looking for a marked man." Hawk tried to remember whether he had been gesticulating. Suddenly he thought of his father rehearsing his sales pitch in the garage, perfecting his moneymaking English and his gestures and style, varying diction and accent to suit his audience. It was a delicate matter to impress black prospects with his business prowess without alienating them by sounding too white, and to persuade white bankers by sounding just white enough.

"Damn! I do the same thing! Just today I —"

While practicing his speech for the BSA he spoke in one idiom, and in conference with his professor he unconsciously tempered his style.

"Unconscious till you were conscious of it!" *Temper your style* and what happens to your soul?

He was in the dark now, passing one mammoth elm stump after another on his left, while on his right the uphill terraces made a kind of wall to the sidewalk. The car was still pacing him. "Tac Squad looking for somebody to rough up."

He forgot that his hands were stiff and cold, and perhaps they were not. His face burned and he looked straight ahead.

He heard with relief the change in the engine's tone and watched the red tail lights pulling away before him. He felt absurdly happy! He was sweating in his clothes and the wind passed right through and chilled the sweat and wrapped him in a sheet of wet cold. He kept his eye on the red lights all the way to

First Street, three blocks ahead, where the car turned left into the blue-white glow and the traffic.

He thought of Gram Taylor, his mother's mother, a woman of the South before the '60s. She had never heard of W. E. B. DuBois but she knew about "the temptation of Hate." One of her principles was: "Hate a whole race, shut your whole face." To be Christian to the bottom of your feet was not always possible but to act like a Christian, while not easy, always was. And the right action when you feel hatred of a race is to be silent and to search in the silence for your error. The whites are often morally wrong, but hatred recoils on the hater. (Gram Taylor's gospel.) To hate them all is to fall into their own peculiar error and curse. Hawk agreed. "But Gram, I reserve the right to hate evil individual white men." To which Gram would have replied: "Pray for guidance, Hawk." Now that he was growing intellectually and prayed no more, he knew that hate was not a right; it was a vice.

There is no right to hate any more than there's a right to be an addict, only a privilege, like the privilege God allows his creatures to commit sinful and shameful acts. Gram's idea was that a man may be justified in sheltering the fires of hate in his soul, but justification isn't the most important thing. Hatred is a fever and like any fever it's a sign of sickness. Gram had preached all this to him for the last time two or three years ago, about the time Hawk was starting college, when she was already on her deathbed. She believed in his special gift. She wanted him to preach and inspire his congregation. She said the difference between a right and a privilege was that claiming your rights makes you a greater man; taking your privileges makes you small.

It was Gram who gave him the name Hawk, for the way he sat in his high chair holding his motionless spoon aloft, keeping severe watch on every plate as it was brought in from the kitchen.

"I don't hate you bastards," he thought, "but you hate me." He wished he could get another look at the three monkeys and blaze his eyes, and turn their eyes to glass.

But he hadn't really looked into their eyes, to find hate, contempt or anything else. "My man, they don't go around hating *all night long.* I looked and saw a cartoon. White cops in a dark car. They gouge your eyes with their badges, stick you with pins, club you with clubs and shoot you with guns, and then stomp you cause you didn't shine their shoes. Hey man, wake up! Think not in stereotypes. I don't want to live in the same body with a stereotyping mind." But thinking again of the cops, especially the one in the passenger seat, whose face he saw so clearly, a face so undeniably twisted by contempt, he grew excited with a seething animus — a spitting, recoiling enmity. "White-bread bigots! Honkies!"

As he reached First he heard a siren somewhere behind, not on Majestic, somewhat to the right, towards the river. Probably he would never have noticed this most unmusical sound had he not heard another coming from ahead and left. The second grew louder, a commanding but slightly crazy noise, and he watched as an ambulance streaked across in front of him. He could follow the wail as it converged with the first one — towards a point not far from where he had come.

He turned left into First, an arc-lighted commercial thoroughfare long since abandoned by half its business owners and landlords. Many of the shop doors he passed led to dark, littered rooms open to the weather. A few businesses persevered under the siege lights, and First Street was in fact the place where Hawk's father made some of his money. Three or four blocks ahead there was a Shipman barbecue that stayed open until one in the morning. It was now about midnight and Hawk had tasted no food since six. The faster he walked the colder he got. Between himself and the barbecue there was another of his father's enterprises, a tavern whose legal owner was probably somebody else, but John Shipman Senior had gained control by making loans no bank would dream of. Hawk believed his father had acquired interest in six or eight taverns this way, even though the city code permitted only one per licensee. John Shipman also owned a legal tavern, a car wash downtown and a barbecue in a white suburb. But his first and still most profitable business was the barbecue in the Jonathan Creek section. This was the area about two miles away, no longer a neighborhood, where the elder

Shipman grew up and won fame as a wingback for Dunbar, the black high school. The section lay across the creek from Majestic on a point of land where the creek met the river. Walking the streets over there was almost safe now because even the predators had moved out for lack of anybody to mug, rob, rape and murder. Many of the houses had been leveled, burned, boarded up or abandoned. Here and there a family or two survived in stubborn isolation. Some of the factories were still working behind chainlink fences surmounted by razor coils, but the employees all went home exactly at quitting time. On the arteries the stores weren't literally closed since most had been ripped open and ransacked of plumbing and fixtures. There were a few junkies and drunks making statues on the corners even in winter, mostly drunks, with their wasted arms and shoulders dangling and their little rounded bellies bulging inside their ragged jackets.

In this napalmed "neighborhood" some institutions still enjoyed a vigorous life and drew the black people from better neighborhoods two, three or four miles away. One such oasis was the Catholic hospital, St. Claire's. Another was John Shipman's barbecue which was more than a barbecue. It was also a boot joint. In a better part of town it would have been shut down but in Jonathan the police let it be and the local alderman was glad to see it thrive. Drugs, weapons and whores were excluded. Here respectable men who had moved their families out of the desolation could come home to drink and gamble at any hour, beyond the reach of creditors, bosses, police or women. The games were private in that there was no house and no house cut. John Shipman himself was a member of this club as well as its proprietor, taking his winnings and losses like any other. He was not a very good cardplayer and it was better for business if he lost more than half the time. He was good enough to be sure he did. And he was an artist at spreading the profits of the boot joint across the books of his legal or quasilegal businesses.

"That's no way to be," thought Hawk with a scowl. "It takes away the whole point. If he knew where to put black he wouldn't do that. 'What do you expect me to do about it?' By god, everything you can. Only one life, there it goes. Could be worse. He could be a wino or a string-o-beads man, could be poor, poor as cinders, have a welfare queen for his mama. He could have left his kids, including me, in the city dump. Could be a ne'er-do-well and a junkie and an over-age dude in alligator skins, with a wide-brim hat over his white-top. Damn! Yeah, sure, *could be worse.*"

Hawk was just passing the tavern in which his father was a silent partner. On a summer night the air conditioner would exhale a nauseating stream of a cloying gas into his path. "Definition of a tavern. Bar. Place where they sell the worst drug of all to those who can least afford it." Including his brother Winslow who got it free. He had seldom thought of his father except as he was; only rarely did he think he might have been something else.

"A boy can turn into a man overnight. All he got to do — all he — has — got — to — do — is decide. Do I serve myself? Do I serve my family — my own family, and you know it doesn't exist yet. Do I serve the dream of a family of my own? Do I serve, say, this corner of a neighborhood? Do I serve 'Nobody Home' up in the sky? No sir, no thanks. Blood, flesh, bones, 'the souls of black folk,' and the emergence of the ex-slaves — yes sir, I serve all black people in this country. They are my con-stituency. They are my judges!

"By God Almighty or by 'I ain't here,' either one, I don't care which — I serve black people landed in America. If that be pride make the most of it. And so you become a man, by decision, by decree. Be a businessman pushin ribs and booze in a crowded smoky hole of a blind pig for drunks and card sharps, or *write it.* Write your History and follow up with, uh, *The African Bridge* or something — work on that title — African element somehow —

"Hey the definition of a man, right, some dude with the organ swinging in his britches who decides to be a man."

He stopped — physically stopped and froze — and said: "Your daddy payin your tuition, what you kickin at him for?

"Fine, I do take the money and I'll take a whole lot more before I get my PhD. If I didn't, where'd it go? So don't heap that on me. All I know is, I got an idea, by God, or it's got me by the throat. You must climb the longest road!" he burst out, like a preacher. "There are no shortcuts. Passion, even black passion, is no substitute for learning. A classic education, classic study, years of it, years! *Course* it was all written by honkies! So what. All that proves is — blacks need a voice! *I know why I'm alive* and woe unto me if I forget because now, now that I know, I see how pointless it is to live without a noble purpose. You're at sea without a compass, adrift and alone and stupefied. I have a standard, I have a staff, I have an end, an inspiration. Everything else is waste. Tell the truth! The cause is the black cause and the method is truth, and the truth will serve because the cause is just. By Jesus and by Judas, I'm dying of hunger. Gimme Superhot Ribs with Mankiller Sauce and a cold milk."

He was only a block from the barbecue, passing a row of dark stores that must have been built in the 1920s. One was closed in with gray plywood, the next was grilled over, the next was a lighted but deserted laundry and dry cleaning shop. One storefront stood agape, and shards of glass stuck out of the window frame. Ahead he could see the sign projecting over the sidewalk, red letters on a white background with a circling glow surrounding: "Shipman's."

Now came the first warning of his sixth sense. The car was pacing him again and he could see (without looking) the face of the one in the passenger seat — the chubby beardless rounded inquisitive and contemptuous face. Tac Squad for sure. In his turbulent imagination he could see Lucas, a friend of his father's who was the security guard at the barbecue. Like his father, Lucas was a veteran of the Korean War, and although hobbled with arthritis, Lucas had a gun. He would be sitting on his high stool in the passage between the kitchen and the front of the shop, where he could see all the doors and the cash register. And Lucas would occasionally take his "Abraham turn" — his "Here I am" perambulation — from the cash register to the east door and back to the west door, thence to his stool.

Thinking of Lucas and the barbecue, Hawk thought once more of his father, saw the elder Shipman's formidable, decisive features. Here was a man who had made up his mind a long time ago. "What do you want me to do about it?" Hawk did not see the self-taught accountant, the "owner," the driver, but he saw the former wingback, veteran of the fighting in Korea, who had done a thousand things before Hawk was born. He saw — he didn't know exactly who — Pop — whoever he —

Now the jury assembled in a rush: Gram Taylor and Lucas, Hawk's elder brother Winslow, Professor Vanevery and Joe Yoshida. In actual life they had never been together but in Hawk's mind they convened during crises to judge his actions, to judge him. Is this boy brave? What's he made of? Winslow was clean and sober, as he used to be. The professor was Hawk's tutor and adviser for his senior honors thesis in American history. Joe Yoshida had been his swimming coach at the YMCA. This was the jury before which Hawk would willingly stand to be judged: Gram Taylor, Lucas, Winslow as he once was, Professor Vanevery and Joe Yoshida. Especially Lucas. He was like an uncle, different from a father.

It was unlikely that in the presence of this jury he would ever betray himself. Before these, he would steel himself against the temptations of intellectual sloth, against a craven desire to be popular, or against the menace of the knifers, the predators, those utterly indifferent young men who didn't seem to know that they were the heirs of a tradition of perseverance, courage, loyalty. Before this jury he could not fall or falter, whimper, whine or say yessuh, not even to the bullies of the Tac Squad.

For one short moment the jury loomed in his mind. Then he thought of shouting to Lucas. Thirty or forty steps to the barbecue and here was the car. He thought of his mother. He saw her, felt her enveloping, loving, powerless presence.

Chapter 3
He Don't Make
Polite Conversation

When Temple got there Ruthenbeck and Banes had backed the actor into an indented doorway between two deserted stores. Ruthenbeck was saying, "Hey, man, we gotta have speaks."

Temple observed that the actor did not have a medium Afro. His hair was cut close. He wore a dark brown tweed sportscoat, jeans and brown leather shoes. His skin was rather light.

The actor said: "You what?"

"Have speaks, man. You deaf?" cried Ruthenbeck. "Flappin de jaw. You-me grunt grunt. Where you been? Where you comin from? Pardon me, sir. *Freeze*. Know what I mean?"

The young man made a motion as if to walk away.

Temple wasn't quite sure what happened then. Somehow he missed a detail. He heard a kind of thump and saw the actor lurch backward, and Banes drive him against the frame of an old wood and glass door. It was dark in the alcove. Temple stepped in and placed his hand on Banes's shoulder, felt the flak jacket under the windbreaker. Temple said: "Cool down." But Temple himself may not have been so cool.

Ruthenbeck was very easy, having something like a good time. He said: "Don't make a big mistake, my man. Atta fella. Back up slow, turn yo cracked ass around, hands high, face the wall. See this young fella?" He indicated Temple. "See how motherfuckin big he is? He's a motherfuckin pro football player that squashed people for a living. People twice as big as you he'd fold up and put in his pocket. And this here young gentleman with the face like a rat" — indicating Banes — "he ain't much but he got him a stick, do you see? What we call a P.R. 24, a head-breaker. So even a little shit like him — excuse me, partner — can whup the black off your ass. See what I'm sayin?"

The actor did not face the wall.

"My man," said Ruthenbeck in a tone of amused patience, "what did I say?"

The actor replied: "Why are you stopping me?" His voice was not quite in control. Temple heard his pronunciation of the word "stopping." He had not said "stoppin."

Temple said quietly: "Tell us your name."

"My name is John Shipman Jr."

"Wow!" said Ruthenbeck. "The barbecue man your daddy?"

"He's my father," said the actor.

"And he own twenty hundred taverns when the city code says one to a licensee?"

"I don't know about that."

"You don't *know about that*. Well my man I know about that. And your daddy got him a boot joint over in Jonathan, right? He be a boozin gamblin whorin moneymaking rogue, right?"

"He's got a club," said the actor.

"Oh a *club*. I done thought it was a motherfuckin boot joint, is how dumb I am. Now spin like a top, Mr. John Shitman Jr., put your hands on the wall and spread your feet and waddle em back this way."

"I'm not carrying a weapon," said John Shipman Jr., and didn't move.

Talking white now Ruthenbeck said, "God damn it, did you fuckin hear me?"

Banes swung his stick. Ruthenbeck lunged and tried to grab the actor round the head but the young man evaded him and tried to break out.

Temple grabbed him and spun him around, making him face the wall, and lifted him several inches off the pavement and held him aloft, and he soon ceased struggling under this display of power, and Temple set him on his feet and said, leaning towards the back of his head, "Spread out." Temple took each of the man's hands and spread the arms out, slapping the hands against the door frame.

But the actor was resisting every step of the way.

"God damn, boy, spread these fuckin feet," Ruthenbeck pleaded, laughing. "Oh my! He won't spread his big foots," and Ruthenbeck took Banes's stick saying, "Hey partner gimme your P.R. 24," and thrusting the stick between the man's knees he lifted it smartly into the groin. The man gasped and struggled for breath.

Temple saw the stick fly up to the crotch and it somehow woke him up and he said: "God damn it, no more of that."

"Right, partner, no more of that or he'll be a *it*," Ruthenbeck replied. "He's clean, we can now proceed with the field interrogation. Turn around, my man, for your very own f. i. We gonna ax you questions and all you gotta do is answer the muddafuckin questions, see what I'm sayin?"

The actor turned — still struggling to breathe — and he looked at Temple — bent low, looking up, his mouth open wide. It was not clear whether he thought Temple alone had the gift of reason, or that he was as bad as the rest. He said to Temple: "Why are you stopping me?"

"You shut the fuck up," Ruthenbeck said, talking white. "I ask, you answer. Here's your book," and he gave over a paperback book he had taken from the side pocket of the sport coat. "I want your O.L."

"I don't know what you're talking about."

"Oh Jesus, he is a moron. Do you have a driver's license?"

"Yes."

"O.K., now let me see it and don't ask why. Get it!"

Temple thought Ruthenbeck was not quite as easy as before.

The young man took out his wallet and Temple saw the trembling hands, the slender brown fingers unable to extricate the operator's license.

With difficulty the actor took it from the wallet. Ruthenbeck snatched it and read it in the glow of his Minimag.

"John Taylor Shipman Jr.," said Ruthenbeck. "You got any aliases?"

"No."

"No nicknames?"

"No."

"You mean they call you John Taylor Shipman Jr.?"

"They call me Hawk," said the actor.

"Oh *Hawk*. Well if they call you fuckin Hawk, then fuckin Hawk is your nickname. How come you said you didn't have no nicknames when I motherfuckin axed you if you had any motherfuckin nicknames, eh? — How'm I doin, Mr. Hawk?"

In the actor's eyes Temple saw a kindling hatred.

"He don't want to make polite conversation," Ruthenbeck said. "Now Mr. Hawk Shitman Jr., you be a student I bet. Can't go nowhere without you take yo book along."

"I am a student," said John Shipman Jr.

Ruthenbeck flapped the O.L. as if fanning himself and seemed to ponder. Without speaking he passed it over his shoulder. Temple took the O.L. and stepped back and dropped his head to his left shoulder. He keyed his microphone and contacted the records office.

As Temple read the O.L. data to the records clerk and asked for wants and warrants and for a national crime information check he watched Ruthenbeck and Banes, who, it seemed to him, took on a slouching, round shouldered hovering aspect against John Shipman Jr. And Temple saw the man's inexperienced eyes appealing to him over the shoulders of his two partners.

While the records clerk was feeding the data into her computer Ruthenbeck was saying:

"How much you spend for your coat, there, my man?"

"I don't remember."

"Mammy buy it for you, did she?"

"No, I bought it."

"And don't remember how much. But it's a nice coat ain't it."

John Shipman Jr. said nothing.

Over Temple's radio speaker came the voice of the records clerk saying, "The O.L. is valid. No wants or warrants. N.C.I.C. negative."

Said Temple, "Thank you." He passed the O.L. over Ruthenbeck's shoulder to John Shipman Jr.

Everything stood still. Nobody was aware of the traffic passing on First Street, nor did any of the passing drivers bother with the unmarked car spread across the sidewalk. Everything that was said by the dispatcher downtown was repeated on each officer's belt speaker and on the speaker inside the unmarked car, with its doors hanging open; so that a passer-by might conclude the four men were pausing to listen to these staccato broadcasts that were mostly numbers and addresses — but they were not. A snake of light streaked in perpetual circles round the border of the Shipman's Barbecue sign only a few paces up the walk from the dark indented doorway.

"And what students *do* is, they study," Ruthenbeck speculated after a minute. "And you been studyin tonight, haven't you."

"Yes."

"And yo po little belly start a moanin and you just went on a pelvis'n down Majestic on the way to yo pappy's barbecue to get you a free Superhot with Mankiller Sauce and a big glassa sodypop."

"Yes."

"Cause you do live on Majestic."

"Yes I do."

"And cause we done saw you on Majestic, didn't we."

"Yes."

"In front of the Irish Video."

"Yes. I was on my way here." And he indicated the barbecue shop whose red and white sign he could see obliquely through the smeared glass of the abandoned store where they stood.

"But you was alone for sure."

"Yes."

"That's why you was flappin your arms like a damn mental when we saw you."

"I was alone, it's true."

"And what were you fuckin doin!" cried Ruthenbeck raising his voice.

"I was — talking to myself." And here Hawk lied and said: "I was practicing a speech."

"Wow! He be a politician."

"I'm not a politician. I was just — I told you."

"Right, speakin to everybody who'd listen which was nobody, so you was by your little ole lonesome and that's why they won't be nobody to say, Why yeah, man, this here student was studyin, he wasn't out rapin and beatin the snot outa some po black girl in the fuckin alley behind Majestic. — Ain't that right Mr. Shitman Jr."

Shipman said slowly: "Now I see."

"Right. Now you see. You is fuckin *caught*. Show me your hands."

Shipman extended his hands. All eyes were drawn to them, including his own. Temple had to move forward for a view of these trembling light-brown hands. Temple looked at the young man's face as he gazed down at his hands. Then suddenly, unexpectedly their eyes met and they searched each other's eyes but only for a second.

"My hands," said John Shipman Jr., "are shaking."

"Right," Ruthenbeck interposed, "they be ashakin. Bet you could get you a good-payin job at a hardware store shakin paint. No need to study in you little ole room till yo po stomach start in ahowlin."

"But I haven't raped anybody."

"I ain't casting any racial asparagus," said Ruthenbeck ignoring this and running his light and his careful gaze over Shipman's face, "but why can't you people leave each other alone?"

John Shipman Jr. struggled through a statement. His jaw threatened to collapse and Temple thought he almost sobbed once or twice but he said every word clearly enough to be understood. He said:

"My hands are shaking . . ."

Temple looked at his delicate, finely chiseled features. He saw the close-cut black-man's hair, the limpid whites of his eyes, the smooth unblemished complexion.

". . . but I'm not afraid of you white cops."

"Cut the shit," said Ruthenbeck. "You're afraid. You fuckin stink with fear. Now tell you what, Mr. Shitman, I don't see no scratches on your hands or face. That's good, sir, you done passed a test."

"That's because I didn't rape anybody. I've been in my room studying since seven o'clock."

"Man! You must be starved. I bet yo mouth just be awaterin fo tha ole pork shoulder. Take down your pants, sir," said Ruthenbeck shifting suddenly to white, "that's your next test."

"What?"

"Wha-wha-wha happnin, man?" Ruthenbeck did a little dance. "I'm saving you some trouble, sir, I'm doing you a favor cause I like you so much and cause you so motherfuckin *rich*. See, man, the girl said her assailant ejaculated. We had us a little pornographic broadcast on it. Raper done come, boys. Mean he got jizzm in his pants. Had hisself a real hot time. Ole jizzm still be adrippin outa his big black dong maybe. Now you drop your pants and Officer Banes here, our super-qualified come sniffer, he'll examine your drawers. If you're clean, off you go to the barbecue shop and you can report to the Detective Bureau in the morning like a free man and tell the dicks everything you done tole us tonight."

"You're insane," said Shipman.

"That's been said before, but you were in the wrong place at the wrong time, weren't you? And you're wearing a dark jacket and jeans, aren't you? Pardon me for being so technical. Hey, Officer Banes won't touch your precious person, he'll just stroke around with his flashlight for the telltale signs is all. Stroke around your little ole weenie but only with his light, know what I mean? Purely as a matter of convenience so you don't have to spend the night in jail and get yoself butt-fucked by all them dirty negroes down at City-County Consolidated."

The actor was not a large man and again Temple felt there was something almost delicate about his features — and he had such clear eyes it was really remarkable, such pure white and dark-brown eyes.

Temple said with finality: "He's not the guy, Beck."

As if he hadn't heard, Ruthenbeck said: "Listen, O.K., you're a real champ at staring me in the eye, but right now either you drop the pants or we put you in the back seat with the big guy and he reads you the Rapists' Bill of Rights on the way downtown. And here's your last chance, Mr. Shitman. Look at it like this. We take you to City-County Consolidated and you *know* what's goin down. You take it off down there, my man. I guess you know that. They search you right to the bone. The City-County boys stomp on your socks, put their fingers in your shoes, and by the way they look at your motherfuckin drawers. What a wonderful job those boys have got. Don't you wish you had a job like that? And if you got soiled undies they write it down. Inmate had gorilla goo in his underwear. They might even get out a warrant on your skivvies. So what's the difference, Mr. Shitman, and what'll it be?"

Shipman looked at Temple first and then said to Ruthenbeck: "I have not raped anybody, or broken any law."

"Bracelets," said Ruthenbeck.

Officer Banes let his stick fall into a metal ring on his belt and pulled out a set of chrome-plated handcuffs that danced in his hand like a man being hanged.

"Stop it," said Temple. "He's not the guy."

Temple saw the actor looking at the cuffs.

Banes groaned and doubled over. The actor shifted his body. He recoiled from a blow he threw at Ruthenbeck's heart, holding his hand and hissing with pain. Temple understood he had smashed his fist against Ruthenbeck's flak jacket.

Ruthenbeck lunged at the actor to get inside his swing, and tried to throw his arm around the man's head, but the black man must have ducked. He came out above Ruthenbeck and hugged his head and brought up his knee with a low grunting sound, driving Ruthenbeck's head down into the upcoming knee. There was a muffled cry from Ruthenbeck — just as Banes swung his stick, landing a glancing blow on the man's head.

Temple's mind hadn't broken through a nerve barrier, a film of nervous denial between his eyes and his understanding. So Temple didn't know what was happening when he heard a sound of splitting window-pane. The little alcove filled up with a storm of shattered glass. Temple pulled on Ruthenbeck and Ruthenbeck yelled at him. Banes disappeared into a jagged opening in plate glass and John Shipman Jr. pursued him with another blow, then wheeled to face Temple. The cascading glass represented a kind of triumph for him and there was no fear in his eyes.

Their eyes met for a split second. Temple saw the kid changed into a fighting nigger. The kid saw Temple changing too.

In one or two quick advances Temple surrendered his reason. He could feel it happening and he didn't resist it. Here was this crazy black shit beating on cops. It was a surge of fury he knew of old. He kept only so much cunning as he would need to fight smart — and he used this minimum of cunning to fake a left. It was too simple for words. The kid fell for it. He seemed at one and the same time to try to dodge Temple's left and to get out of the trap, but the left never came. Temple launched a right, and it was like winning the World Series with one hit. The kid hit the doorway and cracked the glass. As he came flopping back Temple caught him near the point of the jaw with a left. Each was a thrust straight from the shoulder with Temple's weight behind it.

The actor stood suspended, ready to die. Temple might have struck again — he thought later with terror, "I almost hit him again," which would have been three times — but Ruthenbeck came up from somewhere and hit him twice in the face, blows he never felt which hardly turned his head. And he slid down, struck his head on the low sill of a window, and lay at their feet.

Banes came back for a kick, still unable to stand upright, staggering, and Temple held him back. Ruthenbeck kicked the slumped body while Temple held Banes. Temple was the first to speak, a wild shout: "Don't!"

The three men stood there and looked at the actor lying in the glass.

They could have moved. But they wanted to breathe, they wanted to know what was going on. They stood there, all three, gaping for breath, in a fog of witlessness, watching the actor, each man trying to see his eyes. But he lay in a half-sitting posture, propped in the angle between the door and the windowsill, slumped, head down, hands on his legs. One hand was turned palm up. Temple could see this because of the lighter color of the man's palm.

Drops of blood, some of them as large as quarters, were strewn around the alcove in an abstract way. The ones that showed reddest were the ones that happened to land at the edge of the sidewalk where the light was better.

There was blood streaming off the ends of Banes's fingers, dripping steady as a ticking watch.

Temple said: "See if Banes is O.K.," and Ruthenbeck said not a word but bent and lifted Banes's hand in his own, then held out his fingers to look at the blood.

Temple crouched. He knew he was kneeling in glass but the crackling in his bad knee bothered him more. (It had not been easy for Temple to squat or kneel for several years.) He put his face close to the face of John Shipman Jr. and saw the eyes, which were not in good focus. A faint squeak issued from the man's open lips. Temple took him by the shoulder and shook. He waited for a response but the only movements he could elicit seemed to be connected to his shaking the shoulder. Temple listened closely.

He brushed the chips of glass from the low sill, braced himself and stood. He went out of the alcove and watched Ruthenbeck examine Banes's hand. An idea came to him. He knew it was late coming, but he immediately keyed his microphone and asked the dispatcher to send a sergeant and an ambulance. He gave his location as First Street, two doors east of Shipman's Barbecue. He looked into the dark indentation.

Now he was able to move fast because he was merely doing what he'd been trained to do on a dummy. He crouched and put his ear up against the actor's nose and mouth. He heard nothing.

He took the man by the wrist and pulled him free of the wall in a single fluid motion, then slipped his arms under both shoulders and dragged the man out to the sidewalk, where he laid him down and knelt beside him. Now he could see his eyes.

It was easy to concentrate on one simple step after another but it happened that while Temple was looking at the eyes of John Shipman Jr. they changed from the eyes of a man to those of a corpse. But Temple had never seen this happen before, and he thought it couldn't be true. Still, he thrust his fingers into the side of the neck just below the jaw to find the carotid pulse, and found none. He tried for a radial pulse and found none. He said, "Mr. Shipman." He opened the coat and ripped open the shirt and placed his head low, beside the face, and looked at the chest. It did not rise or fall. He said, much too loudly, "Shut up!" to his partners, who were jawing about the "crazy black shit." He listened and heard no breath sounds.

Then Temple put one hand under the neck and cocked the head back, to open the airway. He pinched the nostrils and made as tight a seal as he could over the man's cold lips, and blew. The chest rose. He blew again. It rose again.

In the procedure Temple was mechanically following — somewhere between ventilating the lungs of John Shipman Jr. and compressing his chest — there lay in wait for Temple a small revelation. It was that this had been a man; and now it was a thing like a practice dummy.

Chapter 4
Buckle Up

"Buckle up please, it's a rule."

The words reached Temple's mind from out of the singing and wailing of the siren and from the dazzle of the headlights and from the unstable fields of darkness and the red lights going bright as cars cleared the path ahead.

" . . . two . . . three . . . four . . . five," then a rush of air, an exhalation, followed by a pause and then a female voice coming from behind: "No pulse. Resume compressions." And then: "One . . . two . . ."

"So where'd you get your medical degree? Do you know dead from alive? He's knocked out, you knocked him out, what are you afraid of?"

And from the driver: "St. Claire this is Rescue Twelve."

"Rescue Twelve, St. Claire."

"Coming in with a head injury Code. ETA four minutes."

"We'll be ready."

"Why do they say Code? Code means dead."

" . . . four . . . five," and a rush of air (more likely oxygen) before the counting resumed and the siren pealed out again its desperate signal that waved a path through the traffic and went into Temple's mind through his ears, a penetration that felt like little needles of electricity going in to collide in the center of the brain-mind and make it impossible to tell what's going on.

"He's not dead. He's unconscious but his heart is pumping blood everywhere. He's got a concussion or something whatever a concussion is but you don't *die* just because somebody punches your face. He did have a kind of a little light-weight body. Didn't weigh much more than say one-fifty, bones like match sticks compared to —" He was thinking of the Packers, of naked men in the locker room, necks thicker than telephone poles; and some of these men, the skeleton alone would outweigh the black kid's whole body.

"No! Don't be ridiculous. The guy threw Banes through the window and almost knocked Ruthenbeck out with a shot to the nuts."

Had Hawk's knee found its mark Ruthenbeck would be rolling on the sidewalk this very minute. So Temple concluded he'd missed. Temple mused on this and decided Hawk's up-driving knee had struck thigh or chest and not the head or the organs of increase. One light blow there and you've got nothing but trouble for ten minutes anyway, maybe for weeks. Temple went off on this tangent for a few seconds with " . . . three . . . four . . . five" accompanying his thoughts.

Suddenly Temple rolled down his window and began spitting into the night. He felt the driver's hand on his shoulder and he thought: "He's O.K. This guy's all right." Temple said:

"Have you got a towel?"

"Hey Betty, give us a towel or something."

The counting in the back stopped. Temple dimly understood what this meant, and a second later he wanted to scream: "Don't stop for God's sake!" A hand from the back passed forward a roll of paper towels and Temple said: "Go on, don't stop!" And the counting resumed. "Christ! They stopped to give me a paper towel." He wiped his mouth till the flesh burned. "Yes it's possible but only if he had a glass head and that's not my fault and I didn't hit him in the *skull*, my god I hit his — hey! His head bounced off the sill of that window down there, that must be it, the window sill, he hit it on the way down — but God it didn't

look like a very hard blow, did it? You know what this means,"
he thought as if taken by surprise. And here no words came to
crystallize his inchoate thoughts about what this means.

"God what's wrong with you?" he cried.

When they reached the hospital he headed straight for the
men's room

"Guard him!" he exclaimed. "I'm supposed to guard him?
He's going to run?" He was lifted by a sudden rush of rage at
Ruthenbeck, who had given this absurd order.

"Temple you go in the ambulance. He's your responsibility."

He rinsed out his mouth a dozen times and rubbed his lips a
hundred times with wet soapy hands. He splashed his face, and
after a moment of resisting it he looked in the mirror.

He saw lips swollen red from rubbing, eyes shot with horror
and fear. He looked into the eyes and tried to change their expression. Even while still looking at his own face he ceased to pay
attention to it and saw instead the handsome but delicate features
of John Shipman Jr., especially the clear eyes when he had said
he'd not raped anybody, the clear white background to the gold-
brown iris and pure black pupil. Once when the kid looked over
Ruthenbeck's shoulder into Temple's eyes Temple saw something he couldn't identify. At first he thought it was fear but
maybe it was — hope.

A physical jerk shuddered through Temple's chest and shoulders. He said: "I must have broken his skull."

There was something else stirring in a zone too deep for
words. It was that the body was ghastly, the body was a medium
of life from which all life had been withdrawn. His brain went
into a stupid daze. One minute the kid throws Banes through a
window and the next Temple finds himself dragging a limp *young
man* through broken glass, and the glass crunching.

He straightened his back (and then could see only the front of
his uniform jacket with its badge and the silver name plate with
the word TEMPLE), put his right hand to his gun and felt the
usual reassurance offered by this gesture, but it didn't last.
Nothing that was good lasted. Nothing in this life that he wanted
or loved, except maybe Robbie, lasted; but this night had robbed

him of any right to joy in his son. He looked at the name plate and the letters spelled what they had never spelled before.

The records clerk called.

"Yes, Records," answered Temple, "go ahead."

"I've been trying to raise you for half an hour," she said. He recognized the voice of Mary, a young woman who had begun to show an interest in him after he and Sandra separated. The news of this separation could not have spread through the Department faster if it had been broadcast.

Mary said: "There is no rap sheet on your subject."

"Thank you," said Temple and for him the question of the kid's guilt or innocence was settled from that moment.

Mary continued: "Six forty-one unit R has been calling you."

Unit R was Ruthenbeck, so Temple called him.

"How's your subject?" asked Ruthenbeck.

Ruthenbeck and Banes had stayed on First Street to meet the field lieutenant. Probably the lieutenant in charge of Internal Affairs would have been called from his home and he too would be on his way to First Street, or already there. Banes and Ruthenbeck would wait for him so Banes could make a gaudy display of his cuts before they were cleaned up.

"How's your subject?" Ruthenbeck repeated.

Temple was standing in the ambulance chute and not noticing the cold. He could see across an empty parking lot to the cross-cutting light stream of the highway. The light over the lot spread an almost blue haze through the air. Temple sat down on the back bumper of the ambulance and felt an instant relief in his feet. He thought about taking his shoes off then noticed how cold he was.

"I said how's your subject."

Temple shut off his radio and went into the emergency room. In one of the cubicles they were still crowded around the kid, and Temple signed to a nurse named Rita, who came to him and said:

"He's going up to surgery."

Temple followed her back and came quite close, to the point where he could look between the shoulders of a doctor and a nurse and see the kid's face, or at least his cheek and one ear. Without knowing what color the skin should be under these intense lights Temple knew this was not it. The boy's hand hung over the edge of the table swollen and dark with a tinge of blue.

Standing outside again a minute later Temple noticed that his feet were covering the same few inches of ground as before. There was a nameless and unknown twisting within him.

A squad car entered the ambulance area at a steady speed and its lights went out before it stopped. Sanderfare got out and approached Temple at his usual pace. Sanderfare was a black officer who was working on the rape and would milk it all night to stay off the street. He walked so slow it was impossible to see how he covered any ground. This pace was called "the City employee's sprint."

He said: "Heard you cats had to subdue an unruly member of the oppressed minority. Heard you stopped a m'fuckn revolution."

"We . . . I . . ."

"Heard he was dead," said Sanderfare, pronouncing it "dade."

"The ambulance crew thought he was dead," said Temple.

"Ruthenbeck told me he was," Sanderfare declared. "I wanted to stand him up in front of the girl."

"So did Ruthenbeck but we're not supposed to do that."

"No, if he's out. He don't look the same, eyeballs swung up an all."

"He wouldn't look the same, and we're not supposed to do one-man show-ups."

"Oh we can, you know, if we grab him near the scene," Sanderfare argued, "no lapse of time, victim still lyin there, so forth and so forth. I'm talkin to the girl now. You got any questions?"

"I'd like a more detailed description," Temple said.

Sanderfare smiled. With his moist and dissipated eyes he looked as if all the lives he was leading exhausted him. "That you'll get," he said and repeated the phrase as if it were funny: "A dee-tailed dee-scription."

"Yes," said Temple carefully.

"Gotta boogie," and Sanderfare started to go but turned back and stepped a little closer than before. "Musta been a tough mud-dah," he said quietly.

Temple looked at the strange bloodshot non-revealing eyes of Sanderfare, a man whose features seemed to have been hung on his face at random, whose teeth would make a good nightmare for an orthodontist. Temple didn't respond and Sanderfare lifted his hat and tilted it back, freeing his Afro, then slid the hat forward so the bill almost concealed his eyes.

Sanderfare said: "Musta been a fuckin volcano of a nigger, eh Temple?"

"He threw Banes through a plate-glass window."

"Ah! Oooh! Po little Banes! And that must be when he pulled his sword out his boot and start swinging at you boys, endangering safety by conduct regardless of life! Is that the way it was? That was the pree-cise moment when this armed and dangerous nigger done dropped his disguise and start paddlin you boys ass with his muddafuckin sword. Eh? Temple? That when he pulled his knife and went for Ruthenbeck's family jewels? Mercy me!"

Temple said: "What are you talking about — knife."

"Sword! Ten foot long double-edged razah sharp ball-cuttin sword! Hee hee!"

As Sanderfare entered the hospital his voice boomed out: "Nurse Rita, you talk to our All-American, honey, he need something feminine in his life."

A woman came towards him out of the lighted entranceway. She had thrown her coat over her shoulders and drawn it close about her. She hesitated and called out, "Temple!" and he said:

"Here, Rita."

She said after a look around: "They were going to open his skull but the surgeons said there was no point. They turned the cart around. Actually he was dead before he got here. You can pump oxygen into dead lungs, you can stimulate a dead heart . . ."

"He was already dead?"

"Yes. What did he do?"

"He resisted. He — had a knife and he —"

"Yes," said Rita, "but what crime?"

"Maybe rape and aggravated battery, maybe no crime at all."

Rita said, "You can come in, to the staff lounge, and have something to eat. Are you hungry, are you cold?" She stood beside him until he said:

"I'll wait for my partners."

When Rita was gone Temple said in his mind: "My God, if he had a knife —" And he didn't quite say, but he felt the swell of it: If the kid had a knife —

Chapter 5
<u>Switchblade</u>

"Listen, Big Guy, you don't go off the air like that," said Ruthenbeck. "You keep the channel open at all times."

Ruthenbeck and Banes had strolled up like a pair of cocks, having parked the unmarked car next to Sanderfare's cruiser. Banes was sporting four or five pure white wound stripes on his face and had one hand wrapped. They had been to the hospital on the hill, which was whiter than this one — this was St. Claire's, the Catholic hospital in Jonathan Creek.

"Ruthenbeck, if you ever make sergeant," Temple said, "people are going to slash your tires every other month."

"I'm just telling you — keep the channel open at all times. That's the rule and there's a reason for it. Watch out somebody don't slash your own tires. Drop it, drop it. — So — he's DOA?"

Temple said yes.

Banes interjected: "Dead on the Applecart."

"Where's Sanderfare?" Ruthenbeck asked.

"He's inside talking to the girl."

"Hey, Banes gets a week off," Ruthenbeck exclaimed.

"Yeah," Banes confirmed. "Line of fuckin duty."

"For what? Those cuts?"

Banes snickered and dipped his head up and down and said, "The hand," holding up his white paw.

Temple asked Banes whether his tendons were cut, thinking: "What do I care about his tendons?"

"Just the frog's web," said Banes.

"His *frog's web* is cut?" Temple said to himself.

Banes showed his uninjured hand, extended the fingers and flipped the thumb back and forth. It seemed to Temple he must be indicating the flesh between the thumb and index finger. This was apparently his "frog's web."

"I got him back. It wasn't my frog that croaked," said Banes with a writhing little laugh.

"Jesus, Temple, I admit it, I'm impressed," declared Ruthenbeck. "I know some extra-big guys, they're useless in a fight. And for a second there I couldn't tell, you know, whose side you were on? But lose your temper, wow, Fourth of July for the suspect, right? I never saw anything like it. Ka-boom!"

"Yeah, yeah, but the zigaboo was all kick and spit. I'da trashed his mug with the sidewalk," Banes said.

"Hey look, I'm not accusing you, Temple," Ruthenbeck said with a glance towards Banes. "You lost it — sure — but maybe we all three got a little unprofessional."

"We're human," Banes contributed.

Ruthenbeck said thoughtfully: "I mean, you know? He wasn't exactly a citizen taxpayer out there. Well O.K., a citizen, yes, but I think of a citizen as somebody who'll stand there calmly and answer reasonable questions. Mutual respect, members of the community. — When he pulls a knife —"

"And goes for your gut," Banes interjected.

"Then I say the guy's a noncitizen."

"A menace," added Banes.

"A guy with a knife swinging at my testicles, I just say, he's lost his status."

"Wear him out first, read him his rights later," said Banes.

"Necessary force," Ruthenbeck went on. His rounded body hardly moved as he talked. "But the way it turned out, we keep our balls and the knife puts us in the clear.

"We're doing our job, respecting his rights, and he starts running his mouth. No provocation whatsoever and all of a sudden he's got a knee in Banes's crotch, and there's hate coming out of his eyes. It all goes back to being white. I don't know about you, but I was born white. Nobody asked me. I got white by accident."

"Fuckin lucky accident," Banes said.

"But no. Kick, bite, scream, foam at the mouth — and all I'm doing is trying to keep the guy's foot out of my groin — and click — I hear the knife open. I don't know if you guys heard it."

Ruthenbeck put a hand on Banes's arm and the smaller man, who had been about to speak, was silenced. Ruthenbeck almost seemed to be crouching, and there was a luminous expectation in his eyes. "Did you hear it, Temple?"

Their eyes met and Temple felt a flicker of doubt.

"Me, I distinctly heard it click open," Ruthenbeck calmly affirmed. "The guy changes from a black nonhispanic male suspect to a nigger with a switchblade. And I confess — I'll confess to the D.A. and to Internal Affairs that I lost my cool just like you did, Temple. I thought he was going to kill me. It's possible I may have acted somewhat irrational because of that. I don't know how it'll look in the cold light of day, when people are safe and having coffee in their office, you know? Where there's plenty of light? But I remember how I felt when the spliv swung his blade in the dark. I imagine Banes was in fear of his life too. Were you, Banes?"

"Yeah. Was I."

"But we couldn't run," Ruthenbeck said. "You can't let a rapist go howling down the street waving a knife. Anyway the fight was on. One step back and there goes your balls. You don't have to say anything, Temple, actually. Do you understand that part? You don't have to say a word. Just what you saw. You heard the click? Fine. You didn't hear the click? No problem. Banes and me, we heard it. Two heard it, one didn't. You weren't up against him like us."

"There wasn't any click," Temple said without thinking, "because there wasn't any knife."

"Ah, now, be careful. You're not thinking clearly, a college graduate like you, gonna be a lawyer some day and all. You didn't hear the click. That doesn't mean there wasn't any knife. I saw the knife. Banes saw the knife. So there was a knife, Temple."

"If there wasn't no knife," Banes asked rising on his toes and craning his skinny neck, "what did Crowley put in his envelope?"

Temple turned to Ruthenbeck as if he could kill him and Ruthenbeck said quickly:

"Sure — didn't you know?" Then he continued blandly: "If you kept the channel open, Temple, you'd know what was going on. We called the E Crew and they took their pictures and scraped around, and Sergeant Crowley put the knife in an envelope. It'll be on the D.A.'s desk when we get there in the morning."

"Oh — God," said Temple.

"Sure. Standard operating procedure. The knife, a little glass with cop's blood on it —"

"Yeah," said Banes.

"— the regular evidence report and lab-work request slips. Why not?"

"You searched him," Temple said. "Do you remember that? You patted him down and there wasn't any knife."

"Sure, I feel ashamed of myself, I guess we missed it. We went too fast."

"You didn't miss it. It wasn't there."

"How do you know that, Temple? Did you search him?"

"No."

"Banes and me, we searched him and I guess we —"

"Maybe it was in his boot?" Banes asked.

"He wasn't wearing boots, you idiot," Temple said.

Ruthenbeck said: "Look. I know how you feel. I know what you're thinking. You're thinking this is some point of no return. The Blue Code. Like it was something really awful. Like it was — dangerous. But this isn't a Blue Code thing, where you stand behind your partners, where you keep faith, you know? I mean like keep faith because this is war and we're all in the same army. That's not it. This isn't any test of your honor or anything. This is easy. All you do is tell the truth, what you saw and what you didn't see, what you heard and didn't hear."

"That's what I intend to do," Temple said.

"That," resumed Ruthenbeck, as if Temple hadn't spoken, "and nothing more."

"I intend to tell the truth, and I do not recognize a Blue Code or your code, Ruthenbeck."

"Sure, buddy, right. But you can tell what you did without describing your state of mind. If I was you I wouldn't describe that. I mean we say, 'I struck the suspect with my P.R. 24' — better say 'stick' — some of those young assistant D.A.'s don't like police jargon — 'I struck him with my fist when he grabbed my stick — I knee'd him in the wherever, I bashed his fuckin head' — I mean we're not afraid of the truth. He was a one-man zoo. He was out of his skull crazy. Let's face it, he was an aggravated mental, a ziga-boo nut case, and he hated honkies. That ain't our fault. But what you don't have to do, you know, is tell anybody you lost control, you went apeshit. Banes and me, we know it, but we can't talk about your state of mind. Every word out of your mouth can be a true word, isn't that right? What's wrong with that?"

"Nothing," Temple said. "Nothing, you god damned — fool."

"Now wait."

"I know what knife is in that envelope," said Temple.

"Sure. The knife the nigger pulled."

"He didn't pull a knife."

"Temple, control yourself, really. You're a good cop but you're nothin but a rook. Anyway, you missed the knife? So what? Nobody sees everything in a fight. Some guys after a fight can't tell you anything about it, like they were someplace else. Here's a guy got a broken nose and he can't remember why. Another guy's standing there with the end of his stick in his hand and can't tell you whose head he broke it on. By the way, Temple, where was your stick? How come you had to throw those big fists around? Nobody blames anybody, don't get me wrong. This particular rughead assaulted Banes, that's all we know for sure, and then —

"The important thing is, keep a clear head," Ruthenbeck went on. "You can blow up on the street and it'll be O.K. if you clear your head before you go downtown. Know what I mean? You're not in football anymore, Temple. This is real. That girl," Ruthenbeck said, gesturing over his shoulder to the hospital, "is real. And our man raped her, stomped her, choked her, scared hell out of her for the rest of her life maybe — disrespected her, you know? She's somebody's daughter, Temple. He took his thing and forced it into her. Do you know what the courts do with guys like him? They say, 'How naughty you are, Mr. Defendant.' They let Mr. Defendant go, Temple, they release him after a couple of hours or days, and he does it all over again. He does it again as much as he wants. The reason is because nobody cares, Temple, did you notice? She's in there all messed over, probably a nice respectable black girl, and she's one of the lucky ones — and the criminal justice system, pardon the expression, doesn't care."

"It's the knife you took from the fat lady," Temple said.

"Temple, have you been listening to me?"

"What color is the handle?"

"Jeez, I just don't remember."

"You took it away from that black junkie who was crying out-side McDonald's. I remember it, Ruthenbeck. You showed it to me and you asked me if I wanted it."

They had been in the parking lot at McDonald's on First. This was a few weeks ago when the weather was mild. Temple was driving, Ruthenbeck was in the passenger seat keeping the night's summary record and Banes was in the back. Banes went in to get their dinner. A large black woman came rolling across the parking lot. There were tears on her face but no sorrow in her eyes. Ruthenbeck confronted her and told her to remove her hand from her pocket. Temple thought: "Why is he doing that?"

"You're going to turn that pocket inside out, and then you can go," Ruthenbeck said.

She was in a cotton house-dress, of which she was not the first owner. At first she didn't look at Ruthenbeck: she was look-ing farther than that.

She took the knife from her pocket and handed it to him, looking at him with impotent hatred.

Ruthenbeck said, "O.K., Mama, go home and take a bath," and returned to the car and said to Temple, "Want a knife?"

"I saw that knife in the glove compartment of the Chevy two weeks ago," Temple said. "Wrapped in Saran Wrap."

"You're a suspicious guy, Temple."

"And I saw you cut a peach with it."

"Cut a peach? Christ, let's stick to the point."

"That knife was your throwaway."

"Throwaway? Banes, do you know what he's talking about?"

"No. Hell no."

"Listen, Temple, I try to use the right word. Some people don't like it. You're a candy ass, Temple. O.K. you were All-American and a pro and a terrific coach, city champs and all that, but this is different. Here you learn to think. And I don't care how it looks on First Street, it's how it looks downtown. The judges and lawyers downtown have never been here, Temple, because this is too nasty. I'll tell you what they know, they know even less than you. Do you think they give a shit about the girl? Do they let rapists go? O.K., they don't give a shit about us either. We're animals just like all the other animals. That's the downtown mentality. There are black animals, Appalachian animals, a few native-born white animals, and cop animals."

"It has a yellow handle," Temple said slowly, and he felt the accumulating force of his recollection, "bone, or more likely plastic, a slide switch, a strong spring, a four-inch blade —"

"Temple, did I do anything wrong tonight? Did I have good cause to stop him? Yes. Did I have the right to search him for weapons? Yes. Did I have the right to interrogate him? Yes. And when he refused an evidence search, did I have the right to arrest him? Yes. Did the son of a bitch resist arrest? Did he go off his nut? Did he assault Banes? You hit him and he went out like a bad light bulb, which isn't my fault, and you listen to this, Candy Ass.

"When you and the medics were putting the body or whatever it was into the ambulance I found the knife in the gutter. I picked it up and closed it and put it in my pocket because a crowd was gathering and we didn't have officers to move em back."

"Very bad procedure," said Temple, "for a man of your experience."

"Hey Temple," Banes interjected, "why'd you hit him the second time? Huh?"

"Because," Ruthenbeck said, looking at Temple, "he lost control. Am I right, Partner?"

Temple answered, "Yes."

"Tac Squad got themseff a nigger tonight! Done busted his hade." It was Sanderfare, who had approached unseen. "I got the dee-tailed dee-scription," he said, taking his notebook from the breast pocket of his blue jacket. His policeman's hat was clamped down on his overgrown Afro and looked as if it might fall off.

Sanderfare read from his notebook: "Black. I mean, black *of course*. Blue jeans. Sneakers. How *bout* that *sneakers*. Your suspect wearin sneakers? Dark windbreaker. Ah — she say — tight Afro, light skin. Very light skin. What color skin your boy have, Tac Squad? Two front teeth gone. She say *teefs*." He let out a cackling laugh. "Smelt like onions too. Medical examiner gonna find onions in your boy's belly, Hack Squad? You wanna check them teefs? Ha ha — hoo, Mama!"

Chapter 6
Father and Son

The long black bony finger of John Shipman the elder touched a key. A spreadsheet appeared on the screen. Earnest and studious at first, his quick young-looking eyes lit up with a calm satisfaction as he scanned the sheet and found three numbers that were low enough to bear a little increase. He was looking for a home for five hundred dollars. The more he studied, the more confident he was he'd found it. Displayed before him was the record of receipts of the First Street barbecue shop, a perfectly legal operation and a safe place to make a cash infusion so long as he kept his figures within realistic limits.

He had last buried money here more than three months ago when the shop was running a satellite stand downtown during Fall Shopping Days. None of the receipts from the outdoor stand were recorded on a register tape and he could add to them just about as much as he pleased. Shipman hated to run false entries into a register tape; it made him feel like a crook. "I am not a crook!" He chuckled as he pictured the former president dripping sweat and guilt. "Not guilty as charged," said Shipman, "but guilty as not charged." If the Constitution had said a president *must not be a cockroach* they could have charged Nixon with that. Then he would have jumped to enter his plea. "Guilty, whine, but not my fault. I was born a cockroach!" Then came Carter. (Like everybody else,

John Shipman forgot the presidency of Gerald R. Ford though he liked Ford best because he'd been a football player.) Carter said the tax code was "a disgrace to the human race" but was too weak to do anything about it. Shipman was something of an expert on the tax code. He certainly didn't employ an accountant. "When all the preachers lined up behind him" — meaning Carter — "I should have smelled a rat." And now Reagan. Shipman was prepared to believe Reagan must be right about something since the entire "black leadership" denounced him. Not that he was any damned Republican.

If the world were reasonable it would be easy to assign the profits of illicit enterprises to legal ones in order to pay the taxes, which was all he was doing. All he wanted to do was pay his fair share of income tax so he could say "I am not a crook." He had determined a long time ago that it was all right to break laws that had no basis in ethics, such as those against keeping a gambling house and selling liquor after hours and without a license. These weren't laws but regulations, like Army regulations. Anyway, what he kept was a private club, and it was clear as daylight that his club was a better place for a grown man to spend his time, excluding home or church, than anyplace else in the Jonathan Creek neighborhood.

Some people wouldn't understand Shipman's version of the Internal Revenue Code but he didn't give a hoot since nobody knew about it anyway. And if at first glance his rationale seemed a little twisted, actually it was simple. He disapproved of most of the uses the government found for his money — farm subsidies, aircraft carriers, and most of all welfare. He believed that whoever takes a handout takes a master, that you can be flogged and still be free, but accept the Man's check and you just surrendered your brain. This word *brain* wasn't quite right but Shipman avoided expressions like soul or spirit. He had a terrific abhorrence of preachers.

What made it simple was this, that he couldn't cheat on his taxes and still feel free. He knew this made him some kind of freak. He could give to the government but he would hate to cheat it. Once he had this figured out it was clear what he had to do. He

had to calculate his real profits, distribute them among his legitimate enterprises — three barbecues, a tavern and the downtown
car wash — and pay up. The problem was he sometimes had to do
things that might look queer to the IRS. He took the chance, and
the computer made it easier. If necessary he could destroy the
illicit disk. His legal tavern could absorb all the liquor debits and
credits from the boot joint and the three taverns of which he was
the real owner but not the licensee, and he could talk his way out
of any discrepancy between the register tapes and the computer
accounts because the IRS thought blacks were stupid. As for the
South Town barbecue shop, which was in a white suburb, it was a
fine money-loser and a convenient repository for illicit profits. It
proved whites didn't appreciate good barbecue. John Shipman,
who was not a racist, stopped right there. He wasn't going to say
that whites were prejudiced against red sauce because black hands
prepared it. Although it was true. Any fool could see it.

He was working in the office of his business establishment on
Western Avenue in Jonathan Creek. He had just left a card game
in his blind pig to work at the computer, which was his new toy.
The office was a small crowded room with only one window. It
was located near the center of the building, between the light side
and the night side, between the legitimate barbecue and the illegal
booze and gambling hall in the back.

The light side as he called it had gleaming white walls and
tiled floors that were meant to be a world away from the greasy
dark corridors of the old apartments some people lived in. The
personnel wore white uniforms with "Shipman's" across their
chests in large red letters. Laundry was a big piece of the overhead. The barbecue had closed at one o'clock but the night side
was still humming. The house had originally been a tavern or gro-
cery with the store in front, a small loading dock in the rear and
living quarters on the second floor. When Shipman remodeled he
did the front in a way to hurt the customers' eyes at night, and
added a large club room at the rear. He cleared a parking lot by
felling an ancient elm and knocking down a garage. The night side
got its barbecue and coffee from the light side and its booze from

a closet with a wet bar just behind the office where John Shipman now worked.

The upper storey was rented to Lucas Jones, his boyhood friend, who lived there with his good-looking wife and her two daughters and son, and his mother's blind sister. Lucas Jones would prefer to work here in the building where he lived, but with a manager always on duty in the club and himself so frequently in the office John Shipman got along without a security guard in this place, and sent Lucas to the First Street barbecue. To tell the truth, and he did tell the truth to himself on this score, he liked carrying a gun. Right now he had a Smith & Wesson .357 Magnum revolver with a four-inch barrel. That was one reason he wore a button-down-the-front sweater. Another reason was he was cold.

His feet had been frozen in Korea and no matter how he wrapped them they were a problem in the winter. Sometimes it was just discomfort and sometimes it was pain. He walked with a noticeable lurch for lack of half his toes. These troublesome feet were the reason he kept an electric heater under his desk, which cycled on and off with a click that he seldom heard. If he heard it, his noticing the sound meant the thermostat was too low and he would reset it.

There came a click and he got the tingling in his feet and reached down to turn the heat higher. The motion brought his face closer to the keyboard, blurring the letters.

Here was the point of conflict between the father and his son. It wasn't simply that Hawk had once asked in a critical way why he had fought in Korea, as if anybody had a choice in those days. "Was I supposed to act like it was 1970 when it was 1951? Aren't you studying history, boy?" Incidentally the kid never asked Lucas Jones the same question; Lucas was Hawk's friend and almost uncle, and Lucas was above criticism. Lucas too had fought in Korea.

It wasn't simply that the son rejected his father's idea of manhood. That was his privilege. He had to live in his own generation no matter how screwed up it was. It was worse than that. The kid evidently thought every character on Majestic Avenue was a man, just so long as he was a human being of the male sex. But the first maxim of John Shipman's philosophy was that a man creates himself. A man is an act of will. He works with his luck and the deal of nature. A man doesn't just happen, and can't be created by a decree of Congress or the Supreme Court. Shipman believed he had created himself during seven months of infantry combat in Korea. He may have started earlier and finished later but combat was the place.

Hawk seemed to believe men were created at birth. He didn't see that this forced him to believe also that a man is passive — that he owes not only his life, which anybody would admit, to an outside force, but his essential character as well. John Shipman couldn't agree to this new doctrine because his experience denied it and the idea made him sick. He hated to see his son confuse life with politics. "Your brother Winslow is a dead loss. Why is that?" Winslow Shipman was a ruin, a thief and a drunk. A drunk was a human being who couldn't or wouldn't be a man.

"He's still my brother," Hawk said.

"Ah shee-it, boy, who cares?"

"Don't call me boy, and I don't like all this *man* shit."

"Who said you had to like it. Don't like it."

There were thousands of male human beings just like Winslow all over the West Side. Some were the same male human beings Shipman had worked with in the car wash downtown after he got out of the Army. (That was the car wash he now owned.)

Shipman had come home from Korea a soldier but the whole West Side still thought of him as a football star. They said he was the best wingback Dunbar High School ever had but they talked as if he were a creature from another century. At the car wash he was one of the crew. Inside he knew who and what he was. The start of it was that he was a soldier, or had been one. For about a year, though, he lived the same life as the rest of the crew, meaning the life of booze, gambling and women — actually the bodies of women. He was oppressed by the idea of white superiority because he half believed in it. Yet he was still a soldier. Everybody was saying, "Why should we fight for them?" His sense of finished manhood began to leave him. He realized that if it left, nothing remained.

He remembered 1954 as a very bad year but also as the year in which he started to redeem himself and take back what he had a right to keep. The big discovery was that booze gave him a headache. "This is my biological luck," he said. He didn't try to take credit for it. He started going to night courses in business law, public speaking, business mathematics and salesmanship. He bore down hard on public speaking. He practiced at home in front of a mirror and read aloud from the Bible. He did this to exercise his mind on difficult but familiar language, and in the process decided the whole book from Genesis to Revelation was a piece of white lunacy. He met Odell Diann Taylor, mother of Winslow and Hawk and his wife to this hour, at the night school where she taught the business math course. "I teach mathematics," said Odell Diann pausing to let her eyes touch every person in the whole class, "which has no color. If you flunk this course don't talk to me about prejudice."

John Shipman's mother had been a maid, as they called her, for white folks. His father was a laborer who labored mostly at concealing his bottles and the smell of booze on his breath and body. His mother stole from her employers, came to work late and left early and dragged her feet in between, until she saw who she was hurting. Then she quit being a maid and started her own business in Jonathan Creek, and expanded to cover the whole West Side and the villages west of town where black people still lived as in the South. After a few years she took her business into white neighborhoods where there was more money but she saw to it that the hire was worthy of the laborer. She painted and hung wallpaper and became a jack of all trades, keeping her tools and equipment in the trunk of her Hog Buick. At first she made allowances and then she made mincemeat of the old drinker, and John Shipman, even before he was drafted into the Army, saw the worst thing of all — that his father didn't have anything left to fight for. If the mother said, "He's a drinker," she meant he had no life outside of his bottles. The old man was a bottled human being of the male sex, which is not the same as being a man. Shipman understood that a man cannot be bottled. Not knowing or caring what his father got from booze, Shipman concluded it was better to be

dead than drunk. He began to get a false sense of having conquered temptation. Behind the falsity lay a new conviction that at
least one of the Biblical forces in the world he had been hearing
about since he was born was a thing he must respect. The force
was "temptation," which is more than a word; temptation is not
the specious invention of a preacher with a wet face, flashing
glasses and an Oldsmobile parked behind the church; it is an element, like lead. You had better watch out for it.

His reason explained what he felt. If two thirds of the city was
disposed to deny he was a man because he was black, or "Negro,"
in those days, that was their problem. It was external. External
factors can hurt, of course; they can impede. But they must not be
confused with the essence, which is within. And who shall define
a man? I shall. Who stood up to locate the enemy when everybody
else was making a little ball in his hole? Who fired back when others were paralyzed with terror? Who was free of fear? Who shared
his rations and his water with black men and white, who walked
on crippled feet, who continued, without hate but without hesitation? I. I. I.

If he was working in a car wash for a dollar and a quarter an
hour — "I don't care." If a monkey could do the work — "I don't
care." If some people looked right through him because he was the
wrong color, and others set him up as a has-been high school
wingback, and if literally nobody knew what he had done in
Korea, "I don't care." And nobody did know, except Lucas. Only
John Shipman and Lucas. Even Odell Diann didn't really know
because he wouldn't tell and she had quit asking.

He began to save money without a specific goal but with the
belief that it would free him. His mother announced out of the
blue that when he had built his account to one hundred dollars she
would add twenty-five and would do it every time he accumulat-
ed another hundred. His first business venture was a loan to a
painter who sometimes worked with his mother. It turned out to be
a bad loan but it was a beginning. On his next loan six months
later he made fifty dollars in a week. He began talking with Gram
Taylor, Odell Diann's mother, about a barbecue business even
before he married Odell Diann. He set up a daylight car wash in a

vacant lot, using water from an adjacent apartment building at five dollars a day, and cleared a hundred dollars the first weekend. The owners of the lot kicked him off and he set up in a new place. Gram Taylor got fired up about a barbecue stand, and they made their first dollar at a lodge picnic, kicking back ten percent of the gross to the Exalted Grand Ruler.

Yes he had a philosophy and it seemed necessary to renew his covenant of manhood in combat, but there was no more combat. He also knew that men who slipped into an obsession with this renewal were sooner or later killed or outwitted. In Korea the men who had to "prove it" every day or every week were killed; in the city their life and masculinity were drawn from them by *temptations* having the look of dangerous exploits or exercises in power. They would slug the boss, get drunk, shoot up, gamble away their money or beat a woman, and think this was the ever-receding renewal. Shipman established the spheres of his action: the duty to himself, the duty to his family. He put the race question behind him. He realized there was nothing he could do about it and he said so.

His conclusion and philosophy was that white superiority and white prejudice were a white sickness that had nothing to do with him. Being a businessman he recognized economic and social realities and the forces of the market, some of which depended on race and racism. He recognized these, he didn't recognize limits. He didn't have to be a barber if he could be a businessman. He would make a little money then see if he couldn't make a little more. He would marry this alluring, strong, maybe too-religious woman, who was a few years older than he but all the more magnetic for it, and they would make babies and progress. It never crossed his mind that money was another temptation until Gram Taylor warned him. His reply was: "Money is freedom, Gram." The old woman was lying in her deathbed. She rolled her head from side to side on her pillow. He saw the brown skull through her thin white hair. Her eyes searched him but she was too tired to argue.

Chapter 7
Amber Lights

"They's a po-lice in the lot," said the drink man. He was a squat blue-black young man with bulging cheeks and hardly any hair, and his hairless eyebrows jumped up and down as he waited for instructions.

"Did you tell the customers?" Shipman asked.

"Customers tole me."

Shipman looked at his watch. Ten past two. He touched two keys to save the spreadsheet and rose from his chair, took off his sweater and unstrapped his gun, and put gun and leather in the top drawer of a file cabinet which he locked. Putting the sweater back on and buttoning it, he looked solemnly at the drink man — who saw a lean stooped figure rising erect before him — and said:

"Wait here. No more service till I tell you."

He followed the dark hall toward the light end and could see the door framed in yellow lines from the half-light that burned throughout the night in the closed barbecue shop. He went to his right through the kitchen where another light burned, and out a door into the cold. He stood in the dark slit between his building and the derelict next door, and listened. "If I were going to raid this place I'd put a man here." Shipman looked up between the walls at the sharp edge of the adjacent roof against the pink-black sky — then he went silently forward and stood at the front of the slit, behind a chainlink gate and still in the dark, and watched the street. There was the burned-out laundry across the street, the drug store with its armor in place, the ratty tenement with a few lights showing in the second and third stories, all under the expensive lights the federal government had paid for, nobody knew why — and no police anywhere in sight. Shipman had never been raided but was always expecting a demonstration of official bravado. He stood still in the dark. His sweater was a gray cashmere; his sleeves, he now noticed, were blue Oxford cloth, a little too light but luckily not white; and his trousers were dark gray. So he stood on watch confident no one could see him. If the police were anywhere they were behind buildings, no doubt in their cars with the heaters on — but he began to suspect it was just one crew with nothing better to do. Maybe they were copying down the license numbers of the cars in Shipman's lot or maybe they were planning to wait mutely for a bribe.

If so they would be disappointed. Shipman maintained his business by more sophisticated, rational and safer means, but sometimes new cops on the beat had to be educated.

For a second his thoughts moved to his son. Lucas Jones saw Hawk oftener than Shipman did, since Hawk usually ate a midnight meal at the First Street barbecue after studying in his apartment on Majestic. On his way to the upstairs flat Lucas would lean into Shipman's office and say, "Well, Professor stopped by." But if the time was 2:15 — he looked at his watch again — Lucas had probably gone upstairs already and there would be no news of Hawk tonight.

He told the drink man to continue serving and walked calmly through a room where about twenty men were playing cards and dice and drinking. Several looked at him over their cards as he passed through. They expected him to keep the police off and undoubtedly believed he paid bribes to do so. He left this assumption undisturbed since it served to justify his price list. "Big John!" called one man and smiled knowingly. This was the standard greeting of the place. Another croaked out, "Big John!" and so did a third, and Shipman was out the back door looking at the amber lights of a police cruiser parked where the alley touched his parking lot. He walked down a row of cars gleaming dully under his floodlight. Beyond this lot there was nothing but devastation in three directions. He approached the car.

A keen wind whipped at his sleeves and sent the exhaust whirling away through the beams of red light behind the car.

All he could see was that there was one man inside and that he was black. There wasn't enough light to see any more. He leaned toward the car. He didn't touch it because he knew it would be cold. The window came down and the cop said: "Big John."

Shipman moved his body to shift the shadow away from the face of the policeman. He recognized the overfleshed features, the small chin, crooked teeth, heavy lips and liquid eyes of Augustus Sanderfare. The familiar voice had sounded strained or submissive, and John Shipman had not recognized it.

Shipman said with suspicion in his heart, "My man Sandy."

"I didn't want to come knockin," Sanderfare explained, "and rile the dudes."

It was painful to think Sanderfare might be here for money. He shouldn't need a loan. He was one of the "retread" cops who had been hired under a federal court order to integrate the police force, and had spent two or three years in nasty conflict with his superiors. He had finally been dismissed on charges of incompetence, unauthorized absence from duty and lying. He charged discrimination and sued the city. After two years the court had ordered Sanderfare and six other blacks reinstated with back pay less their interim earnings, and each of the complainants had recently been issued a substantial check by the city treasurer. If he wanted a bribe that would be very distasteful. Augustus Sanderfare was the son of one of Shipman's oldest friends, a man with a neverending need to prove it who had died last year in a knife fight. The elder Sanderfare was what Shipman called a man in spite of everything.

"John — say — I got to talk," Sanderfare said.

Shipman heard a profound reluctance in the young policeman's voice and thought it was shame. He went around the front of the cruiser and in the passenger door. The seat was forward to accommodate the short legs of the driver but Shipman's knees pointed toward the windshield and his shins pressed against the radio suspended from the dash.

Sanderfare squelched that radio and the one on his belt. All was silence in the car save the soft blowing of the heater fan, and farther away the idling of the engine. John Shipman sat there with his big hands on his knees and his face turned left, his head tilted slightly back, waiting for Sanderfare to speak.

The dash lights cast a twilight kind of shadow pattern over Sanderfare's black face, as irregular as the surface of the moon, and his round eyes gleamed like nacreous pools in the midst of it.

"John, this is bad. I been workin for you. You better get ready, John."

Shipman held his peace. More than one cop had claimed to be protecting the blind pig when Shipman knew his protection came from higher up. So he sat with his head on one side staring with patient contempt at this unworthy son of his friend, yet wanting to hold back the contempt.

A man can't control his sons, he thought. Sometimes he cannot even reach his sons.

Sanderfare said he had news that he hated to bring, and Shipman held his peace. He said he had intervened to stop a telephone call, and Shipman held his peace but he did begin to wonder. Possibly somebody in City Hall or the Police Department downtown was out to close him and had set a trap, sending this young man to prove he was a real cop by luring his father's friend into a bribe. Sanderfare said: "I'll help any way I can," and Shipman could now hear the wind outside and feel its buffeting of the car body.

Shipman thought: "Keep your help."

There was a silence between the two men. If Shipman said something like "What are you talking about, Gus?" might they not play it to a jury and interpret it as follows: "Mr. Shipman using his private hints and gestures proposed to bribe Officer Sanderfare with vague language which had a clear meaning: 'How much do you want?'"

John Shipman watched the dim gleam of Augustus Sanderfare's eyes and saw pain. The young man's almond-shaped convex eyes brimmed with evidence of Shipman's conjecture. "Man I hope I'm wrong," thought Shipman, and he felt a stronger emotion towards this boy's dead father than he had felt in his lifetime. This boy's father had slipped away while trying to "prove it." A battler, a struggler, whom John Shipman had known since they were boys together in places like Jonathan Elms Park, and down he goes. Both men had been born in the North but in a deeper way were sons of the South, where their parents came from.

Sanderfare turned to face Shipman and said: "Cops kilt your boy tonight."

"Winslow," said Shipman instantly.

"No — the young one."

"Winslow," Shipman repeated.

"Tac Squad caught him up against a wall on First Street by the barbecue and cracked his hade. Thought he was a suspect and punched him up. Not Winslow."

John Shipman could see his son Winslow lying on the ground and a white cop with a club standing over him complaining, "He's nothing but a damn drunk."

Sanderfare reported that he had told the woman on the hospital staff that he would notify the family, so John needn't worry about his wife being awakened by a telephone call.

Then Shipman saw his wife. Odell Diann would be asleep in her red flannel nightgown with her arms outside the covers "because I sleep hot," her Bible on the stand and her poodle on the rug. There she is. "Tell her in the morning, let her sleep."

"Are you sure they won't call the house?" Shipman asked.

"Lady said she wouldn't."

Sanderfare said that initially he had known only that the Tactical Squad had killed a black kid. Then he learned the kid was innocent. Then he asked the hospital clerk for the name.

"And what name did they give you?" Shipman asked as if they were starting from the beginning.

"John Shipman Junior."

"Did you see the body?"

"I seen it. It's him."

Shipman said: "I can believe that. If one of those two had to die young it stands to reason it'd be Hawk." He revolved this thought in his mind. "For sure it'd be Hawk!"

Some power capable of thinking independently, some uncensored power, declared within him that this idea too was trash, just like his "philosophy." Nothing like this death had ever happened in his family and nothing could prepare him to believe it. "You don't believe it," the power said, "but it's true."

Looking to his right Sanderfare saw the big bony hands on the knees, raised almost as high as Shipman's chest, an elevated chin, the profile of a flat flaring nose, an eye fixed, focused and seeing, a comprehending eye.

"What they gonna do now," Sanderfare said after another minute's hesitation, "is make it right, you know? First thang they sayin he had a knife. I hear the talk on that, settin it up. This one honk say, 'Yella handle, switchblade, four-inch blade,' gettin it right down. Your boy have a switchblade, John?"

"No, hell no — I don't know."

"Switchblade's a plant, I bet on it. They usin a throwaway, a dropsy, found property, some such bull like that. Without no knife this a college boy and a 'credit to his race.' With a switchblade he a nigger punk. Next question, John, this boy live at home?"

"No."

"Have his own place?"

"Yes."

"With a lady?"

"I think not," Shipman said. "His girl might stay there some nights."

"So she have a key?"

"I don't know."

"You got a key?"

"No."

"But the gal maybe," Sanderfare said optimistically.

"Yes, maybe," said Shipman.

"Medical examiner's boys, D.A.'s boys, I.A. fruits, everybody like to know what's in that apartment by morning, John. S'pose they's drugs, guns — then we got a different boy. We got a punk, a pusher, a plain ole jagaboo, see what I'm sayin?"

The father said after a pause: "Yes."

"They plant a knife, they can plant anything. See what I'm sayin?"

"Yes."

He walked back through the club room and pausing at a table he flashed a confident smile and said laconically, "Nothing at all. Nothing at all." There was subdued laughter around the table and the room. One man a good deal older than Shipman lowered his cards, looked up and uttered in a solemn bass addressing the whole room: "Safety, Order, Trust," which was the motto encircling the city seal on the doors of police cars. A surge of laughter swept the half-dark room. Shipman opened the door to the stairway that led to Lucas Jones's flat. He mounted the stairs one by one and his heart began to work.

Standing before Lucas's door he said to himself: "If I knock loud enough to wake him I wake everybody."

He knocked softly and then again loudly. The blind aunt whispered from beyond the wood: "Who's there?"

"It's me. It's John." The name seemed to resonate back through the years to his childhood.

The aunt summoned Lucas. Inviting him into the hall Shipman told him that Hawk had been killed by the police. His words were: "The Tac Squad beat Hawk to death." The simplicity of this sentence allowed it to penetrate the speaker's brain to a certain depth. His was the mind of a man who had always known that life is a chamber of calamities, yet no calamity had struck till now. He got through Korea with the loss of a few toes. He didn't think of his elder son Winslow as a calamity because he had smothered Winslow in contempt. His mind recognized the news about Hawk as the long-anticipated event; it was a purely intellectual recognition.

He said: "Get your badge, leave your gun, come with me."

Lucas stood with the lapels of his bathrobe hanging loosely
open and his hands on the belt to keep its knot from slipping, his
head cast somewhat down and forward by arthritis.

Lucas stood like this for a minute with eyes raised to meet
Shipman's. He turned, then, without speaking, and came back in
a few minutes dressed in his brown guard's trousers and brown
nylon jacket with "Security" on each shoulder, his "Certified
Security Guard" badge on the left chest and an American flag
sewn on the right. The two men went down the stairs and
Shipman stopped at his office. He reached for his coat, and
pushed the switch to turn off the computer.

Shipman and Lucas left by the service door at the old loading
dock without passing through the club room.

John Shipman could think. It felt as if somebody else were
doing the thinking and communicating with him through a third
intelligence, but he was thinking clearly enough. He was even
clear about this, that there was a separation between him and
whoever or whatever was doing his thinking for him.

"If they planted a knife they can plant anything."

Actually he did not know they had planted a knife but
Sanderfare knew these cops and that's what he said. So there was
an audience, somebody who was meant to see, handle and think
about the knife. Who this audience was Shipman didn't know.
Maybe the D.A.'s office. But if the audience were presented with
another piece of physical evidence indicating that Hawk was
someone who could be safely discounted then there wouldn't be
any justice. Shipman heard this word justice in his mind. He
heard "justice" and "somebody who doesn't matter," a no-
account black kid.

He was driving his Lincoln sedan at the legal speed down the
mercury-lit corridor through that darkened part of the earth that
had once been the Jonathan neighborhood — new amber-tinted
lights in the street to dazzle any eye that should try to penetrate
to the desolation beyond. Lucas sat beside him.

If they searched Hawk's apartment they would either find
something that could defame him or they wouldn't. If they found
such a thing they would remove it. If they didn't Shipman would

leave Lucas in the apartment with instructions to prevent, delay or witness any search by the police.

The risk was that by searching the apartment Shipman would arouse the suspicion that Hawk's own father thought he was a dealer and had removed evidence. But in that case Shipman could say he searched the place to establish that Hawk was clean, because the police couldn't be trusted. And if the police had nothing physical to present out of the apartment they would have only the knife, which they had already. If Shipman did nothing and the police came out of the apartment with a sack of cocaine from the trunk of some narc's car the evidence, however false, would be overwhelming. There was the possibility the cops wouldn't search the apartment. In that event nothing was lost by Shipman's searching it.

So it wasn't a problem of whether he could think. He was doing that. It was more like a problem of walking on frozen feet.

They crossed the creek into a better black neighborhood and drove uphill into an even better one, where some of the old houses were now owned by black doctors, lawyers, government officials and a few businessmen. They were very near Shipman's own house. It was about three o'clock and he had to be home before Odell Diann awoke at six.

Chapter 8
What Do You Want
Me to Do About It?

Shipman turned up the collar of his leather coat against the wind and woke the house at last with a steady thunderous pounding on the door.

A curtain in a side window moved and he knocked again, more gently, on the little leaded-glass window. When the door finally opened a chain's length Shipman looked again at the side window and saw, within one inch of the glass, parting the curtain, the muzzle of an Army semiautomatic pistol pointing at his head. He said to the teenage boy whose eyes he saw in the crack at the door: "Tell your dad it's John Shipman," and he turned to face the pistol. The two men conversed in low voices and five minutes after he had ascended the walk to the house Shipman went lurching back down to his car with Lorraine's key in his pocket.

It was now a five-minute drive down the hill and a few blocks north to Majestic.

Lorraine was rolling on her bed, whipping her head from side to side, breaking her father's desperate grip and crying, "No! No!" These words were a scream and not distinct words. They transfixed her little brother and filled him with a terror of life. It seemed to him that an evil spirit had jumped into his sister at the signal of three short words, "Hawk is dead," and was devouring her from within, exulting in the triumph of death and waving aloft the rags of her personality.

The key slid home with a neat sound and John Shipman rotated it in its socket, the door gave way and Shipman and Lucas Jones entered Hawk's apartment where a green-shaded lamp still burned at the desk. Lucas closed the door and hooked the chain and the two men looked at each other, listening, and looked around. A creature of some other species would have thought they were listening with their eyes.

Lucas moved from room to room, bent as he was, he looked like a fighter ready to spring. Shipman turned all the lights on and with each click the place seemed more desolate. A grid of brown fibers appeared in the rug. The light was strong enough to reveal a grayish brown stain on the wall and several thicknesses of paint on the window frames. The kitchen was primitive and there was practically nothing in it, not even a coffee pot. In the refrigerator were apples, milk and cheese. The cabinets were clean and empty.

There was a new mattress on the bedroom floor. The bedding was neatly arranged, by Lorraine's hand, he assumed, and turned diagonally back, and the sheets were fresh from the laundry. Against one wall a folded sheet had been spread on the floor and Hawk's underclothes, socks and shirts were stacked there. The closet contained a pair of shoes, leather gloves and a fake fur hat. Shipman paused before the closet and took the gloves in his hand.

As he went back to the living room he passed the bathroom and saw Lucas lift the lid of the toilet water-box, look down, and turn the lid over to inspect it. When Shipman reached the desk he heard the squeak of the medicine cabinet door.

It was a massive cheap old desk whose surface easily accommodated several stacks of books, a typewriter, a glass holding pens and pencils, and a picture frame with a sheet of blank paper in it. Shipman picked this up. "What's this?"

Shipman didn't need his glasses at computer-screen distance but he did at book distance. He put the frame down, took his leather coat off and draped it over his son's chair, and put on his over-and-under reading glasses, which he then straightened against the bridge of his nose.

Again he held the frame at arm's length, looking over his lenses, and could see nothing but a blank piece of paper. He brought it close and looked through the lenses and now he could see the texture of the paper, a little dust on the glass and the grain of the frame, but there was nothing written. He laughed and put the frame down.

Here was a spiral notebook. On the first page there was a title printed in blue ink: "Degradation and Dispersal of the Hurons." There followed fifty or so pages of notes and references written in ink.

Now that he had his glasses on he could approach a long sheet of computer paper hanging in a three-foot strip on the wall between the two windows. This strip would be directly in front of a person working at the desk. It bore four quotations, each outlined by a square of 8's and dashes. The sheet had been printed by John Shipman's new computer. With his head back Shipman moved forward, rested his hands on the desk and read:

"A man without force is without the essential dignity of humanity."
— Frederick Douglass

"When I trip I get up. I been all around the ham bone three, four times."
— Lucas Jones

At that moment Lucas himself said: "Ain't nothin in the bathroom," and Shipman heard him starting in the kitchen.
Next he read:

"No man liveth unto himself, or ought to live unto himself."
— Frederick Douglass

"What do you expect me to do about it?"
— John Shipman Senior

"God damn, why did you twist it?" Shipman exclaimed.

He read the last two quotations again: "What do you expect me to do about it?" and "No man liveth unto himself" — and felt a knife-like cruelty in the way Hawk had set them together.

"Why didn't he say, 'Let's debate it, let's talk it out, tell me what you really meant'? Jesus!"

Shipman sat in the chair and his tears obscured his son's possessions, even the blank page. His eyes burned; his heart thudded and expanded under the injustice of his son's attributing to him such a complete and stupid indifference. Shipman went weak with pain and rage.

"Jesus! Jesus!" he cried in a whisper, "I must have said twenty million words and these are the ones you put on your wall." The quotation kept repeating itself in his head. "Why didn't he ask me to explain what I meant?" he said — and then that question repeated itself. "Why didn't he ask me? Why didn't he ask me?" — and on and on.

There was an eager stress in Shipman's eyes as he bent over the desk and searched for any sign or souvenir the boy might have kept. Shipman and his wife had given him a black and gold pen when he started college. Shipman's long-fingered hands stirred through the middle drawer and its little compartments, but he found neither the pen nor any other gift he had ever given his son.

Now Shipman flipped the pages of the notebook on the Hurons and saw to his surprise that the last two or three pages were written upside-down. He reversed the book. The last page, which was the first page of a journal on a different theme, was titled: "Finding the Path."

"After many years — too young or too careless — one disciplined hour opens the path. Chaos of black in America. Black hand searching for the way in the night. Disciplined mind educates the groping hand. Where the path leads. Sure! To a question! Which world do you choose? A little money-world of businesses legal and illegal?"

John Shipman conquered his pain and read on.

"A family as a refuge? Or a people? A whole people? Black people landed by hook or by crook in America. Choose a world, see a task, see a life: *write the history of the black people in America!*"

Turning a page Shipman read:

"Speech to the Black Students' Association. The activities of our group have to start somewhere, otherwise we won't understand what it is we are doing. So what are we doing? Why does the BSA exist and why should it continue to exist after we have passed through this institution?

"That is no easy question but I have an idea of how to answer it. We must begin with a fact, a fact around which others converge. The *fact* is that we in this room represent the most fortunate segment of the black population of the United States of America. I will go farther than that. We represent the most fortunate black group ever to exist in the whole history of the country. Can anybody deny it? Further still: we are — you and I in this room — are the luckiest black people who ever existed in the history of the world.

"Every black man or woman who ever endured slavery, hunger, torture, oppression or discrimination endured it for us. Every lash that ever hissed across a slave's back and every hunger pang that ever bewildered an innocent child was a stroke of suffering so that someday, somewhere, a group of black men and woman would have the privilege of holding a meeting like this to ask one momentous question: How should we live?

"More on how lucky we are — great chain of martyrdom, struggle, suffering, and hope. Got to mean something. Search for meaning — today's meaning to be derived from black history. Lift Every Voice and Sing. More on how hard it is to answer the question: How should I live? BSA as a forum to debate this. No holds barred. *Truth* not propaganda.

"The Jury idea. — Let me offer this suggestion. I suggest each one of us choose a jury of twelve. We can nominate eight members of our own choice but the remaining four are chosen for us by history. Those four are Medgar Evers, Martin Luther King Jr., and the last man to be lynched in the South and the most degraded prostitute in the city. So each of us now has a jury. Face the jury. Eight members chosen by you for your jury and me for mine, plus the historic four, equals twelve. On my jury Gram Taylor, Lucas, choose 2 more.

"Now we can explore the question of how to live. Let us live our lives *as if in the presence of these twelve*. If we do that, if we decide as if they were watching and if we *act* as if they were watching — etc. etc. — then the six-point BSA program and the —"

The medical examiner's assistant lifted the sheet, and the shape of the face disappeared from the cloth in a kind of billow as it was lifted and then settled on the air. And when the billow settled John Shipman was looking at his son's face.

Shipman's heart wanted to leap with joy because at first he couldn't recognize the face and he said to himself, "The god damned fools have made a mistake!"

But the assistant — looking not at the body but at Shipman — drew the sheet farther down, exposing the thin neck, the prominent collar-bone, the wide but skinny shoulders, the small nipples, the flat moderately powerful pectorals and the thin dark-reddish fuzz in the middle of the chest. All this looked as it would if the fools were right.

The face had been knocked out of shape. There was an unnatural rounding of the jaw that changed everything, another isolated swelling at the right eye and a third along the lower lip. There was no blood in his hair, nostrils or ears, but the chin looked odd each time Shipman's eye returned to it. He studied his son's face. "They cleaned him up," he thought. "They beat him smart so it wouldn't make a mess." Yet there was a mark that he now discovered on the right temple and forward of it, as he parted the hair with his fingers, a faintly stamped pattern, sandy in texture. If a close-up photograph of a sandy beach had been projected on the skin it might have looked like this.

"I want to see his groin," Shipman said and the sheet descended.

Here Hawk was unbruised and unharmed so far as the father could see, but now he wanted to see the feet, to determine if they had crushed his toes — he didn't know why this occurred to him — but the feet appeared unhurt too, except: they were laid out at a cockeyed angle, discarded, one to the left and one to the right, because they were useless. On the big toe of the right foot a stiff paper tag was tied with a green string. Shipman did not look closely at the tag.

Shipman knew Hawk had muscular arms for a boy of his size but lying on his back like this the biceps receded. The bones stood out in his shoulders and made him look smaller.

The lids were closed over the prominent eyes and the lips over the prominent teeth. The forehead curved and shone, as if it could say there was too much pressure behind it. The brain was now too large for its case, but the fatal case held.

Touching his son's shoulder, first, with his fingertips, and then resting his palm on the cool shoulder and curving his fingers over the top of it as he might have done when Hawk was a child, Shipman felt that his son was not present in this abandoned body. But it had a power of speechless eloquence, and other powers exceeding any that Hawk had possessed in life, for example the power of silent reproach and the power of the last word. It had too the power of being nothing and yet claiming him as its father; and the power of wounding him. As the sound of his own bones breaking tells a man he is made of substances similar to wood, reeds, gum and the sap of trees, so the feel of this shoulder told Shipman how it was that his son could be dead.

Shipman stood before the body instinct with love, and dumb when the medical examiner's assistant asked, "Is this John Shipman Jr.?"

On his second attempt Shipman said "Yes," and all at once he did see his son again in those features so like his own — the high curved brow, the prominent eyes, flared nose, imperfectly aligned teeth, and square protrusive jaw. Shipman was heavier and more powerful, his hair was iron gray, his face was a philosopher's or a soldier's face. His son was smaller-boned and the color of his skin was lighter, his hair had a black luster, his features were smaller; his face was the face of one who thinks and is sensitive. There was a touch of the feminine in his face; it was almost beautiful. But in the features of John Shipman the elder there was no trace whatever of femininity. But the son had inherited his father's face. Knowing how the shoulder felt, Shipman didn't touch the boy's face.

He signed an identification form, exhibited his Operator's License and gave his address and telephone number. When he left the Police Administration Building the sky was still dark, but the street-lights seemed unaccountably weak; the early traffic had already begun to flow.

He went to an all-night diner on First Street near Majestic to get a takeout breakfast for Lucas. And after placing his order he sat on one of the stools and began thinking. If only one small fact could be changed. Of course it was pointless to wish Hawk were still alive, and everything else was pointless if he wasn't; but in his dark interior mental world it seemed implausible to the father that he would never be given a chance to explain what he had meant.

He worried this "fact." He went at it like some dumb, stunned, crippled animal being stoned by malicious boys, when the animal tries to get back in its hole and the boys cut it off with a hail of stones. If only his son had not walked where for no good reason he did walk.

The waitress was an old white woman, skinny everywhere but in her little bulging belly, too worn out to stay on her feet through her entire shift. She sat at a table to the side and a little behind Shipman waiting for the black cook to ring his bell. Shipman, the waitress, and nobody else. She had been indulging her resentment over the 25-cent-an-hour night differential that was supposed to make up for the tips she sacrificed by working this shift; and seeing the full-length leather coat her customer wore, a black coat with a light tan belt and tan shoulder straps that gave it a kind of military look — and seeing his wool trousers and polished shoes, she thought: "Made out of money."

He seemed to be striking a pose like a politician, a minister, a lawyer posing for his portrait. Suddenly the figure came into her head: $5,600. That was all she got from Social Security. How can anybody live on that? How could it happen to her, that a black man should be better-off than she was? She studied him from her perch on the edge of her chair. If the owner came in and found her sitting he'd bawl her out. She hated being bawled out and she knew that nobody ever bawled this guy out, this guy in the leather coat.

The way he laced his big black hands together like he was a preacher, the tilt of his gray head — she couldn't pull her eyes away. He was perfectly still but now she didn't think he was posing. He was unaware of her, or of the cook whistling "It's Howdy Doody Time" behind his slide hole. She believed that when she walked behind the counter to pick up the order she would see tears in his eyes. What had suggested this improbable image she didn't know. She watched closely, watched the slope of his shoulders. He wasn't weeping or anything, he was barely breathing.

"Who's there?"

"It's me. John."

The door swung open and Lucas saw there was no need to ask his question.

His eyes followed the white paper sack smelling of coffee and eggs as Shipman placed it on the desk under the green lamp. "I done made up my mind already," said Lucas still watching the paper sack.

"So have I," said Shipman.

He tore "Finding the Path" out of his son's notebook and all the while he was folding the pages and tucking them in the inside pocket of his coat the two men were looking at each other, but they didn't say anything more.

Shipman drove up the hill towards home.

Chapter 9
A Call from a Friend

Whatever else he could swallow, this was hard — knocking on your own damned door!

He stood in the empty hall and surveyed its familiar length. He did have a key and Sandra hadn't changed the lock. If he beat on the door loud enough to wake her he'd wake the whole building. If he used his key and entered her bedroom (their bedroom as it used to be) to wake her quietly he'd be intruding on her precious psychic space. Where exactly was this so-called space? Was it in her finger, her brain, or was it the apartment itself?

"This isn't your apartment any more, Jeffrey. I live here with Robbie, it's our apartment. When you come to pick Robbie up, or for any other reason, and I hope you won't come often, please knock."

She had asked him every week for a year to fix the doorbell but he never had. Now she couldn't ask him and he couldn't volunteer — "because that would be groveling," he said to himself. And he felt the sting of this word *groveling* even though he hadn't groveled.

He could feel the key ring in his pocket. At the same time he sensed the pressure against his right buttock of his light-weight, hammerless, off-duty gun. The thing had not become a part of his personality but he suspected Sandra of believing it had.

Her bedroom door would be open. She would be lying on her side, probably her right side, with her arm extended and the fingers gently curled. Her other arm would be concealed behind the rise of her hip, lengthening the line of her breast. Her blond hair was short and never quite disheveled, and it would look as if a breeze had disturbed it and then let it settle softly. There would be a perfect peace over her eyes and brow, and her lips would be closed, as if she were formed by nature to be beautiful and touched with dignity in all attitudes. Her face in sleep expressed peace and innocence.

She would not care why he came because she could not. How could she share his trials and be his wife when this was exactly what she was teaching herself not to be?

"Turn around!" he commanded but he did not obey. Instead he rapped on his own damned door.

To his astonishment it opened and Sandra stood before him and said, "Come in, Jeff."

"What are you doing up?"

"I'll tell you in a minute. Come in."

"Expecting somebody?" he asked involuntarily.

"Oh sure, Jeff, at three in the morning in my pajamas. It is not your business whether I'm expecting anybody."

Actually it was his business. That's what he should have said.

She was trembling, maybe because she was wearing those thin cotton pajamas. She went down the hall and closed Robbie's door and stopped at the thermostat to turn up the heat. She glanced strangely at him as she passed and went to the closet and got her coat. She threw it around her shoulders, a heavy wool coat of dark plaid, and he thought of Rita, the nurse at St. Claire's, and of how she threw her coat over her shoulders with a gentle twist of her upper body. He thought of Sandra's superiority to Rita and every other woman who ever attracted his notice.

Rita was younger but Sandra was more youthful. There was sincerity in Rita's sarcasm, and a certain wonder at the center of her broad knowledge of the world. Sandra had all this except the wonder. Rita's work had immediate value whereas Sandra's had none (so he thought) but she used her money to create a home and continuity for their son, beyond Jeffrey's contribution. And during the year and a half when Jeffrey had been an insurance "advisor" Sandra supported them all. This in fact had marked the start of her turning from fill-in work to that force he called her career. Three years ago she had been a part-time advertising saleswoman for a bubblegum-music radio station, now she was sales manager for a company that operated a television and six radio stations.

However predatory this force might seem, however willingly she submitted herself to the alien influence of this career, he could still see their whole life from the beginning until now in her face.

He had but to look at her and the world fell into a secure order. This wasn't because he was in the same kind of love as at the beginning. She was his life in this special sense, that if she were removed he didn't know what kind of man he would become. He knew where she was bound, in her career and her life. What about him? She was working on "Sandra of the World." What was he working on?

"You came to tell me something awful," said Sandra, "some big unbelievable mess."

He looked at her searchingly and she explained:

"It's written all over your face. 'I'm in trouble!'"

"We killed a man tonight."

"Of course, a black kid. You reared back and let him have a dose of the Temple temper."

Jeffrey stared and she added:

"You don't carry a stick — no, that would be too macho, so you gave him a shot from your cement fist instead, but a stick would just give him a bump on the skull and instead you had to slug him and so now —"

Jeffrey couldn't believe what was happening. Her mouth grew all distorted and tears sprang into her eyes and she struggled to control her voice as she sobbed:

". . . so you killed him and now you're — for Christ's sake! Didn't I beg you not to become a cop?"

He was struck with horror, a physical fear of what he was witnessing.

He tried to hold her but she writhed in his arms and screamed him away. He let her strike at him but defended his face and made a circle with his arms to try to control her. Strangely in the center of this storm he found himself calmly recognizing he had only one way out, and that was to tell the truth. This gave him the strength he needed to comfort and console her, to speak soothingly and to lead her to a chair at the kitchen table.

She sank down uttering quick despairing sobs, steadying herself with both hands on the arms of the chair, thus involuntarily exposing all the suffering in her face, while he tried to console her. She spread her arms and rested her cheek against one arm, and stared away along the table surface sobbing softly. Soon she lay there motionless. Jeffrey watched her.

He looked at the fall of her ash-blonde hair around her flushed skin, at the part which had formed at the crown of her head, at the tender nape of her neck. He wanted to say he loved her but he knew better.

He felt the embedded psychic signature of a hundred other conflicts and revelations, sought and resisted over the boards of this same table. It was the first piece of furniture they ever bought. It had cost exactly ten dollars, on a day when Jeffrey possessed twelve dollars and some change; when she was pregnant.

Jeffrey sat across from her. He passed his handkerchief and she took it, wiped her nose, blew her nose and held the piece of cloth crumpled up in her hand while she stared down at the table. At length she got up and disappeared down the hall. When she returned Jeffrey asked:

"How did you find out?"

"Ruthenbeck called," she said.

"What? Called here?"

"Yes."

"If he ever calls again," Jeffrey began, but Sandra cut him off: "Please be quiet. It is not up to you."

"Right, of course, we're separated," he said with an ugly sarcasm.

"Exactly," said Sandra.

"What did the little shit say?"

"Tell me — is he that stubby, tank-like person with a peach-fuzz mustache? Did I meet him at the P.B.A. dance?"

"You've met him. 'Peach-fuzz,' that's it. — So what did he say?"

"Just what you've told me."

Temple brooded on this. He said: "Look, I want to know why he called."

"He wanted to tell me you were in trouble. He said he knew we were separated and being your friend and your partner he thought he —"

"Ha! Friend!"

"Keep your voice down!" she cried, glancing toward Robbie's room. "And something like — oh, like he had to tell me the consequences could be serious — that you and he and Banes had stopped a rape suspect, a black kid, that he attacked Banes or something like that — and you put out his lights. Those were his words."

Said Temple: "I wonder why he called."

"He thought you might need help, figuring out what to do."

"I've already figured it out. I know exactly what to do."

"And I was the best one to give that help," she added.

"Ruthenbeck," said Jeffrey as if coming unexpectedly upon a simple truth, "is scum."

But Sandra shook her head, and appeared to imply the problem lay with Jeffrey.

"What's *that* mean?" he demanded.

"Jeffrey — it is the plainest most predictable thing in the world. In fact I did predict it although not out loud."

He felt as if he were being sucked into an old argument. He protested: "Right. You wanted me to be the assistant to an old tenured loser who I had beaten on the field five times!"

"Oh God let's not — *please*, I get down on my knees! — not again."

"You brought it up. And you're thinking right now I wrecked my career with the Packers — I should have been more careful — I should have gotten x-rays."

"Ah — so that's what I'm thinking."

"Yes. And you're sure I lost my temper and threw one at this kid when I should have said, 'Please, sir, excuse me, but is it necessary for you to throw that officer through the window?'"

"Ah well, now I know what I'm thinking."

"And Ruthenbeck told you I went nuts and pasted this kid to the wall by his lips. Is that what Ruthenbeck said?"

"Yes, precisely."

"God damn! — God damn!"

He heaved to his feet, his thigh hitting the table and making it jump. Sandra gave a cry of alarm and he saw in her eyes a spontaneous fury, because he had startled her and made her heart trip. Her face went all red again, and here came the icy confluence in her gray eyes of indifference and contempt. She wasn't looking at him; there was no point in that. This was a look that kept him away, reserving herself for herself. It went deeper than anger and he couldn't stand it, neither could he do anything about it.

It was at this point they always began talking in code phrases that had no literal meaning but were sharp as knives or blunt as stones. There was nothing, or next to nothing to be saved, but they inflicted suffering and suffered as if their very lives depended on this conflict.

Why had he wrecked his football career? Crazy, careless, *deliberate neglect*, that had ruined him. No! A bad break, a piece of bad luck. No! He just got carried away by an urge to save the poor downtrodden — Oh and what a brilliant career it could have been! You loved the money! So what? Didn't you? And his coaching jobs — city champs, and then the Board of Education closed down Benedict High, another bad break. Oh yes, such a piece of luck and such stupid blind pride, to refuse the assistant's job. And you and your career, your "Sandra of the World" outfits, your two-hundred-dollar briefcase —

All this history and anguish was distilled into bitter pellets carried in sentences that began with "You always" or "Why do you have to . . ."

She said at last: "Sit down, Jeff."

He sank exhausted into a chair and she slumped down in her chair, letting her arms stretch out on the table and watching him with a trace of a compromise in her eyes, not quite mercy, rather a glint of desire at the center of the indifference.

She said: "Ruthenbeck told me you were going to go to law school. What on earth."

Jeffrey took the letter from his pocket, unfolded it and gave it to her.

"Night school?"

"Right. Anything wrong with that?"

"For how long?"

"Three years — four years — I don't know, maybe five years."

"I see, another fresh start."

"As a matter of fact, that was the idea."

"That's always the idea, isn't it. Tell me what happened."

"Why do you care?" he said. "You're not my wife."

"Why did you come? You're not my husband."

But they both knew he would tell her and he did, repeating himself more than he knew, yet Sandra sat patiently through his repetitions, only noticing that the details that obsessed him all had to do with the way the black kid had looked over Ruthenbeck's shoulder in some kind of appeal.

When he seemed to be finished she said:

"Let's pretend that I've said everything I'm supposed to say about the death of a human being. But how much sympathy am I supposed to have for a rapist? Who not only raped this poor girl but beat her almost to death."

Jeffrey responded morosely: "Not much."

"And if he had a knife and tried to slash Ruthenbeck."

Jeffrey sat looking at his hand which lay on the table like an inert object. With this object he smashed the kid.

"So I don't understand why Ruthenbeck —" Her voice trailed off.

"Why Ruthenbeck what?"

She shook her head and closed her eyes to fend off the query.

"O.K.," said Jeffrey, "number one, he wasn't the rapist."

"Oh — you know that?"

"I know it now."

"But you didn't know it then?"

"No."

He told her what Sanderfare had said outside the hospital about onions and so forth. He continued:

"So Ruthenbeck disappeared. I looked around and he wasn't there. Banes said, 'Where the hell is Beck?' Sanderfare jived around for a while snickering and then he went back into the hospital. Last thing he said was, 'You honkies is hard on my intestines, you know? Now I gotta go inside and throw up.' Then he was gone and I stood there with Banes. Eventually we sat in the cruiser and after a while here came Ruthenbeck wiping his fingers on his trousers, and he got in and slammed the door and told us he had pulled on the corpse's front teeth and they were real. He must have found the body and pulled the sheet back and —"

"I don't need a picture."

"Then he closed the lips."

"Please —"

"That was the proof he was not the man we wanted," said Jeffrey. "Ruthenbeck turned around in his seat and kind of snarled at me, 'Now are you glad he had a knife, you stupid son of a bitch?'"

Sandra ruminated on all this, never, however, looking at Jeffrey. Her eyes glowed with a concentrated effort and betrayed a doubt. She said: "I don't understand. If he hit first, and knocked Banes through a window, and drew a knife, and if it's obvious you didn't mean to kill him, since if you do mean to kill someone I presume you don't hit him with your fist to do it — I mean — aren't you in the clear?"

Jeffrey replied: "We are not in the clear. We were, but not now. All we had to do was tell the truth and we would probably have been O.K."

"Well you said you intend to tell the truth, and that's what Ruthenbeck said. 'All your husband has to do is tell the truth.'"

"Now look at me."

She did so.

"Now — what else did he say. Tell me exactly."

"He said — this may not be exact — 'Tell Jeff all he has to do is tell the truth. Tell what he saw, and no more.' Something along that line."

Jeffrey had been leaning forward watching her. For a minute he had a wife again. He gave a little snort of contempt and commented: "He said the same thing to me."

She continued: "And then he said, 'They'll crucify us for beating on the poor oppressed black man.'"

Jeffrey grunted.

"But I don't see — the urgency — I don't see —"

"There wasn't any knife," he said.

"But Ruthenbeck said he found the knife in the gutter after you left in the ambulance," she insisted. "He said he, or somebody, must have kicked it there."

"There wasn't any knife."

"Ruthenbeck said that in a fight it's not unusual for people to see different things — for one man to miss what another sees."

"True, but there wasn't any knife."

Sandra said, "If there were a knife —"

"Right. Everything would be a lot better."

"But I don't believe you're thinking clearly," she protested. "You were gone! They found it in the gutter after you rode away in the ambulance."

"They put it in the gutter."

"But why would they do that?"

"Because he's half right, plenty of people downtown will go after any white cop who kills a black suspect no matter what."

"But," she said stubbornly, "it wasn't Ruthenbeck who killed him, it was you."

"So we think. But we all hit him, and he bashed his head on a sill on the way down. Ruthenbeck couldn't afford to take a chance on what the autopsy will show. And he was senior man, he was the M.I.C."

"I wish you wouldn't use police language that you know I can't understand."

"Man In Charge."

Sandra seemed to have withdrawn into some deeper intellectual process.

"What he wants," Jeffrey said believing he was enlightening her, "is he wants me to lie for him. But I know that knife."

"How can you know it," she burst out, "when you haven't even seen it. Ruthenbeck told me the evidence technician took custody of it."

"My God, what didn't he tell you?"

"I don't like what you're doing," she said. "I don't see why you should go off on a crusade at this particular rather awkward moment."

Jeffrey said: "As soon as I see the knife I'll be sure."

"I wish to God —"

"What do you wish to God?"

"Leave it alone!" she cried.

Temple was stunned. Sandra half rose from the table and bent towards him and hovered in a barely controlled fury, hissing out: "Just leave it be!"

And this loveliest of all faces he had ever beheld, this most tantalizing mercurial nature, this white heaving breast on which he had lain — this woman, wife, Sandra —

She could hardly speak and he could hardly comprehend.

"Stay out of it," she said still in that damning voice that filled him with despair, and she sat slowly down in her chair and looked across at him and began to move her head from side to side, looking at him all the while with her outraged eyes. Somewhat more coolly she said: "Tell the truth since you apparently need to make some kind of success out of this, but don't talk about what you didn't see."

"I think it's the knife he took off a junkie at McDonald's," Jeffrey said calmly.

Her answer was, "Jeffrey, you are a fool."

"Who cares? 'The truth shall make you free.'"

"And what do you think Ruthenbeck will do?"

"He'll be squashed."

"Why shouldn't he and Banes simply testify that you did it all? Why are you so sure people will believe you? No, Jeffrey, the truth will not make you free, it will put you out of work again."

"Well, you can support me again."

"You are so funny."

This felt like an ending. Temple endured the descent of the "thing of negation" upon his mind. Yet he knew or wanted to know that all those who had preached across the ages the identity of freedom and truth were right. If the truth didn't set him free he never would be free. This surely was the profoundest wisdom even if he couldn't quite understand why.

"I'll do it," he said to himself. He waited for the thrill of reassurance and it didn't come. He was searching within himself. "The truth shall put you on the street."

"And so Ruthenbeck went in and found the body," Sandra mused, "and tested the teeth."

Jeffrey scarcely noticed her — except that the vision returned, of Ruthenbeck's wiping his fingers on his pants. Temple thought: "That squat little tyrant."

"Ruthenbeck also said," Sandra began, "— I didn't understand at the time — 'your family will be better off' — 'it will be better for your whole family' — if Jeff tells the truth."

"Good," said Temple.

"Oh yes, *good*, that's what you plan to do, tell the truth."

"Right."

"Jeff, are you really such an innocent?"

"No, if you mean don't I see that the little man is making a threat, no I'm not so innocent. He's trying to scare you so you'll pull me back."

Again she looked as if he were a hopeless case — contempt, derision.

"He's bluffing," said Jeffrey. "Ruthenbeck is scum and he walks with scum. He sees threats work every day on the pathetic people we push around so he thinks they'll work on me."

"He does not think that," Sandra declared. "Maybe you'd better not be a lawyer after all."

And into Temple's mind for some reason a stray fact made its way — that Ruthenbeck used to work on the kiddie-gang unit.

"The threat," said Sandra, "is directed at Robbie."

"Aaah —! No — I can't believe he'd touch Robbie."

To which Sandra replied: "This is the man who pulled on the dead man's teeth."

They tried to sleep, Jeffrey on the living-room couch and Sandra in her bedroom, but the night was spent.

As the winter light filled the room he lay under the blanket waiting while first Sandra and then Robbie used the bathroom. Then he could find nothing to shave with, all his implements being at his own apartment. He looked among the things in the medicine cabinet and in the cabinet under the sink, but could find nothing belonging either to Sandra or himself that would serve. His hand moved slowly among Sandra's cosmetics and the other things belonging to her that he hadn't seen in two months.

Jeffrey had offered to take Robbie to school (Sandra usually did this and Jeffrey picked him up) and there would be no time to stop by his apartment to shave and still dictate his Use of Force report by 8:45. For a time this simple problem of the shaving gear quite baffled him and he stood there in his undershorts, a great living sculpture of a muscled athlete, picturing himself skulking unshaven around the "bucket room" at the District.

Sandra at least had not closed her bedroom door and Jeffrey went in to ask her. She was by the window in bra and panties; the light strained its way through the curtains and she seemed to be judging whether a blouse she was holding to the light harmonized with the suit laid out on the bed. The rays of the sun shone upon, and his eyes observed, her slim ankles and the cleanly defined muscles of her calves, and the trim inconspicuous muscling of her shoulders and arms.

She searched and found among the miscellany under the bathroom sink an old shaving kit of his. This time he managed to hold her eyes for a little longer than she wanted, but all she said was: "You better take this with you."

When next he saw her she had turned herself into Sandra of the World, a woman of business affairs — deals, motion, confidence. She wore a pale green wool suit fastened with two buttons low in front, with a narrow V of black rising to suggest an unspeakable femininity and softness —; a severe hair style, the breadth of her

forehead being accentuated by a parting of the hair on one side and
a sideward sweep of blond color and luster; eyes quick and clear as
if she'd slept all night; and her broad, somewhat emphatic features
complemented in their plain simplicity by a thin gold necklace.

Jeffrey looked up at this apparition from his bowl of fruit and
cereal. Robbie looked at her and said, "Hi, Mom," and Sandra said:

"Jeff, may I speak with you?"

Robbie, aged twelve, bent his blond head to ignore the rico-
chets of whispers and tones from the parental bedroom.

Jeffrey followed Sandra down the hall into her bedroom where
she said:

"Do what he wants you to do."

"You mean Ruthenbeck?"

"Yes. Tell what you know, what you saw, and keep your suspi-
cions to yourself."

Jeffrey looked into her eyes, and she did not flinch.

She said, "If you grandstand this, Jeffrey, and Robbie is hurt, I
will despise you for the rest of my life."

Temple drove his son to school and watched through the car
window as the boy ran onto the playground where a group of black
kids were playing basketball. They took Robbie into the game, and
Temple saw his son pass to a skinny black boy, break, take a return
pass and dash in to score. Temple drove to the District. A vise was
tightening around his mind.

The cops' lot was strewn with cinders that must have come from
the station furnace in the old house in coal-burning days. Under a
dirty gray sky Temple walked across the lot to where a row of
bleached old telephone poles lay on the cinders to form a border
with the alley. He stepped across and went into the squad lot, where
the unmarked car he and his partners had used last night was one
of the few sitting there idle. The rest were on the street. A shaded
light with a single bulb still burned over the six cement steps leading down to the roll-call room. Temple went down and along

between the two ranks of tables and chairs, past the lectern and the radio locker, and turned right into the men's locker room. This too was empty.

He spun the lock and opened his locker and sent an image of the room flying past his eyes. He avoided the mirror, and retrieved his clipboard from a hook. Without this he could not write his report.

He noticed now for the first time that his uniform trousers, hanging before him, were ripped in the knees. Yet it was not "for the first time" at all because now he remembered how the wind had found his knees while he stood in the hospital lot. And tumbling after this recollection came another, that while changing clothes here last night, before going to see Sandra, he had re-opened a bunch of little cross-cutting scratches on his knees, and they had bled. And looking down at his khaki civilian trousers he saw the dark stains at the knees. He did not understand how he could have forgotten all this. He clearly remembered what a relief it was to decide to go see Sandra, partly because he knew Ruthenbeck and Banes would be upstairs in the "bucket room."

A sentence, clear, complete, hit him out of nowhere: "You are going to end up in a rooming house" — alone, of course. Not till he became a cop had he ever seen rooms like the one that now seemed to be reserved for him, with hideous noises filling the filthy halls at night and a communal bathroom and a smell that made all these places seem like one place. If his father saw him in that room he'd die all over again. Temple's father had been a high school band teacher, had organized a marching band among the best in the state, 120 kids in red-and-blue uniforms marching and tootling in a half-time show that was almost as famous as the football team. Temple's father was the only teacher in the school whom the kids called "Prof." The English and math teachers were not pleased.

In the "bucket room," which he had avoided last night, he now sat at one of the chairs and thrust his head into the sound-deadened, box-like cubicle and dictated his narrative over a phone line connecting him to the stenographic center at the Hub. Then he read off the printed number on the blank form in his hand titled "Use of Force Report."

He heard people passing through the room behind him and once somebody knocked on his head with a hard set of knuckles, but Temple bent to his work. All he could see were the little perforations in the soft walls, and as for hearing, after a while he heard nothing at all.

He wrote at the top of the narrative box, as he was required to do, the time he'd dictated his narrative. He proceeded to fill out the rest of the form, till he came to the section titled "Was suspect armed?" Under "No" there was a blank area but under "Yes" a column of boxes, and the answers waiting to be checked: gun, knife, club, chain, knuckles, missile(s), and other.

"I do not recognize a Blue Code or your code, Ruthenbeck."

He knew who had said these words. He knew how it felt to say them.

"You are going to end up in a rooming house."

He wasn't quite sure who had said this but he knew how it felt to hear it.

Something was beginning to happen in his body and it was so alien he didn't understand it for a second or two. It lifted through his center and enveloped his heart and tried to pull it in all directions. It was fear. Later he would be ashamed. For now all he felt was fear, which made him helpless, impotent and unstable.

His pen was suspended over the page. He did not check "Yes" and he did not check "No." He looked farther down and encountered "Did suspect have visible injuries?" but immediately his eye jumped back to "Was suspect armed?" and Temple realized — he recoiled from the knowledge — that he was afraid to check "No."

The body fell, the head bounced off the sill. He dragged him through the glass, taking him under the arms and lifting with one quick and easy move — pulling him out of the dark doorway, seeing his feet flop this way and that. He cradled the head in his palm and lowered it to the sidewalk. The head had weight, yet it was light and easy to handle. He tilted the head back to open the airway and saw the eyes, the teeth, the bleeding mouth, the swelling chin, the slender neck, the light-brown skin.

Bending closer he smelt the human-being smell of a man with no food odors on his breath (no breath at all). He watched the chest.

He put his ear up against the mouth and nose, in direct contact, and he heard no breath sounds. He plunged his fingertips into the warm notch under the jaw and probed for the carotid artery and encountered no pulse, only a firm resistant wall of muscle under and behind the hard ridge of the jaw bone. He looked at the face again and it did not look back. The eyes were indifferent, although wide open. The face didn't care what had happened.

Temple pressed his mouth against the boy's and wondered if he would vomit. He sealed the two sets of lips and blew and with his head straight but his eyes looking aside he saw the chest rise. He straightened up and wiped his mouth and almost retched. When he pressed the lips with his own again he felt nothing at all, he was too crazy with the job — now he felt their yielding softness as they slipped off the teeth. He bent down again and kissed lifelessness.

Dropping his pen, covering his face, he said: "He's dead! He's dead!"

Chapter 10
In the Garage

Shipman was in the narrow space between his Lincoln and Odell Diann's old Buick, both parked in this ill-lighted garage. The daylight was already pressing its rays through the dusty windows.

"Laid out, laid out, oh damn, damn." His throat contracted as if closed in a pincers. "And what was that about the seats in the car?"

His enlarged eyes tried to bore into the cement. He thrust his hands deep into his overcoat and braced back, and he was very erect, too erect, stiffening.

"Trap closed. Snap!" As if his mutilated feet had been thrust into a trap.

"I just don't want it," he said. There was "something" he didn't want. It was something to do with the all-night diner — while he sat there waiting for the shriveled-up white woman to bring Lucas's breakfast. Something happened in his mind, during those minutes, without his knowing. It was then he looked at the wall. Not earlier, when Hawk died, but while he sat on the stool hunched over the counter, thinking.

"You can *take* the thing," he cried and beat his fist on the hood of the silver Lincoln. Which was real? The *snap* of the closing trap or the plush seats in this superexpensive car? Money, cars, TV, good booze, good fellowship, and the oceanic dance with his wife, all unreal.

Life is over. He had realized it when he paid the skinny woman for Lucas's breakfast, and he didn't care. He scarcely noticed that part of it. His mind did a search as simple and final as the arithmetic performed by the cash register when it spat out his tape. You owe this much and exactly this much for the breakfast, and so much and precisely so much for the murder of your son. Pay the skinny waitress; pay the cops. So the life of the silver Lincoln is at an end; and if you add it up a thousand times it will always come out the same.

He stopped and looked at the seats in the Lincoln and even opened the door and touched the velvety material.

"It's not a trap," he said. Now something had come over him and he was rational, attaching one link to the next. "You could sit on these seats naked and it'd feel good. All that's over." This seemed to be the first link, that all sensuality was ended.

He groped on. "All right say snapped. But a trapped man can't go anywhere, he's on a chain." That was the difference. "I ain't on no chain." He was going somewhere.

He tried again to connect the links.

"Standing at the register —"

Shipman pronounced the word *standin*. This was one of the few traces of Alabama English, which he had imbibed as a boy here in the North, remaining on his tongue today. He was a son of the North, grandson of the South, and father of black sons. He could talk to bankers in a conference room where every chair cost as much as an Alabama shack, talking banker language to raise $200,000 for his franchise plan, and he could talk to the men in the blind pig. He could talk to preachers, teachers and liquor salesmen. He could talk to Lucas Jones in the idiom of their boyhood on the West Side. He could talk to the barbershop crowd and the old YMCA crowd. And he could talk to the kids on the street and the ones wearing their "Shipman's" shirts in the barbecue. He could not talk to his son

He saw it plainly again, as simple as arithmetic. There was one sum, and one only, that would settle the account. He had to pay the sum. It was equal to his life, and to the lives of the cops. This was the only kind of "racial equality" he could recognize.

This explained why his life was over. It was simple and final. Otherwise why would the car have seemed so strangely repulsive when he left the diner carrying that little white sack of breakfast and coffee?

At this point his mind leapt forward and language tried to catch up. What he discovered was not that Hawk was dead — of this he still wasn't sure — but that since he had to kill the cops Hawk must be dead.

Nothing else could make him decide that, and nothing else could turn him back into a killer. His mind now was saturated in an atmosphere of crime and blood, as if he were back in Korea. It was the feeling of being a killer. Not the feeling of killing, not that exploding frenzy that was so easy to justify by necessity. No, not that. This permeating, cool, dripping consciousness wasn't about something he did but about something he was.

Once you're a killer everything you do and every thought you hold up to the light is something a killer has done; you do not ever escape it. It brings its own consciousness and style of living. A man who has been tortured and left to shiver in a wet cell, and is released, and after years of freedom is stripped and thrown back in, who hears the tramp of the guard's approaching boots, lives in the same atmosphere.

"True," he said quietly, "but I got the feelin in my chest of a mistake someplace. — Think, search." The light from outside was making its way through the high windows and revealing his gardening implements hanging on their nails, his spade, hoe, rake, fork, his socket wrenches in a graduated array, the red metal cabinet with little square drawers for screws and nails of all sizes, and the vise on the work bench waiting to seize and hold some object. He saw all this but he said:

"If my boy were white he'd be alive now. I saw the body, I touched his shoulder." He remembered but it was only a memory. "He feels alive." Under his hand the boy was a corpse. In his heart he lived.

John Shipman saw his leather portfolio hanging by a nail driven through the plaster into a wooden stud that he had located by tapping on the wall. He had wrapped tape around the nail to prevent its damaging the leather-sheathed handle of the portfolio. This was a folder of good leather and brass, and so big it only fit by inches into the trunk of the Lincoln. It held the architect's sketches and color photographs that John Shipman used in his sales presentations for the franchise plan, and he had carried it this fall and winter to Cleveland, Columbus, Indianapolis, St. Louis, Gary, Chicago and Milwaukee.

" . . . so don't ask yourself if you can make money on this franchise. I guarantee you can. Ask whether you want to work seven days and seven nights a week. Ask whether you want sixty or seventy thousand dollars that much. Whether you want to give your children the means to build a good life by honest work. Do you want — I want my son —"

His teeth bared themselves. He looked like a mental defective grinning and stooping his way down the street.

"I never explained, I couldn't talk to him, he wouldn't listen, I didn't try hard enough, I wasn't patient enough — He didn't want to hear all this *man* shit."

Suddenly he realized his mistake.

"Keep Lucas out," he said. "You let him in. That was a mistake. He's my son and I'll die for him."

He turned violently and paced back the other way, seeing nothing. He said: "Don't need no *Lucas* on my conscience." With one stroke they had killed Hawk and himself and cursed Odell Diann. "That's enough!"

Lucas would surely be abused by prison guards. Not beaten perhaps but scorned and denied the aspirin tablets that were his only relief. Shipman could see him in prison, his old face and white hair, see him bent forward, his upturned eye's bleary with unrelenting pain, knuckles swollen and fingers twisted —

"I know he loved him," he thought, "but I can't let him spend the rest of his life in jail. He's old and sick. He's no older than I am! Never mind. He's got a new wife and her kids, and the blind old aunt. He's the best thing they've got. The girls could grow up to be — ah —" For a moment it didn't matter what they grew up to be, or if Lucas threw his life away. "He loved him, let him decide for himself."

Shipman pondered, even stopped. He said quickly: "No, I have to come out clean. I have to act within the law." Meaning the real law. "I can't let Lucas sacrifice himself. Let him express his love some other way." Immediately that phrase "express his love" struck him as insane when he had a vision of Lucas leveling his pistol at the buttons of a cop's jacket.

"That's not insane," he said. "I'll tell you what's insane. All the people who do nothing. 'Oh they raped my wife and murdered and cut my grandmother in pieces and stabbed my son, why they *do* that?' They know as well as I do, they'll never get justice in a court. 'Hey nigger, we got the monopoly of force, you the piece of shit, so whatever you get you better call it justice, and then you better shut up and adjust your mind.'

"I know why they don't do anything, it's simple, it's fear. Ha!" he exclaimed emitting a jet of steam in the frosty air. "But for me it's all possible, courtesy of the US Army and it is for Lucas too. We did it before and it feels like last week. Do I have any compassion for all those men, any pity?" He suddenly veered off on this odd tangent. A quick glimpse of something in Korea, he didn't know what, maybe something as harmless as a map, and for a moment he was back there, his brain was a combat brain.

"You're supposed to feel compassion — 'those poor bastards are human beings' and all that sort of thing — but you better 'repel the advance' and 'pursue by fire' — and then, man, 'shudder' a minute and 'pull yourself together' and go through a bad night every few years and shut up about it. Be a man! What garbage!"

He wondered if he could do it alone. The way he felt, the killer mind, he knew he could. "When I kill those killers," he said and again stopped in his tracks. He stood straight and his eyes were staring.

"When I put that thing against the motherfucker's heart and his eyes can't believe it, I pull the trigger and he bounces back! His whole body chasing its bullet, arms and legs —" Where was the wrong? "You did the wrong, you motherf—"

He cut off the profanity. To call a man motherfucker because he had killed Hawk would be a profanity itself. "This is no time for gutter talk or going crazy." It was a time to be cold and kill. And to punish his wife with a glancing blow.

"I can't help that," he declared. "She's already been sentenced. Pain," he realized, "isn't the most important thing. I didn't sentence her and I can't lift the sentence. I can change the form it takes by lying down and whimpering, then she gets one kind of punishment. I do what I must do, she gets another."

But he did feel her throbbing body in his arms. He had to go to the house but he was scared of her tears, he couldn't bear her sobs.

He felt her body withering in his embrace. Stricken. What a word! "She be stricken in her grief." He didn't know where the words came from. She would collapse, as if falling through his arms. He couldn't hold her tight enough.

"This!" he thought, "— is what you did to my wife. Killed my son. Done this to my wife."

Another thing a killer is is some man without a future. "I don't give a damn for any future!" They had turned him back into what he never wanted to be. What did he ever care about communism, whatever that was, and why should he kill those "gooks"?

A tide of hatred, tide of fury, licked at the moorings of his intellect, and the intellect struggled for its life as Shipman tried to say what was true. He spoke aloud and slowly, his eyes shining and racing over the cement, over the cars, the walls, the hanging tools, the dust- and light-clogged windows. And by a supreme effort he connected one idea to another because he had to know where he was.

"They killed our boy. She be stricken in her grief. This is a lot to bear, a heavy burden." Here he was distracted: she would "wither in his arms."

"Aaah!" he cried. Whatever else he could do, here was one thing he could not: relieve or release her.

"Go on!" he said. "So next you kill the killers and do what? Double her burden!"

Some quick reasoner in his mind wanted to act as if this were a step in elementary logic: if it doubles her burden, don't do it.

"I can see two lives for her after this. I lay back and let the honky motherfuckers — quit! *Do not degrade your mind.*"

He spoke aloud and became his own listener. "Do not degrade your mind with filth and race hate. 'Hate a whole race, shut your whole face.' These are not 'honky motherfuckers' I am going to kill. I am going to kill the murderers who killed my son and I would do it even if they were black." He paused over this new idea and his eyes were fixed on nothing — stark, enlarged, tortured eyes.

If Hawk were white he'd be alive right now. If the killers were black . . .

Shipman's eyes grew sharper and lighter as he said: "I'd kill them just the same." But was this true? Brown and black eyes swimming in the bloody red of the "whites" of his eyes.

He snapped out of it.

"I lay back and do nothing, I see her future clear as anything. She lives the rest of her life with a corpse, a eunuch of the Pharaoh, a drunk, a stinking drunk just like my old man. Or, the other life, *I do what I must do* and she pays her share of the price. How could it be otherwise. They already assaulted her. And I live with a killer's mind — but only for a little while," he added with a smile.

He opened the door.

Some soldiers can do anything because they know they won't be hit. Shipman had been this kind of soldier. Others do things only gods ought to do because they know they are already dead. This is a rarer kind.

Shipman walked out of the garage believing that he was already a dead man and for this reason could do anything. Except maybe tell Odell Diann.

Walk toward a machine gun, through a minefield, over a frozen battlefield in bare feet with the frozen toes cut off, naked over a frozen ocean with the wind swirling around his cock and balls — but tell her? Say to her: "Our boy is dead"?

Chapter 11
She Stands Watch

If Odell Diann Shipman awoke at two in the morning and discovered herself in the bed there was nothing remarkable in that. But waking again at four in the same solitude disturbed her. She flung back the cover and sat on the edge of the bed sinking her toes into Tillie's coat, and Tillie, a mere smudge of gray light hovering at floor level, didn't even wake up.

Odell Diann arose and went downstairs, turning on the stair light but no others because she was still hoping for more sleep. And so she wandered the first floor undecided. Whether it was her age or some other unknown change in her body, she needed a full night's sleep more than she ever had. In the last couple of years she found she would lose her good-will more quickly if she slept five or six hours instead of her basic eight. The kids set her on edge; the whole school with its chaos ready to break out in the halls at any minute jangled her nerves. And she didn't feel like her best self. She felt, if she got too little sleep, that life was a struggle and she was running short of food and water.

The coffee pot was ready and she had but to turn the switch to set it going. She stood before it still doubtful.

"Maybe I should say my prayers" — meaning go to the sewing room that was her chapel and pray now instead of later. In other words get it over with. Not such a good attitude.

Sometimes God didn't seem very real, or herself very worshipful. The Rev. Mr. Beecham had told the congregation only last Sunday that while praying on his knees he complained inwardly of the discomfort. He reported that his unbelief was so strong it had taught him to listen to the traffic passing under his study window even while he prayed, or pretended to pray. "That's me," Odell Diann said. She turned on the coffeemaker and went to the powder room to wash her face. By the time the coffee was ready a pale light had begun to put the kitchen things in their assigned places. The darkness still prevailed but this night was ended. The black triangle of the garage roof rising into the sky began to acquire familiar details such as shingles and the vague rectangles of windows and the pedestrian door. Blowing calmly over the steaming surface of her coffee, Odell Diann watched the garage as if for movement, and waited for a sound; and none came. The building was a silent wedge against the sky. She carried the cup into the living room and eased herself onto the couch. She crossed one leg over the other and glanced at her calf. Looking at the calf and the calf alone a person might guess she was thirty years old. She drank her coffee slowly and the gathering light showed her the room. There was only one old chair. All the rest was new and even opulent, chosen in the last five or six years after John's businesses had started pulling in the money. Before that, they had lived partly on her teacher's salary. They had been working hard and making no headway. Now they could buy just about anything, except there was nothing else she wanted.

The television and music system had a kind of chateau of their own in one corner, and there were speakers planted inconspicuously on all three floors of the house. Most of the chairs were leather, the carpet was a pale green wool contrasting with the red and charcoal leathers and the mahoganys, and the windows were "draped in dignity" — according to the decorator.

Above her as she sipped her coffee the triple portrait came into view — John F. Kennedy, Martin Luther King Jr. and Robert Kennedy painted in stronger-than-life colors on a background of black velvet. All three men had the same look of courageous hope. With a few flecks of the brush the painter had planted nobility in the eyes of each man. She heard the sound she wanted to hear, the lifting of the garage door, the low hum of its electric lifting device whose throbbing labor pulsed its way through the walls to reach her eager ear. She rinsed the coffee cup and went upstairs.

She stood at an upper window, a tall brown woman waiting, keeping watch. Nothing she heard downstairs or saw in the back yard suggested he had left the garage. She saw what must have been his form pass a window, so she kept watch. He must be working on some project yet she heard neither hammer nor saw. Maybe he was measuring some piece of wood, or maybe he had taken down the big portfolio and spread it out on the warm hood of the Lincoln to examine the visuals, while he prepared to rehearse his presentation.

And if he really was working in there at this hour, no matter what work it was, she could dismiss all the agitating possibilities that had crowded her mind while she sat on the couch. Forget about fire, collision, heart attack, stroke and gunshots; quit imagining some bloody accident killing one of the boys; forget that John was a prime candidate for every form of black-man's early death and that the boys crisscrossed hell every day and night — forget her fear, the fear amounting virtually to a certainty, that Winslow's habits would catch up with him and sweep him right away.

There was however one possibility she couldn't get rid of. It was the ugly, humiliating renewal of John's affair with Clarabelle or whatever her name was, an unknown, never-seen woman who pretended to need a lot of advice before signing a franchise agreement, but who actually had in mind a more intimate kind of connection. There was a question whether this woman existed but a friend had spoken and Odell Diann's night-thinking took it from there.

Odell Diann Shipman was a woman in the prime of a mature beauty, more aware of her age than of her beauty's effects on her husband. That somebody pressing as close to sixty as she was could seem like anything but an old woman to a man of John's energy did not enter into her thinking. When he told her she was beautiful she loved the lie and the liar. Obviously John could have as many Clarabelles as he wanted. She almost said, Have anybody he wanted. Do such potent aggressive men pass it by? She knew a woman whose husband's entire defense in the catastrophe of their marriage was: "Do you expect me to pass it by?"

She might believe he was true, and lack all evidence that he wasn't, and find nothing in his lovemaking that had any other stamp on it than their own — but all the same she dreaded something. Far back in her mind. Like the claws of a snapping turtle she had seen once in Alabama crawling through the dirt and dragging its spine-tipped tail and lunging forward first with one forefoot then the other. The longer John gave her reason to think he was true the more amazing it was. Could this man be different from all others just because she loved him? The turtle heaved his weight forward pulling its back-curved taloned feet through the dust.

What disturbed her perhaps was the belief she was too lucky in her marriage and family (despite Winslow's boozing). The thought was cruel to Winslow. She knew his craving and suffering and sometimes in her prayers asked whether he was the sacrifice to her unspeakable happiness. To be married to "Big John" — to have two living sons and nobody shot or stabbed — to be surrounded by the comforts of a fine big house and all this fine furniture —

One day last summer while on her knees gardening she happened to think about being on her knees praying; she thought of a simple prayer that reached as far as any she ever uttered. She asked: "What must I do?" — if John was indeed deceiving her. Not "Poor me!" or "Teach me to swallow ashes," but just: What must I do? Next morning in her chapel she deciphered the answer. Trust him. It was not John but the snapping turtle who was her enemy.

Now suddenly the man she trusted was lurching up the walk from the garage in the strangest way, as if he had needles in his knees. It flashed through her mind that he must be drunk. She hurried down the stairs — "Big Boy drunk?" — with little white Tillie struggling to pass her. Tillie reached the kitchen door and began springing up and touching the knob with her nose, covering it with a little sheen of moisture. Rather than scold the dog and wipe off the knob, Odell Diann opened the door.

John stood still in the walkway, about half the distance from the garage to the house, leaning forward and swaying to one side, with his hands out as if to grasp some support. He saw his wife and seemed to stare amazed at her, as if she'd risen from the dead; he seemed almost terrified. Then he took a series of staggering steps toward her. She helped him across the threshold, with one arm around his back and her other hand clutching his hand. The dog worried their feet and she shoved it away. In this manner they passed through the kitchen and hall in silence, to the living room, where she guided him to the couch. Neither spoke a word. Each heard the other's breathing.

Seeing him halted on the walk, about to topple, she had been pierced with fear but now she was thinking: lie him down, raise his feet, loosen his clothes, call an ambulance. And she could see herself a few minutes hence, with the ambulance already screaming into their street and John breathing deep and calm, see herself kneeling by the couch whispering to tell him he was home, he'd be all right, she was there —

"I'm here, Big John."

"Del Honey."

"Yeah Big Boy, lie down first."

"Del."

"Lie down, then you can tell me."

She saw fear and confusion in his pain-stricken eyes. The pain must be terrible to frighten him so. She embraced him and felt how broad and powerful his shoulders were, and it seemed like an awesome act of God that a man so strong should tremble and stammer so incoherently. He was trying to speak but choking on his words which were not words at all, they were not coming in a language she could understand, and into her heart crept the cold belief that the worst was happening, that it must have begun in the garage while she stood uselessly watching and it was continuing right now, and that it would lead on to paralysis and total loss of speech, to the loss of every faculty but the ability to suffer. She saw him in some hospital bed with tears filling his eyes, evidence of emotions he couldn't otherwise express, his mind clear, life still surging through him and he couldn't say it. She saw how this silence sharpened his suffering — and for some reason she thought of Winslow, of how she would bring Winslow to his side and join their hands —

This word — " . . . dead!"

She understood it. She faced him and looked into his eyes and it was she who couldn't speak.

"Our boy's dead."

Her inner voice declared: "Hawk!"

"Our boy's dead," said John more clearly, in his own voice, and he tried to take her in his arms but she tightened her hold on him. She pressed his head down. She felt his unshaven face against her neck and she forced it even harder against her flesh and felt a kind of snap, a throb, and heard him begin to sob. All she could make out was "cops" and "dead." His whole massive body trembled and then shook within her embrace.

At the same time she seemed to be tumbling into a deep space of water, like somebody who is pitched off a boat in the rapids. Had she been somersaulting down into deep water this is how she would feel. Her luck has run out. The best explanation is not that John is suffering a stroke but that Hawk has been killed by the police. And yet she kept trying to get around it, just as if she were under the boat being swept downstream, waiting for the inevitable rocks, and whenever she would swim to the surface she'd strike the bottom of the boat, which got to wherever she went just before she did. The water in the shadow was darker, approaching black. This is how people drown.

A sound reached her, the cry of a stricken animal. It might have been John's howl or her own. She tried to rock him, soothe him, but she was going as wild as he, and the sound only increased.

Chapter 12
Sam Lovico,
Deputy District Attorney

Sam Lovico closed the door of his office and went to the old green safe behind his desk. Sending his chair rolling away on its little brass wheels he squatted and began to spin the dial. This business of squatting was difficult now, and impossible to do for long. The tumblers fell and the thick door swung open. From the fascinated look in Lovico's eyes anybody might have thought he had never seen the things in the safe before.

Rising from his painful position he took a turn around the office to make his knees feel better, then he looked at the book he had taken from the safe. It was a paperback copy of *The Jesuits in North America in the Seventeenth Century* by Francis Parkman, a copy much used, much studied, but still hanging together. He opened the cover and read the name of John Shipman Jr. written in blue ink.

He consulted a report on his desk and noted that the book had been in the right pocket of the sportcoat. He put it in the right pocket of his own coat and walked around his office pacing slowly and with a false air of detachment, as he sometimes did during conferences with his subordinates or when defense lawyers came in to make a deal.

He added some bounce to his step, such as he imagined might jiggle the gait of a twenty-one-year-old black man. During this imitation of the ghetto walk he was unaware of the book. He stopped and tapped his fingertips on his pocket, feeling the book inside almost as if he wanted to be certain it was still there. He said aloud: "Hm!" He felt natural with this book. He went to the window to look out on Courthouse Square six stories below. The square was nothing but an expanse of cement desolation in winter. His eye found the place, between a potted tree and an abstract steel sculpture, where Shipman's barbecue stand did a thriving business at noon-hour in the summer months. He removed the book from his pocket. He hadn't felt a thing. What he learned by this experiment was that the book going into his pocket didn't change him.

Leaning over the safe he put a hand inside and groped around till his fingers touched a hard object, a yellow-handled switchblade. He dropped it into the pocket where the book had been and it landed with an impact he could feel.

He didn't have to walk around or hold his psyche in readiness for subtle changes. It was already plain that the knife was alien to him and made its presence known throughout his body. Carrying it was like the first few minutes of carrying a gun.

He reached in and took it in his hand, keeping the hand in the pocket. He removed it and pressed the switch and the thing tried to spring out of his hand. It snapped open with a click, transforming itself and making a second change in the way Sam Lovico felt.

He closed the blade and released it again and listened to its clean and evil sound. It felt more lethal than a gun.

Then, closing the blade, taking care lest he cut his palm, he dropped the knife into his left pocket, took the book and slid it into the right, and stood still. He then reversed the objects in his pockets. He put both hands in his pockets and stood up on his toes a couple of times whistling the first few bars of the "Toreador" aria. Each hand held its object.

The conclusion of this second experiment was that placing both objects on his person at the same time made him feel strange.

He returned the book and knife to their place of safety and went out for lunch.

With his gloved hands buried deep in the pockets of his topcoat and the coat buttoned all the way up to the red scarf at his throat he moved along the thronged sidewalks, observing how fast people go in cold windy weather. A wool tweed hat that he had purchased nine tenths for warmth and one tenth for fashion reached down to the narrow ring of white hair that went around the back of his head. His feet in their polished black shoes swung lightly along the pavements. "Just so long as I don't have to bend my knees," he said to himself, conscious of a springy feeling in his legs.

He had a mobile affectionate face. When he nodded and smiled to people he knew, chiefly lawyers, judges and others often to be seen around the courts, including especially the young female clerks and stenographers, and most especially the young women lawyers, for whom he had a weakness that he concealed from them, these people always believed he liked them. They believed that among the run of mankind he liked them more than most. The exception was the criminal lawyers, that small corps of men in the city who devoted their full time to criminal defense work. These men knew that in Lovico's cosmology they were assigned to the same category as their clients, and they resented this and called it unprofessional. Lovico's smile for the members of the criminal defense bar from the richest to the most desperate was a declaration of genial contempt, and he loved to meet them on the street in order to make this declaration. Doing so never spoiled his lunch. In the courtroom he was a master of the silent art of communicating this emotion to the jury by means to which no objection could be raised.

Toward stupid judges his attitude was sympathetic and humane — not really condescending. He saw in their position what his own would be if he were drafted into the engineering profession in wartime and required to design an airplane. He knew these shortfall judges had gotten where they were by voluntary means, by blind ambition and not by a draft, and that they willingly took the emoluments of office and prevented abler

lawyers from rising, but his feeling of fellowship was not affect-
ed. He saw their predicament as something like an accident.
Being endowed as they were they could not have known in
advance what the weight of their duties would be. Toward that
rarest of all the types and individuals he encountered, the intelligent hard-working judge, the truly wise judge, he was happy to
extend all the respect at his command. This was a considerable
amount of respect. He was always ready to respect and to like a
man or woman and see their problems.

He was a stranger to envy. He had decided not to pursue a
political career sometime in the 1950s after concluding he might
waste ten or fifteen years in menial boring jobs and still get
nowhere in the end. He had believed there was a ballot prejudice
against Italian names, while in this city there was no Italian vot-
ing bloc to offset it. This decision may have been an error but it
was not one he regretted today.

He renounced a career in corporate and tax law, and any
career with a big firm, because he wanted life.

He declined a place on the appeals bench when it was offered
by the governor only two years ago because — he said this distinctly to himself — he sensed in every cell the superiority of the
power he already had to the poor unpredictable happenstance
power of a judge.

These renunciations made plenty of room for respect where
respect was due. He could respect whom he chose and like whom
he chose. His only vice was power.

He was the right man in the right job, which was deputy district attorney at the head of a staff of sixty lawyers. He was
responsible to a district attorney elected and regularly re-elected
by the people for his Irish name, his white eyebrows and blue
eyes and his genuine humility. Being responsible to this boss was
like being responsible for one's retarded nephew.

Lovico in his early fifties was one of those men and women
whose days are a stream of initiatives, acts and decisions, whose
influence is seldom felt because it is so pervasive. They live on a
plateau. In one sense or another they are high most of the time.
Events come and go swiftly but their mental speed is faster than

the speed of events; so they learn. They seldom make a mistake twice. The swiftness of their life is itself a teacher. They gradually awaken to a recognition that others know less than they; moving amidst events, by careful and often reluctant steps they see that they can do what others cannot. Over the course of a year or two they test this realization, which at first they are inclined to suspect. They enter into the fullness of their powers when they find it objectively confirmed. This is when they ascend the plateau. There is no mystique, rather the absence of mystique. They use their power without histrionics, and they care about power itself, the pure thing, and not about credit or publicity. These latter may be means to an end but the end is always power.

Lovico lunched this day with another such man, Lieutenant Michael Kennelly, officer in charge of the Police Department's Internal Affairs section. Kennelly more than any other officer, more even than the chief, was guard of the guards. He seemed to be a man without personality; he was all job. Nobody loved Kennelly but his wife. Lovico had no wife.

Neither man took alcohol at lunch and neither noticed that the sauces were out of a jar and the cooking out of an industrial handbook. They talked mostly of politics and the city. Their discussion followed a short tangent to the matter at hand: the death of John Shipman Jr.

They agreed that the mayor would maintain a mountainous silence for hours or days, promising however to answer questions on the subject at his next regular press conference. The mayor did not hold regular press conferences. While the media steamed up, or until they forgot the case, the mayor would test the atmospheric pressure. If necessary he would choose a propitious moment and express his confidence in the police, using the language of loyalty. He would credit the chief with reducing certain categories of crime and say that he, the mayor, like all citizens, awaited the outcome of the police investigation and medical examiner's inquest. He would ask the reporters how far they expected police officers to go in endangering their lives while disarming a dangerous suspect in a dark alley, implying that the reporters would be happy if seven or eight police officers were murdered every week.

The chief of police, appealing to the same majority as the mayor, would confound the reporters and drive the editorial writers nuts with two or three sentences whose involuted syntax only a fool would attempt to untangle. Understanding that friendly newspapers and television stations are more dangerous than hostile ones, the chief's statement would say nothing that could be falsified but would contain, half-hidden in its linguistic labyrinth, a word or phrase addressed to the public, for example "armed suspect" and "the good people of this city." If he were particularly bold the chief might mention "the good people of the West Side," showing he was so broad-minded as to admit under pressure that blacks could be "good." His clear meaning would be that good people would make one thing of the case and bad people another.

Both the mayor and the chief, without of course naming the game, would treat the case as a routine police killing and attempt to muster a constituency in the city that would treat it the same way, or else ignore it altogether, which came to the same thing.

If an organized protest emerged from the black neighborhoods there were two or three black politicians in City Hall and the state Capitol who could be depended on to turn it to personal advantage and thus take away its meaning.

When the conversation reached this stage Lovico and Kennelly went silent for some moments and drank their coffee, looking around the restaurant, thinking silent thoughts and watching women.

"And so —" Lovico began, as if the time had come to say what it all meant.

Lieutenant Kennelly contemplated this animated bust of a political performer. What he saw before him, he felt convinced, was an actor. The man had a legal education and twenty-five years' experience as a prosecutor but he was an actor nonetheless. Kennelly looked at the huge, sagging, sparkling brown eyes, at the unmistakable signs that Lovico was already enjoying the speech he was about to deliver. He stared for a second longer at the teeth which were neither white nor lined up in even rows, but which were presented to his gaze in an unashamed smile. Lovico's was an intellect that saw life as a half-grotesque comedy startled from time to time by gongs of horror.

"And so," Lovico said, "the mayor is not responsible. I mean of course responsible for justice. He could try to lead public opinion if he cared to, but does he care to? Ha. Otherwise he is only an administrative officer of city government. Am I right? The mayor is a figurehead with a bloated figure and a little head. The medical examiner is a mere technician. Now we come to the chief of police, your leader and your role-model. The chief is responsible but depends entirely on you. He will do and must do what you recommend since his mind will be formed by what you tell him. And lastly the district attorney, whose mind cannot be formed, depends on me."

Again by slow degrees Lovico's features were transformed from a solemn to a comic mask. "Now," he said.

"Don't bother," Kennelly interrupted.

"Don't bother what?" asked Lovico shocked and startled.

"Asking what you're going to ask," Kennelly said.

"So you already know. And people say cops are stupid."

"People say lawyers are ghouls."

"If you think I want to take over the investigation," said Lovico, "you're wrong. Each of us must conduct his own independent investigation."

"The chief'll be glad to hear it."

"Tell him, by all means. I respect the chief, I respect the police and I respect boundaries. But there is no reason, you know, that we can't work in cooperation."

Kennelly said: "Here it comes. Do I say it or do you?"

"Why don't you."

"O.K. All you want is first crack at the three cops."

"Exactly."

"Not that you think I'd screw it up."

"No, I do not think that. In fact, Mike, I respect your skill at breaking spirits."

"And I respect how quick you jump to conclusions."

"Well, you're an Irishman and should have been a Jesuit. In fact the three cops will be more scared of you than of me and that's the reason I should go first. My standard of proof is higher and they know it."

"But you have another reason, I think."

"Why do you think I have another reason?"

"The first one is flimsy. Sam, excuse my asking, do we need this fucking opera? What's your real reason?"

"Hmm. My other reason, I'm compelled to say, is flimsy too. I intend to study the boy."

"What boy?"

"The victim," said Lovico blandly.

"What victim?"

"The twenty-one-year-old black male suspect who seems to be dead, and who is no longer a suspect as I am told."

"We arrested another guy for the rape this morning," Lieutenant Kennelly said expressionlessly.

"I'm glad to hear it."

"'Study him.' What does that mean?"

"Just a few hours is all, but I'll do it, is the point, and you won't. This is a division of labor. I'll be prepared to interview the officers in a way you won't, because we proceed differently because we are different men, and exploiting the differences can make a stronger investigation. There's nothing wrong with saying so. You for example can make a credible threat of suspension or discharge to the officers and I can't. They know that. They know all I can do is issue a charge or do nothing, and any charge I issue must be sustained to a jury or I look like a chump. It isn't whether I believe in the knife, it's whether a single member of the jury has a single doubt of guilt because of the knife. That's obviously the utility of the knife to the very clever man who planted it, if it was planted. That is also my great handicap, one which you don't suffer from."

"I also don't suffer from the handicap of prejudging these cops," Kennelly said.

"I am not prejudging, Mike. I am using a hypothesis to structure an investigation. I am aware that the knife has the kid's —

the suspect's — prints on it, or some marks that are probably his prints. We start by believing our cops."

Kennelly reached inside his suitcoat and Lovico said calmly: "You aren't going to shoot me, are you?"

Kennelly unfolded three sheets of paper and passed them to Lovico saying: "Yours."

Then Lieutenant Kennelly watched the big droopy eyes going back and forth and up and down over the three sheets, while the expression of Lovico's face changed from ravenous curiosity to a kind of painful fascination.

The papers were the "Use of Force" reports filed by Banes, Ruthenbeck and Temple, which had reached Kennelly's desk shortly before lunch. The dictated "narrative" was spread across the top of each sheet and the form with boxes to be checked and blanks to be filled occupied the rest.

Lovico spread the three reports like playing cards in a fan and read them a section at a time. He started with the section titled "Type of Force Used." He observed that Ruthenbeck and Banes had checked the box for "baton" while Temple had not, and that Temple had checked "punched" but Ruthenbeck and Banes had not. Tilting the papers and moving down the page he saw that only Temple had answered yes to the question: "Did suspect have visible injuries?" In "Was officer(s) injured?" Lovico learned how Banes had been knocked through the window and Ruthenbeck punched "in face, neck and body." Lovico read each man's narrative last, then looked up to see Lieutenant Kennelly's patient blue eyes upon him.

"Do you see," Lovico asked, "what I see?"

"I'm telling myself it doesn't prove anything," Kennelly replied.

"It proves nothing. It may mean a great deal. Three police officers struggling in a dark place with a man they believe to be a rapist, a pervert, wielding a knife in a desperate final attempt to eviscerate one or all of them, a man who has absolutely nothing to lose — a complete desperado — and one of the officers in his report to his superiors says nothing about the knife. 'Was suspect armed?' He doesn't check either box. He says neither yes nor no. This knife could have had his balls and he doesn't check the box!

"Mike," Lovico continued after thinking for a moment, "you haven't talked to these officers, have you?"

"No. I think they should cook for a day or so."

"Yes. It's remarkable how two nights of bad sleep will affect a man's judgment. Especially perhaps this man," Lovico said touching one of the reports. "I propose . . ." Lovico said. "Hmm. Is this the football man? Jeff Temple?"

"Yes."

"I propose a Flim and Flam approach. Not the Friend and Foe method, that would be so obvious. Instead we simply exploit a natural difference of personalities — you and I, each of us being himself, no fancy dance and no phony roles. Who knows what subtle effects the disparity might have? My message would be: 'In this office we are like chemists in a laboratory, we do nothing more than test for the elements of a criminal offense.' Your message would be: 'I'll slice your balls like pepperoni.' Once we understand this God-given difference it does make sense for me to go first. I just want a few hours to study the victim before I talk to the cops. I want to know who was killed before I try to find out how."

"I don't care who goes first," Kennelly said. "So go."

"I have a third reason, Mike, just as flimsy as the other two," Lovico said leaning so far forward that Kennelly could distinguish the pores in his nose. "I love the sound of a conspiracy cracking open. *Crack-crack.* That's not a prejudgment, only a prejudice. Ha ha ha. What a lovely sound it is. My sensual gratifications are few, Mike. I'm a widower. What else have I got?"

Chapter 13
What the Statute Provides

Sam Lovico parked behind a silver Lincoln. The brown water running in the gutter, the trampled grass and mud in the strip between the curb and sidewalk, the elm stumps and old brick houses — none of these reflected the winter sunlight as the big car did. The sun gleamed with a special affinity on this magnificent object.

Lovico surmised it belonged to the slumlord; he peered into its dark tinted window to see if there was a man inside. Then he read the insignia *JS* on the driver's door. His mind, his stomach and intestines translated the letters. He stood there for a second wondering whether to go on, then mounted the concrete steps as briskly as a man can whose knees have lost their youth. He went up the walk to the house, opened the door and found the slumlord waiting for him by the mailboxes. The slumlord was short white and unhappy.

"Are you — who are you?" he asked.

"I'm Sam Lovico, deputy district attorney," Lovico declared and produced his credential.

"Let's see the search warrant."

"I do not have," Lovico said with the display of artificial patience he always made for the benefit of jailhouse lawyers, "and I do not need a search warrant."

"His property's still in there," the slumlord said, shifting the ground of his objection.

"If I remove anything I will be guilty of theft. You will be guilty of nothing. Please take me to the apartment."

In Lovico's expression the slumlord could see exactly where he stood. At such moments the money was never quite enough.

They went up two flights, Lovico following and observing that the heels on the slumlord's shoes had been worn down on the outsides by his bowlegged style of locomotion. Following this man's revolving buttocks was an unpleasant experience in itself. Lovico dropped back and watched this ball of humanity and textiles laboring upward, raising squeaks and cracking sounds from the wood. This was the sort of building in which Lovico did not put his hand on the banister.

As they went along the third-floor hallway the slumlord began unfurling a ring of keys on a springloaded wire that he drew from a leather case on his belt.

Lovico said: "Just a minute, please. Is this the door?"

The slumlord said it was and made a sign of protest as Lovico raised his hand to knock. The landlord said: "There won't be anybody in. He lived alone."

Lovico listened and could hear nothing except the slumlord's breathing. He knocked a second time.

The slumlord brandished his key and Lovico interposed his hand.

They stood thus, Lovico seeming to restrain the fat man, when they heard the scrape of the chain along its track.

The door opened and Lovico confronted a tall black man of about his own age, more youthful than he but with iron-gray hair, who stood much taller than Lovico even though he had no shoes on. He had been asleep in his clothes which were rumpled but expensive. One of his front shirt-tails was out, the other in; his sleeveless cashmere sweater was unbuttoned.

The slumlord demanded the black man's name.

In Lovico's categories a slumlord and a criminal defense lawyer were pretty much the same. He wouldn't for a minute deny that the legal system needed defense lawyers or that defendants were entitled to their invaluable services. And he would concede that slumlords were necessary too. If the whole fraternity were poisoned and buried at midnight others would fill the ranks by dawn. They were necessary in that sense. If Lovico were driven to the wall on this question he might have argued that Judas Iscariot was necessary for the fulfillment of the prophesies, but it were better for Judas had he never been born. It wasn't just power he liked; he had a hunger for righteousness.

The black man said calmly: "My name is John Shipman."

In that face strained by fatigue and afflicted by — something else — Sam Lovico thought he saw patience, possibly even sympathy for the slumlord who had put his question in a nasty aggressive tone. This was Lovico's first scrap of information on John Shipman, this agreeing to let the slumlord be what he was. The surprise was that Shipman didn't hate him for being white or a slumlord. Lovico thought: "How interesting." And the next surprise was that John Shipman, whom everybody in law enforcement knew by reputation, had a well-defined presence, as a minister or a legislator should. Lovico thought: "This man runs a boot joint?"

"I'm the landlord, your son's landlord. We extend — my wife and I — sympathy . . ."

Shipman gravely shook the man's hand, and turned to Lovico.

Here then was the beginning.

"I am the deputy district attorney, Mr. Shipman. My name is Lovico. L-O-V-I-C-O. I am here because it is my responsibility to make a recommendation to the district attorney in the death of your son. You are the father of John Shipman Jr.?"

"I am."

"It was you who identified the body this morning?"

"It was."

"I came here to look at your son's apartment."

"To search it, you mean," said John Shipman. There was a calm resonance and reserve in the man's voice.

"No I do not mean search it. I mean look at it. To search it I would take it apart, which I have no intention of doing, sir. Nor will I ask my investigators to do so. I want to look at it."

"You can certainly do that, Mr. — will you give me your name again?"

"Lovico." And he spelled it again.

"You may look at the apartment, but why?"

Again Lovico couldn't help noticing the man's calm and rumbling voice which seemed to come out of a cave. He might have been an actor at the height of his career playing Othello. But he was not. Lovico too could read eyes. These were the eyes of a father whose son has been beaten to death. Lovico almost turned away but his conscience told him: "Stay. Go on." He said:

"I want to know more about your son than I will read in the police reports."

"And there will be an autopsy report," Shipman said and the word autopsy had a hissing quality. "You can read that too."

"Yes."

"That will say," the black man continued, "how my son was killed. How they beat him."

"Yes."

"How they cornered him," continued the tall man slowly, with steady eyes, "and beat him and then beat him again for practice."

"It will identify the — pardon the directness of my language, Mr. Shipman, but I will try to respond accurately — it will identify and describe the physiological mechanism of his death."

"The mechanism — we know what that was. Three — white — what you call police officers."

Lovico stood in silence. He did not try to stare the man down. He waited and he looked somewhere else, and after giving the bigger man an interval for reflection he looked back at him directly.

For Sam Lovico this was a problem in physical inferiority. But everybody has one problem or another and Lovico had dealt with this business of being small and weak since boyhood. He could appreciate the greater strength of the other man because he didn't fear it and because the world has been redesigned by smart people to nullify strength.

Shipman stepped aside, still looking reservedly, directly into Lovico's eyes and Lovico returned his gaze without antagonism or fear. The slumlord disappeared. Sam Lovico entered the apartment. He looked around the living room, deliberately detaching

his gaze from Shipman's. He listened to the door close and listened for the chain to slide on its rail, but this didn't happen.

He started in the bedroom, where he saw bedding that was
neat and clean, albeit on the floor. He saw neat stacks of cloth-
ing on a sheet spread on the floor and he observed with interest
the monastic simplicity of the whole place. In the bathroom he
found the same simplicity and economy. Opening the medicine
chest Lovico found it quite empty. He sensed John Shipman following him. He turned.

Shipman stood leaning against the door frame with his arms
folded and an expression almost of derision on his face. The
shirt-tail was still loose and the sweater unbuttoned. Lovico
noticed his skin was very black, but the son's had been described
as light brown.

"Did your son live here or simply keep this as a place away
from home?"

"You mean a place to screw. You think niggers screw all the
time."

"Actually, Mr. Shipman, I do not mean that. Isn't it true that
young men often seek an escape from their father's authority and
the atmosphere of their father's house, while also being not quite
willing to cut themselves off by moving out. That's what I
meant."

The father said simply: "He lived here."

Lovico glanced into the kitchen and then went where he had
wanted to go at the start, to the desk in the living room. He read
the four quotations on the wall, including the one from John
Shipman Sr., and the titles of the dozen books piled on the desk,
then said to Shipman: "Do you mind if I go through his desk?"

The father at that moment was seating himself on the only
chair in the room, other than the one at the desk, swinging it back
between his legs. He leaned forward with his arms on the chair
back, never taking his all-observant eyes off his visitor. He said:
"Go ahead."

There wasn't much in the desk drawers.

Lovico opened the spiral notebook, read the title and turned a
few leaves at random. He read:

"Sneak baptisms. Jesuits flick water and mumble prayers over dying Huron babies and deny to parents they did it. Triumph by treachery of one superstition over another." The superstition to which the writer referred, of course, was Roman Catholicism, Lovico's religion.

There followed two references to a book by Francis Parkman, the same book Lovico had put into his pocket that morning.

Seeing a few shreds of paper caught inside the spiral Lovico guessed some pages had been torn out of the back of the book, but he didn't mention it. Neither did he forget it.

"May I borrow this?" Lovico asked, closing the notebook.

"My son was not a drug dealer, Mr. Lovico. That's his school book."

"May I borrow it?"

"Why?"

"I've told you."

"Maybe I've got a poor memory. I don't remember anything you said about why you need to read my son's school books."

"I said I want to know more about him and this is a good place to look. Mr. Shipman, I will not spare your feelings. The question in my mind is, Was he the kind of boy who would carry a switchblade knife?"

"And even I don't know the answer to that," Shipman said. "Take the book."

John Shipman watched this peculiar man moving slowly about the apartment, not quite understanding where the opinion came from that he was telling the truth. He was a little man with a big head that looked as if it had just been washed and polished. He had a hat in one hand and Hawk's book in the other. He had big features on his face — a huge hooked nose, bags under his eyes, loose red eye sockets, a beard shadow and a wide mouth with coffee- and tobacco-stained teeth. When he paused to read or look at something his lower teeth showed.

"What do you mean," Shipman asked, "you make a recommendation?"

Lovico stopped. He would have unbuttoned his topcoat, being hot, but he was ready to leave now. He tucked the notebook under his arm, pulled his scarf, waved it, and stuffed it into his pocket. He said: "The district attorney is empowered by law to issue criminal charges. I tell him in a given case whether I believe he should or should not."

"If you and your boss agree there shouldn't be a charge, there won't be one. Just you two."

"Just him, in law. Just the two of us, in fact. You're correct."

"If I say my son was murdered, and you say it was self-defense, nobody is charged with anything."

"The statute provides that a judge may issue a criminal complaint in the presence of the district attorney if the district attorney refuses, but I must tell you that never happens. — Incidentally murder, Mr. Shipman, is a compound of two separate acts, the physical act of causing the death of a human being and the prior mental act of forming the intention to kill, the 'mental purpose,' as the law says, to kill. — Yes, it is the district attorney's decision, upon my recommendation."

"Two things, Mr. Lovico. One, don't get hung up on the knife. I don't care if he did have a knife. Two, I am going to have justice."

With that last word justice a look passed between the two men as if an electric bolt had been slowed to zero speed, and suspended.

"Mr. Shipman, I will speak to you in the same spirit. I will not flinch from your grief."

But Lovico stopped. He looked into the eyes of the black man and saw a perfect self-possession.

Lovico said: "I do care if he had a knife. And I care about justice too. Justice is my duty. When you speak of justice, Mr. Shipman, remember I must be able to prove what I charge. I don't go to court with a belief, even a strong belief. If I go, I go with a criminal charge every element of which I must prove to a jury."

Shipman said: "I hear you saying it doesn't matter what they did to my son. I hear you saying what matters is what you can prove in court."

"That's all the justice I can get for you."

"That isn't justice."

"Mr. Shipman, nothing can —"

"Don't tell me nothing can bring him back!"

The perfect composure of the man cracked.

Lovico turned away, placed his hat and the notebook on the desk, and wrote his home telephone number on one of his printed business cards. He took long enough, he believed, to let Shipman wipe his eyes. He took a few seconds more to pick up the notebook and put his hat on. When he turned back to Shipman he met the same black-crystal eyes.

He gave him the card — looking closely at the eyes and being quite sure now that the man hadn't cracked at all — and said, "Call me at any time."

Shipman looked at the card indifferently. He got up, swinging the chair forward with a lithe movement, and led the way to the door.

"Let me add," Lovico said, "that it makes no difference to me that these men are police officers. I am working like a chemist in his laboratory, testing for the presence of certain elements, in this case the elements of a crime. I simply don't care whether the men who might be involved are policemen."

John Shipman opened the door. He did not hold out his hand. He said: "I don't care either."

Chapter 14
What Is a Thing?

Sam Lovico drove down Majestic to First and turned left, and parked behind Shipman's Barbecue. He went in and ordered coffee, standing at the front windows and watching the traffic. He walked to the place where John Shipman Jr. had died and examined every relevant aspect of it. He drove back downtown. Crossing the bridge, with the West Side spread out behind him in the mirror, he seemed to be heading into the high ramparts of a Roman citadel of the future.

He left the freeway on a descending ramp that turned 270 degrees right to enter Harkness Street, which he could follow to the Courthouse. Now the man drove in the foot-trail of the boy. When his mother had first allowed him to ride the bus downtown alone, on his ninth birthday, he had walked up Harkness Street to a hobby shop with a model train room in the back. If there was anything beautiful in the city today, except for some of the old churches, and houses falling into ruin on streets like Majestic, it was hidden like the train room. The river retained its contour and nothing else. Apart from these gentle lines and a few trees surviving along the banks he had seen nothing to gladden him from the time he left the Barbecue. Majestic in the teeth of its filth decay and danger still offered a tint of human consideration. Whereas downtown all was steel, glass, space, cement, and a crude pretense of ascetic power. He drove into the alley between the Courthouse and the Police Administration Building and parked against a brick wall where a sign reserved his space.

He returned the knife to the custodian of evidence but kept the Parkman book and put it in his briefcase with the notebook. He worked until 6:30, ate dinner in a restaurant somewhat better than the place where he and Kennelly had lunched, and read the *New York Times*, the *Wall Street Journal* and the local newspaper. This carried an account of the Shipman case on page one of the second section, including a picture of John Shipman Jr. evidently taken from his high school yearbook. After drinking another cup of coffee Lovico bade goodnight to the waiter and cashier, and went home.

He opened the notebook and read the first two pages by the lamp in his den even before removing his coat and hat.

"They lived on elevated land surrounded by swamps. Slash and burn agriculture. Clear woods, plant corn. Harsh climate. Swamp all around. Swamp! I never saw one. I will find a swamp and take off my clothes and wade in. I will know the Hurons better."

This struck Lovico with particular force because he himself had once sunk into a swamp during a fishing trip to the Menomonee lands in Wisconsin. He was in up to his groin before he could catch a branch and stop his ghastly descent.

He turned a page and examined a photocopy of a map that John Shipman Jr. had pasted into the notebook. It showed the Huron country east of the Georgian Bay of Lake Huron, with firm ground projecting in numerous lobes into a maze of rivers, lakes and swamps.

"Young women sexually free, go with any man they choose. Jesuits condemned. Save these savages from sex!"

Lovico thought: "Maybe it was the Jesuits who had need to be saved." For a few minutes his sexual hunger simulated that of a Jesuit living celibate among the Hurons. He hoped it would go away.

He took off his coat and hat and went to a cabinet, slid a door and selected a tape. Soon the room was filled with sacred music written for the organ by J. S. Bach a century after the Hurons first encountered a white man.

"First insult, their very name. *Huron*: derivative of Old French for lout, knave, ruffian. You can't trust these bristly-headed boar-heads, colored aborigines. Huron equals NIGGER."

A few lines down Lovico read: "Their real name: Wendat."

"*Permanent* Jesuit mission established 1634. Epidemics begin the same year. Population halved in five years. Traditions weakened. Jesuit conversions easier.

"Before the coming of the Jesuits these people did not fear death. Along comes a religion *based on death*. A religion of sin propagated by representatives of the Inquisition.

"In Huron belief a little baby who dies is buried on a path or trail so he may *jump up into the womb* of a passing woman and have a second chance at life. Cool idea!

"Older people die, travel on Milky Way. Meet the brain sucker who makes a hole in skull and sucks out your brain. Not bad, better than Freud. Cross a raging torrent guarded by toothy dog. Somehow get across on slippery log. Enter village of the dead, and live again. What's wrong with that?"

Lovico turned the page and began reading references to Iroquois attacks on the Hurons, the aim being to block the Hurons' access to the St. Lawrence River and exclude them from the lucrative trade in furs with the French in Montreal and Quebec.

John Shipman Jr. had written: "A war inspired by a greed unknown before the French came. Huron tribe divided in factions, pro-French, anti-French. This when unity against Iroquois invaders critical, necessary, vital. Iroquois now burning Huron villages. War aim: destroy Huron tribe, get fur-bearing lands.

"Hurons degraded. *They ask the Jesuits what to do.* Obsequious. Degrading. Don't do that! Iroquois attacks intensify."

A few pages deeper into the notebook Lovico found this:

"Argument. (Magna cum laude by the balls.) Hurons held their own against Iroquois through generations of wars before French came. Sometimes win sometimes lose, always maintain tribal life. What is different now? Iroquois side: intoxication of greed, economics, a new passion. Origin French. *Huron side*:

doubts, dissension, their culture condemned, their religion scorned, their babies baptized. Sources of strength polluted. Origin of these woes and weaknesses *French*.

"The Hurons are scattered. And victory in war avails the Iroquois nothing.

"Plague of smallpox, plague of war, plague of French.

"Tribe dispersed east and west, religion gone, language gone. What did a Huron ever say? Nobody will ever know. They are a lost people."

There followed a list of references, then notes on village life and life in the long houses — and a list of the Huron clans: Beaver, Bear, Turtle, Wolf, Deer, Hawk, Porcupine and Snake. The clan-name Hawk was underlined three times and followed by "!!!!!" and Lovico wondered what this emphasis signified.

"In Huron custom, treason and witchcraft with intent to kill: guilty one placed 'outside the law' and anyone may kill him. Witches who refuse to remove a spell or can't are executed on orders of the council or chief. If these are savages so are the Puritans of Salem."

Lovico thought he would not wish to oppose John Shipman Jr. in a court of law.

Then he read: "Murder must be avenged. *Or paid off.*"

At this point Lovico wondered whether the young man's father had read the notebook. "Murder must be avenged."

He came to a section on torture, under the general heading: "The Iroquois Enemy."

"Captured Iroquois warrior taken to Huron village and adopted into Huron family. They call him brother. Torture begins. Men, women, children. Around a fire and torture platform. Days. It says days. Concentrate their fierce hate on this bound mutilated man. He sings as long as he can to prove the bravery, valor, strength of his tribe. When dead they eat him. Chief gets heart. They call him nephew during torture. Iroquois did this sort of thing too."

Now came a reference to the Parkman book. Lovico took it from his briefcase and turned to the referenced page. Reading back a few pages to get the context he came to a sentence underlined in the familiar blue ink. Parkman had written:

"These Canadian tribes were undergoing that process of exter-
mination, absorption, or expatriation, which, as there is reason to
believe, had for many generations formed the gloomy and meaningless history of the greater part of this continent."

The blue-ink comment in the margin: "Gloomy and meaningless? Like the European wars? Like the religious wars of
Christendom? Like WWI?"

Lovico now approached the referenced passage but his cheat-
ing eye strayed down the page and he read: "Look at me . . . you
cannot make me wince." Here is the passage John Shipman Jr. had
marked, and his comment upon it. The passage narrates the home-
coming of an Iroquois war party.

> On the morrow, they entered the town, leading the captive
> Algonquins, fast bound, and surrounded by a crowd of men,
> women, and children, all singing at the top of their throats. The
> largest lodge was ready to receive them; and as they entered, the
> victims read their doom in the fires that blazed on the earthen floor,
> and in the aspect of the attendant savages, whom the Jesuit Fathers
> call attendant demons, that waited their coming. The torture which
> ensued was but preliminary, designed to cause all possible suffer-
> ing without touching life . . .

> On the following morning, they were placed on a large scaffold,
> in sight of the whole population. It was a gala-day. Young and old
> were gathered from far and near. Some mounted the scaffold, and
> scorched them with torches and firebrands; while the children,
> standing beneath the bark platform, applied fire to the feet of the
> prisoners between the crevices. The Algonquin women were told
> to burn their husbands and companions; and one of them obeyed,
> vainly thinking to appease her tormentors. The stoicism of one of
> the warriors enraged his captors beyond measure. "Scream! why
> don't you scream?" they cried, thrusting their burning brands at
> his naked body. "Look at me," he answered; "you cannot make
> me wince. If you were in my place, you would screech like
> babies." At this they fell upon him with redoubled fury, till their
> knives and firebrands left in him no semblance of humanity. He
> was defiant to the last, and when death came to his relief, they tore
> out his heart and devoured it; then hacked him in pieces, and made
> their feast of triumph on his mangled limbs.

The comment of John Shipman Jr.: "Man is the steadfast creator. At the pinnacle of pain and in the darkest valley and pit of distress, when they are turning him into a piece of meat, when they try to take him away from himself and *thing* him, he creates his soul. This is his highest work performed and achieved in the extremity of pain, desolation and *fear*."

In the margin of the same page Lovico saw a number. He flipped a hundred pages forward and read the account of a Jesuit whose endurance under torture until death was also perfect. John Shipman Jr. had written in the margin: "I recognize in this misguided missionary a *man*." Lovico smiled and indeed Lovico felt something like relief.

Another reference directed him to a page where Parkman had written: "The truth is, that, with some of these missionaries, one may throw off trash and nonsense by the cart-load, and find under it all a solid nucleus of saint and hero."

The commentary here was more difficult to read than usual because John Shipman Jr. had written a few sentences and then crossed them out, started again in a tighter space and continued on the next page. His comment:

"What is this trash you speak of but the religion, the fire, and the zeal of these men? Without all that you would not get your saint and hero.

"In all respect to the greatest American historian: the tortured Algonquin pulled his manhood out of a *primitive superstition*, you would call it. The Jesuit pulled his out of *trash and nonsense*.

"Don't you wonder, as I do, how they created this most valuable essence out of the crazy illusions of their unsophisticated minds?

"I have the answer. I have the answer! It is not the faith so much as the power that creates the faith. It is the power of mankind — the flame of humanity in both the Algonquin and the Jesuit. And in you, sir, and in me. May fate spare me from the anvil of torture and from the rack of disease on which you were stretched. May it also spare me the blindness and malice of racial bigotry."

Sam Lovico woke at three that morning tormented by the absolute certainty that John Shipman Jr. had been carrying the switchblade;

tormented by the missing pages. Somebody had ripped out — the father! — John Shipman Sr. had ripped out something incriminating.

But when he got up at seven he felt tranquil. He took a shower, shaved, relieved himself and, being still undressed, took another quick shower, in order to have it between himself and his time on the stool. He dressed in his lawyer clothes, went downstairs and made himself a poached egg, whole wheat toast and freshly ground coffee. He ate an orange. He sat at the little booth in the bay window projecting into the little back yard, with the sun striking the tablecloth so brilliantly that he had to shield his eyes as he looked for birds at the feeder. His wife had put the bird feeder up. They had used to breakfast here in the months after their daughter left for California, and talk about her, asking more questions about her than either could answer from her infrequent and brief letters, asking What is she doing now? Lovico placed his tape recorder on the table. He wanted to send a letter to John Shipman Sr.:

"Sir — It would be no great crime to carry a knife in that part of the city — but it is illegal — I am fully convinced your son was not armed with a knife —"

Of course he did not dictate that letter. Instead he pushed the switch and talked into the machine to this effect:

"Dear Mr. Shipman: I urge you to delay any conclusions you might feel inclined to reach until more facts become available as to the nature of your son's injuries and the manner in which they were inflicted. I most particularly urge you to attend the medical examiner's inquest which will be held in open session, and to take careful note of all the testimony and exhibits to be brought forth at that time. Paragraph. The district attorney's office serves as special counsel to the medical examiner in cases of this kind. I will therefore be afforded an early opportunity to place all parties to this matter under oath and to raise all questions and explore all material pertinent to your son's tragic death. The inquest will commence within a few days. I will give you ample warning."

Chapter 15
The Fat Lady

Temple didn't have the contacts. If he inquired at the Rescue Mission or a homeless shelter or some place like that they'd cover her trail right before his eyes, because to them he'd be nothing but a racist cop. He didn't know what to do, so he just cruised the West Side. All he had was her nickname, Darlin, which he got from the security guard at the McDonald's where Ruthenbeck had relieved her of her knife. Even if he saw her he wasn't sure he'd recognize her. It was futile and stupid but he kept it up, cruising. He knew what the alternative was.

"Check that box!"

The voice beamed it into his ear like a bee sting. And so he cruised in the oil burner through blocks and miles and square miles of urban Hades and created a fair illusion that he was actually searching for the fat lady.

It had to end soon, when his Relief took the duty at three. They would yank him off the Tac Squad and put him on Traffic; then the great Jeff Temple, All-American, would be passing out speeding tickets and giving safety lectures.

And it happened exactly like that.

He reacted to the insult by issuing only three tickets in his entire shift, and the sergeant reprimanded him. That night Temple slept the sleep of the minor key. Images went outward and played at the borders of chaos even as his body restored itself. In the morning he continued searching. His mind had not restored itself. "Check that box!"

"I'm not afraid. I'll do it — I just —"

It wasn't that he hoped ultimately to see the fat lady filling the witness stand, identifying her knife and exploding Ruthenbeck's lies. He knew she was as good as worthless before a jury. His hope rather was to walk into Lovico's office at the appointed time this afternoon with the fat lady in company and invite her to describe the knife a police officer had taken from her last summer. Whether or not a jury would believe her, Lovico might.

Temple went into the West Side Gardens. He would probably be safe enough so long as he wasn't recognized. He wore blue jeans, an old shirt and a tan windbreaker. He also wore kicking shoes, leather clodhoppers that laced up to the ankles and had hard rubber soles. Each was a weapon in itself. He didn't carry a gun.

West Side Gardens was lightly patrolled; police cars hardly ever went in. The streets were obstructed by asphalt speed bumps six inches high running clear across and slowing cars to a walk. Thus if a cop got into trouble in the middle of the maze and called for help he'd have a long wait.

As Temple's Ford lurched over the first bump he looked in upon his mind and found its workings ludicrous. This odd-shaped Jeff was looking for his friend the fat lady.

"You'll never find her. You don't even know what she looks like."

Here was a man who had scarcely known a black person before he started his career as the "Bombcatcher" at Ohio State. Then he'd known them by the dozens on the football field and in the locker room — seldom as real friends — but to know a man by blocking and tackling him, and by racing away to prevent his tackling you — this was really to know him.

The car came thudding down off the bump. He gave it a little gas and drove past a dumpster where some girls were playing jump-rope, with one end of the rope tied to the dumpster. A girl about Robbie's age was swinging the rope and chanting with her playmates. Her eyes showed that she enjoyed swinging the rope for her friends as much as jumping. Temple couldn't make out the chant. The girl lingered visibly in his mind. The weather was warm and sunny, and everybody was out, dressed in winter clothes and soaking up the sun. They were standing around in groups, sitting on their back steps, and some of them glanced in his direction.

"They see white people in here all the time," said Temple. He was thinking of social workers, probation officers and such. "My God," he couldn't help thinking, "why don't these people work?" He knew some of the answers to that question and had argued the answers to people like Ruthenbeck — but here they stood, in fives and sixes, in tens, dozens and scores — mostly women and kids, it was true, but there were men among them and a great many teenaged boys. Evidently school didn't figure. They looked through him or didn't look at him at all.

He felt it now more keenly than ever, their difference. Everybody is different from everybody else. He couldn't even touch his own wife. He knew she'd be his wife forever and that he'd never touch her again — different, gone. But this other difference —

He crept over the next bump and thought about stopping but he had an idea that he would go right to the center of the maze. The place was a red-brick government-invented slum. It had the atmosphere of an institution without the order, and of a slum without the freedom.

He saw an obese woman who was obviously not his fat lady. She was ordering children around with a practiced indignation and sharp authority. He took the next bump, the Ford humped up and over, and the phrase "my friend the fat lady" went through his brain.

Temple parked and walked to a courtyard where a group of women sat around a swing. He said: "Hello. I'm looking for a woman named Darlin." There were about eight women. Temple could not have described them very accurately. He looked at them as a group. True, if one had been on crutches, or one-armed, or naked, or white, he would have noticed. Somehow he looked at everybody while looking at nobody. There was something coming between him and his senses, which were his only contact with the world.

A woman said: "Darlin?" pronouncing the word just as Temple had done. She turned her head a little and moved her eyes back to take him in.

"She's an addict. She's large, about thirty. I just want to talk. She's not in any trouble."

"Anybody know a Darlin?" the woman asked, and nobody did.

A little boy asked Temple if he was an undercover po-lice and Temple said he was a policeman but not undercover.

"Show me your gun!"

"No. No."

"What's your name?"

He hesitated and said "Temple," a name now well known to readers of the newspapers for a new reason.

He walked around the center of the place if center it had and spoke to three or four adults about Darlin. He found himself talking to a middle-aged man, whose face again he didn't really look at, and whose monosyllabic responses he didn't really hear. He heard his own voice and knew he'd never reach this man. It occurred to him that he wasn't really searching for the fat lady, that he would never find her this way, that it made no difference whether he found her or not, and that he was excited. He went on with his search, approaching a group of boys and asking if they knew Darlin. Again he couldn't quite see how they reacted to him. As for what they suspected, there were two possibilities: he was a dealer or a cop. Temple came out of his warp and looked straight at one of the boys. The boy lifted his chin and looked back without communicating a meaning.

The sun in its infinite power spent its rays to little effect on the bricks and the brown lawns of the Gardens. The wind entered as if through cracks. Sidewalks went off at many angles and Temple lost his memory of where his car was. The slabs of faded plywood covering the windows of the vacant units evidenced the good sense of the people who had left and of those who had declined to replace them. The sun went dull as it hit the plywood.

But still in Temple's mind there was a struggling fount of energy that made him feel crazy.

Rounding the corner of a building that might have been deserted, judging from the plywood slabs covering almost every door and window, walking on a cement strip through a sea of mud newly melted by the sun, Temple came unexpectedly on his car. This heap, parked in a place he had never been, was supposedly his. He went to the driver's side and looked around at the buildings, and found a new perspective. Now he saw the walk he had followed to the first group of women by the swings. Now he pictured the woman who had said "Darlin?" with an inflection and a bemusement that were almost friendly. He could see her sympathetic but skeptical face. He remembered how she had offered to present his question for him, and remembered that she smiled at him. Was it a mocking smile? She might have been smiling at his busted pugilistic nose. People always noticed that.

During his football days, when he became a familiar figure on television and everybody said, "That guy doesn't talk like a jock, he talks like a lawyer," his twice-busted nose was about as famous in the state as anybody's nose had ever been. On television his size and power didn't come across, so people noticed the simple, correct dignity of his answers, and his broken nose.

Opening the door, placing his body in its accustomed position behind the wheel, starting the engine, which started at the touch of the key, he felt a lifting wave of absurd relief. He took the first bump a little too fast and the Ford shivered, the vibrations reaching him through thick layers of Detroit stuffing. He went slower as he came to the next bump.

The car eased itself into this obstacle like a draught horse reluctant to address a hill, and there was a loud, goading bang. Temple thought as if in protest, "I can't go any faster," and an even louder bang thundered on the car. A rock hit the right door and another flung a pattern of cracks across the rear window, which Temple saw in his mirror. The rear wheels rose to the bump and a stone bounded off the hood, hit the windshield without breaking it and was gone. Another hit the car somewhere, and then two or three more in succession, and a big piece of jagged concrete skidded across his path.

The inner voice shouted: "What did you expect? Out, fool, out!"

Driving down the freeway he was still shaking but not with fear.

"What's going on!" he cried.

Because he knew it wasn't happiness, it couldn't be. "Check the box! Check the box!"

Chapter 16
Sister Mary Joseph

Temple didn't notice, of course, and neither did Lovico, but it was a dingy office and it would depress any mind that strayed from the immediate task. The walls were insane-asylum green and the windows, though high in square-footage, somehow excluded more light than they admitted. The top of each was crossed by an ancient yellow fringe of cloth that the cleaning staff never touched for fear of shaking it to pieces. Lovico's safe, visible behind his chair, was colored an olive green suggestive of a post-World War II surplus store. There was a carpet, also best unnoticed, which used to have some kind of pattern or design. And Lovico's desk, though broad and sturdy, was an artifact of the philosophy that "form follows function."

The chair, though, Lovico's chair, which was not county property but his own, embraced the man's small and rounded body in a welcoming mold of rich black leather, and squeaked with muted pride when its owner chose to transport himself from one degree of comfort to another.

Instead of observing these details Temple kept his eye on Lovico, who was apparently toying with him. He seemed to be playing the role of a buffoon, yet this was the man who could charge him with manslaughter, second degree murder, homicide by reckless conduct, misconduct in public office, conspiracy, obstructing justice and maybe a dozen other crimes. And what if Lovico himself subscribed to the Blue Code? "If he does," Temple thought, "I can forget the fat lady."

"I remember the stories when you quit pro ball," Lovico said, spreading a headline in the air. "'Temple Quits Packers.' Giving up all that money, sacrificing a career, to come back to this dull city, which is, however, the place where life really throbs, if you know what I mean, the realest place in the country, to coach our kids, to teach kids — to build character."

Temple said nothing.

"It meant something to me personally," Lovico continued with a respectful smile, "because I'm a Benedict graduate myself. I never played football," he added lifting his arms as if to display the pathetic inadequacy of his body to the demands of any contact sport, "but I'm a Benedict man. I care more about Benedict High School than I do about my college or law school. I think about it more too. Odd, wouldn't you say?"

Temple would say nothing.

"You can tell a man's character in a single action," Lovico mused, adding: "Sometimes."

Temple again felt the pen between his fingers, hovering over the "Yes" and "No" boxes.

"Yes, one action. One revealing decision in one flashing moment. When you came back to town to coach those black kids at Benedict —"

"I just wanted to coach somebody," said Temple.

"Sure. Maybe I think about Benedict because they've boarded up the windows. When I pass it and see the boards it all comes to life in my memory as it once was. It was the best school in the city, you know, in my time, in the late '40s and early '50s. We had a few Jewish kids who went to Hebrew School after classes let out, and it occurred to me that the Jesuits and Jews have a lot in common, and if there was a Jesuit high school in town I would go to it, but I went to Benedict — strange, really, that I went to a public school considering how Catholic — my whole family tradition was against it but my father said, education, education, and as to religion my whole program was the Bible. All you need, you know, is the Bible, Shakespeare and mathematics. But no, Benedict was a hell of a school in those days. It was never tops in sports until you came along." He smiled again and seemed to take a benign attitude toward Temple's silence.

"Character revealed in a single action," Lovico hymned as if to himself. "We can misjudge. I often have. Yet I still seek the revelatory act or statement. I don't care about a person's philosophy or religion, give me action."

Here the conversation seemed to end. Temple sat so long silent, while Lovico creaked back and forth in his chair and smiled, that he believed a radical change in direction must lie just ahead and that the prosecutor would have to reveal his strategy.

"As a young kid I went to Sacred Heart grammar school," Lovico declared. "We had a teacher, Sister Mary Joseph, who took each boy and girl into an empty classroom. There you were, alone with Sister Mary Joseph, who was nothing but a pale face and beady black eyes half hidden in a black cowl, and you could see her hands too — they were pink — well! You can see how vividly I recall it, my own trial before Sister Mary Joseph. Could that be right, a pale face and pink hands? It doesn't matter, it was the total concealment of her body and even her *life* within her habit, that's what mattered. Woo! Do I remember that! It is a great advantage, believe me, in this difficult world, to have lived a Catholic childhood. You didn't have the advantage?"

Temple said, "No."

"Well if everybody had it it wouldn't be an advantage. Do you know what she made us do? Why she took us in there alone? She said, 'You must recite the Our Father or the Hail Mary. Choose which you will recite.' I presume the boys chose the Our Father, I certainly did, and the girls the Hail Mary. She said: 'Begin.' She said: 'I can see into a boy's soul when he says this prayer.' — Do you have children, Officer Temple?"

"I have a son."

"Ha! When those newspaper stories came out I wondered what your heirs were going to think when they realized how much money you were throwing away. But a wrong career — must be abandoned. A man who fails to do so or cannot do so, pardon me, abandons his soul. In the grimy halls of this public edifice, in order to preserve the holy separation of church and state, one should say he abandons his true self, not his soul. To betray yourself, I have always believed, is to leave a trail, an evidentiary trail. What do you think? Wouldn't it be useful if we had Sister Mary Joseph on the staff? 'I can see into a boy's soul when he says that prayer.'"

Neither man spoke for a while, Temple eying his tormentor and Lovico smiling and reminiscing and letting his uplifted eyes dart back and forth across the ceiling. He seemed to be watching happy scenes of childhood.

Then Lovico bent his look upon Temple and said: "You aren't very friendly."

"Neither are you," said Temple.

"Hmm. Hmm. Can that be true? I certainly feel friendly enough. You see that's what I was hinting at when I talked about a single action. You thought it was just talk but look at the case as I do — from the outside. Here's this football player — and they are supposed to be boneheads — and yet he realizes at the age of, what, twenty-four or something, that life must have a purpose, and you took the right action in spite of all temptation. You walked away from millions."

"Hardly."

"Oh yes, don't be so modest. You'll say I'm a flatterer, but you see before you a man who is prepared in all cases to disbelieve, who in your special case is prepared to believe, all because of this one action."

"You're talking about when I quit the Packers?"

"Of course."

"I had an injury. Let's not make a big melodrama of it."

"I know perfectly well you had an injury," said Lovico. "I have a couple of bad knees myself and I read about your troubles from a very personal viewpoint, believe me. But I also remember the interview in which you said something like, 'I want to coach high school ball.' You did say that, didn't you?"

"So what."

"And you could have taken a rest, and come back the next season, experimentally, as it were, am I right? The Packers wanted you to do just that. I remember it well, Officer Temple. I remember the interview with Doctor What's-His-Name. It was a big story. You may not appreciate it, but that's the fact. 'Temple Quits Packers.'"

Temple said: "Is that my Use of Force report?"

Lovico glanced at the paper in his hand, which he had been holding or waving around for quite some time, and said calmly: "Yes, of course."

"Give it to me."

Lovico complied, leaning forward and causing a little cacophony of squeaks.

Temple placed the paper on the edge of the desk, took his pen from his shirt pocket and tapped it several times against his badge while finding his place, then checked the "No" box under "Was suspect armed?" He returned the paper to Lovico, who said without looking at it:

"Yes. Good. Even though it could ruin your career in the police. Let's see, the pro football career is gone, I believe. Your career in coaching ended when they boarded up good old Benedict and you refused the School Board's offer of an assistant's job somewhere else —"

"West High," said Temple. "I'd beaten that guy twice and I'm supposed to be his assistant?"

"Oh, right. I remember that story too — 'Temple Stiffs Board.' And now the career in the police is likely, at a minimum, to be truncated, let's put it that way."

Temple was uncertain of the word truncated but suspected it meant dead end. He said: "Ask your questions."

Lovico replied: "Officer Temple, I don't want to sound too clever, but suppose you ask *your* question."

"I don't know what you mean."

Lovico went gently backwards in the chair without taking his eyes off Temple and rocked patiently back and forth. He said: "Surely your question, Officer Temple, ought to be: 'Are the boy's fingerprints on the knife?'"

The reaction was so extraordinary that Lovico suffered a little pang of conscience as he watched Temple's face lose all character and style. He could almost feel in his own chest the stunning effect upon Temple.

Lovico said: "You do not mention a knife in your Use of Force report. You undoubtedly know the other two officers do. You say in your report that you helped the medics put the body — the unconscious man — into the ambulance. The knife on the other hand went into the evidence crew's envelope at the scene, and never left the envelope until it was removed in the crime lab yesterday morning. These are just a few details I have gleaned. Now then, do you want to know?"

"Yes," Temple said, not very loudly.

"The answer is — Yes. There are partials and partial palms on the knife which appear to a high degree of probability to belong to the dead boy. No-no," Lovico said raising his hand quickly, "don't say anything. If you are a truthful man I want you to be perfectly free for the next twenty-four hours to say to anyone that you have not spoken to me about the knife, not a single word. It might mean a day's delay in the pressures that will undoubtedly be exerted on you. And you haven't said a word. Just ponder this information, Officer Temple. There are prints. Experts if called will testify they are the boy's. For the moment this seems to puzzle you, you seem surprised, you seem not to have expected this, although you should have. Think it through — reconstruct it — every minute, every second.

"The problem is really quite simple," Lovico continued in a somewhat tutorial vein. "The boy had a knife which in the heat of combat you did not see. There would be nothing astounding if that were true." Yet Lovico popped his eyes and lifted his brows as if it were preposterous. "Or one of your partners found opportunity to impress the boy's prints on the knife in your presence without your seeing. That too would be nothing very remarkable. It could be done by a deft hand in a second or two.

"It seems to me," Lovico said, "that you have been thinking of something else."

He'd been thinking of the kiss on the lifeless lips.

"You see, Officer Temple, I care about the boy too. I am not some bloodless scientist conducting tests in a laboratory. Last night I read his notes for his honors thesis. I have looked at his body. I always see in the human form, even in one so misshapen as my own, that gesture of nobility that precedes total disintegration. I am not immune to this gesture. But I must think ahead to the jury. It is not going to seem unbelievable to a jury that a black kid would be carrying a knife on First Street especially if he lived on Majestic.

"I am a man who makes use of his instincts, Officer Temple. I don't say I rely on them but I listen. They are, as it were, a resource. Why cut yourself off from a resource? I say first inform your mind, search not only for answers but for the right questions and listen to your instincts. My instinct tells me you are now a soldier of truth, Officer Temple. You have just enlisted in that army. You see one of my instincts is for fine phrases. Ha! And yet I repeat it."

Temple noticed however that he did not repeat it. Instead he said:

"We'll talk again tomorrow. I should say, you will talk tomorrow. I will now take detailed written statements from your partners and we'll see if they trip over these statements at the inquest. People never trip over the truth but lies often stick to the quickest foot."

Within an hour Temple knew how Ruthenbeck had managed the fingerprints.

In the locker room at the Sixth District station, while dressing for duty, Temple bent his right leg to pull on his blue trousers. He re-opened a cut on his knee. The wound began to bleed freely and to threaten his only remaining pair of winter-weight trousers. He saved the trousers from the falling drops of blood and walked in his shorts to the restroom where he made a compress out of paper and held it against the cut. He was thinking of those minutes when he knelt on the glass-strewn sidewalk, minutes in which, as he placed his lips hard against the lips of the unconscious boy, he had been unconscious himself of any pain from the cuts on his knees. The pain came later — in the ambulance — and returned now. So these must have been the minutes or seconds during which Ruthenbeck, working swiftly behind Temple's back, pressed the knife into the young man's hand, and then perhaps kicked it into the gutter. Temple knew only that he had been concentrating on his own effort during those minutes. Thinking it over now as he held the compress firmly against his knee and saw it gradually darkening Temple remembered that the boy's right arm had been stretched out towards him. The hand would have been beside him but almost behind him, near his knees and out of his sight when he bent forward to close the boy's nostrils and blow air into his lungs.

Temple remembered that Banes had been crouched on the boy's other side and had spoken a couple of words of pointless advice from time to time, probably to keep Temple's attention from veering to the side or back. Ruthenbeck was absent from the picture.

Chapter 17
The Rag

At rollcall the sergeant gave Temple the keys of a radar cruiser. He positioned the car in the driveway of a vacant fire station on Upper Main Street and aimed the radar toward oncoming traffic. He saw a police car approaching, that at first he didn't recognize. Its red flasher began pulsing and it pulled into the opposing lane, easing towards Temple, forcing the traffic to deviate. It was the district's other radar car and Ruthenbeck was driving.

Ruthenbeck put his window a foot from Temple's. The red flashes bounced off the plate glass windows of a car dealer's showroom across the street, and there sat Ruthenbeck in the center of this lightning display smiling at Temple with small teeth under his wispy blonde moustache, rolling down his window.

Ruthenbeck said, "Open your window, partner."

Temple saw Ruthenbeck's pale blue eyes as they must have looked when he was placing the knife and glancing up to be sure he wasn't observed. He saw Ruthenbeck's eyes as they must have looked when they met Banes's eyes, across Temple's back.

Temple flipped into "Drive" and moved away, his right wheels lurching over the edge of the firehouse driveway and back down off the curb. His hands and arms trembled and his right leg trembled so violently he could scarcely drive.

A few minutes before midnight, with six speeding citations in his clip, Temple steered the radar car down the rutted alley behind First Street, between Saxon and Harper. This alley led to the rear of the station. Temple parked in an empty slot among the blue and white cruisers. He turned the switch on the gooseneck reading lamp and completed his log entries for the night, the final lines being the odometer mileage and the time. He shut off the lamp, touched a switch and popped the trunk lid, and went back to confirm the serial number on the shotgun that hung in a rubber rack in the trunk. He had forgotten to do this at the beginning of his shift. His eyes were still accustomed to the bright light of the reading lamp and he strained in the half light to read the number on the shotgun. He slammed the trunk, shut down the engine and locked the car, and started across the lot.

He was walking toward the big old house that had been remodeled to provide a station for the Sixth. One could still read in dark letters embossed over the coach house door: "Boyle Funeral Home." The lot was illuminated by blue-white lights casting a protective glow over the fleet of cruisers through which Temple was making his way.

Across the alley lay another lot, for the Boyle mourners. The lighting here was older and dimmer. It was here the officers parked their private cars and here Temple had left the Ford. It was not quite in his view, being on the far edge of the lot, so he took a few steps into the alley and stood on one of the old telephone poles that lay along the edge. He saw his car, and for the second time that day it seemed to be in the wrong place. It seemed to be facing wrong, with the shattered spread of glass in front, not in the rear. Had somebody moved the car? The idea came to Temple that he would surely kill Ruthenbeck. But he was thinking about the car and he did not seize on the idea to ponder, criticize and reject it. He did feel and momentarily yield to the urge and he almost said: "I should kill him."

He left his flashlight and log book on the ground by the pole and went into the lot. Other officers were returning now, and two or three cruisers were moving nearby, which he didn't really see, some entering from First Street and some from the alley. Behind

him there was a mild tumult of men and women coming off the
street to the security of the station, the slamming of car doors and
the occasional abusive shout of one officer to another; while
before him was the comparative darkness of the mourners' lot,
which darkness was perhaps deepened because the surface was
spread with cinders.

Temple saw what he had almost expected and what he feared
when he had been forced to park so far from the alley. Not only
the rear window but all the windows were shattered and the body
had that sunken look of a car resting on flats. Walking around this
pile of worthless junk Temple saw that all four tires were slashed.
Here was Ruthenbeck pulling on a dead man's teeth, clasping
dead fingers around a knife and pissing his pants for fear of being
seen, and stealing into the lot in a darkened radar cruiser to
assault a piece of inanimate property. Temple wasn't even angry;
he was almost triumphant that his enemy should act like such an
imbecile.

Then Temple saw something that might have been a rag on
the windshield, something like a rag blown here by the wind and
stuck on a shard of glass. He leaned against a fender and picked
it off the point, being careful not to tear his trousers. Here was a
strange sort of thing, a kind of knitted brown and white mess.
There was a hole in it where the point had passed through. A few
threads had been severed and dangled one way and another. He
opened the car door and pulled the headlight switch but found the
lights too had been smashed.

He held the object in both hands and some sense of its identity seemed to enter his fingers. With an increasing need he took
it right under the nearest of the old light poles and held it at the
best angle. It was his son's hat.

Temple ran to the radar car, neither hearing nor responding to
the greetings and shouts of his fellow officers, whom he didn't
even see. He drove into First Street and east to the freeway. With
its massive engine the radar cruiser effortlessly touched ninety
and might have gone faster, but ninety was exactly Temple's state
of mind. He was not out of control. He knew the vital importance
of control. He would get there and see his son. Temple drove

skillfully, as he did all things, and controlled his energy and strength, as he always did except when he lost his temper.

Yet there was evidently some compromise of his mental acuity because he passed within sight of Benedict High School, which stood boarded and blinded by plywood sheets with two or three antivandal lights around it on a hill to his left, and he had no awareness of where he was — only that he was going somewhere on a freeway where despite the hour the traffic remained heavy and seemed slow as he shot through it with red lights blazing. He took his exit ramp as a test of skill and managed a stop without skidding. He followed a commercial street for about a mile, slowing down to fifty or so and screaming the siren as he shot the intersections; he turned into the neighborhood he knew so well. Here he began to look around for police cars, for Ruthenbeck's car.

He ran up the walk holding his gun and radio against his body, and climbed the stairs three at a time. He took a breath and paused and inserted his key.

He went down the hall past the nightlight and into Robbie's room. He could see Robbie lying asleep, his face serene, his arm bent at a gentle angle on the blanket. Temple listened to his son's steady breathing. The light entering from the hall was weak and he could not see the boy's face as clearly as he wanted to, and he now remembered he had left his flashlight and log book in the lot. He bent closer and listened to the same sound he used to listen to when he and Sandra crept into the nursery at night.

He entered his wife's room, looked at her face, and stood beside her bed for a long time.

Now came the vexing problem of getting around the city without a car. He returned the radar cruiser and looked by the telephone pole for his flashlight and log book but they were gone. He found them on the sergeant's desk and faced the sergeant's threats and venom for being late, off his beat and off the air. The sergeant declared that but for Temple's other troubles he would suspend him for joyriding. Temple saw that the sergeant meant exactly what he said. Here was an act of clemency. He was tempted to explain where he had been but realized just in time that the sergeant didn't want to know. Temple filed his speeding citations and went down to the locker room to change clothes.

The shift to civilian dress, from an officer to a man who looked like a professional athlete in the off season, who appeared more powerful in jeans and a knit sportshirt than in a policeman's uniform, was not so affecting a change as it might seem. It didn't affect Temple very much. The reason was the hammerless gun that he put into his pocket, which extended into his off-duty hours the sense of being a policeman.

Ruthenbeck and all the other officers on Temple's shift, the so-called Third Relief, were gone; and the officers of the First Relief were already on the street. Temple was alone in the locker room but if he stood quietly he could hear voices from the Bucket Room. It was there, evidently, that he must beg a ride. Or he could telephone for a cab but he opened his wallet and counted just six one-dollar bills.

He went upstairs and through a set of heavy glass doors into a room bordered on three sides by rows of writing tables. Above each table and attached to the wall there was a little booth or box lined with soundproofing, and in each booth a telephone to downtown. When this room was crowded with male and female police officers with their murmuring heads thrust into "buckets" it presented a truly absurd scene, like a vignette from a drama of the 1960s whose point was that you can't cope with life.

When Temple came in there were five officers from the First Relief doing nothing. Two of these, a man and a woman, both white, were Can't-Work-Alones. They had been assigned to single patrol but had notified the dispatcher that they were at the station on paperwork, hoping that if the dispatcher should assign them to a job he would send them both. The third officer in the room was a black malingerer and the fourth was a white malingerer. The fifth was probably there to do some actual paperwork. In a single glance Temple saw that they all knew about his car.

He asked if anyone could give him a ride to the Hilton, feeling it was better to beg a ride to a taxi stand than to his wife's apartment. Temple looked around, smiled and said: "Really? Nobody?" And he kept smiling because that was how he felt. Their silence didn't seem to hurt him, he felt nothing, unless it was pity. Next they offered a variety of excuses, all of them good, and Temple turned and went out through the double glass doors.

It was not a cold night and he wouldn't have felt the chill even if it were. He walked for a mile on First Street approaching Shipman's Barbecue. He was going toward it from the west; John Shipman Jr. had approached from the east, from the river. Now he could see the sign ahead but he was thinking of his car and he experienced that premonition of calamity that strikes the observer like a bolt at the first sight of a man down in the middle of the street. His car gave him that "man down" feeling in his guts. With the image of his car a thrill of something awful went through his frame. The next moment a pile of inconveniences presented itself, and he realized that he might spend half the night getting back to Sandra's because he doubted six dollars would cover the fare from downtown to her apartment. And he would have to draw money from the bank tomorrow but didn't know if he had any to draw. He would borrow Sandra's car and if she refused he would rent one. He would certainly have a car by early afternoon. He must, because he had to pick up Robbie after his appointment with Mr. Lovico and before work.

He was anxiously sorting all this out when a police car pulled up beside him and Greta Can't-Work-Alone Gabriel signed to him to get in. It was she who had been in the Bucket Room. She said simply: "Where to?" and he gave her Sandra's address. As they passed Shipman's barbecue he looked at the empty parking lot and the half-lit interior. And then he saw the recessed doorway where they had killed Hawk. There was plywood in Banes's window. Temple turned away.

When they reached Sandra's street something happened that Temple dreamed about later that night during the minutes when he lost consciousness on the couch. It may not have been a dream since he may not have slept, but if not a dream it was a vision. He could not remember the vision in the morning but the event that inspired it he could hardly forget, even though it was nothing.

He opened the car door and looked at Greta Gabriel, who up to now had been a mere name and a stereotypical joke. He knew she was a Can't-Work-Alone and that she had a fine body and that was all. He saw in her face, in her eyes, a darkness and a lack of life. He suddenly wanted to embrace and kiss her; in truth he wanted to mount her.

He said as if it were a joke: "Thanks for the ride. I won't tell anybody."

Greta said: "Please don't."

But when he got out of her car, when he entered the building, and even when he finally laid his exhausted and sleepless body on the couch, he still had the physical yearning for her. It was so strong it would have denied him the sleep he needed even if nothing else had.

The scene with Sandra was unendurable. It left a place in his mind bleeding. When she departed holding the hand of their bewildered son Temple walked as if upon sore feet to the bathroom, stripped and showered in very hot water, dried himself on the first towel that came to hand, filling his nostrils with Sandra's femininity, and walked to Sandra's bedroom — to what had been their bedroom — and slept naked in her bed. It was a deep and gothic sleep lasting three hours and drawing him by a chain through a morass. It was some time after the alarm went off before he could remember his arrangements with his wife.

These were that she would drive Robbie to school and even walk with him from the curb to the building; that she would leave her car at a certain garage downtown where Temple could get it after his appointment at the district attorney's office; that Temple would pick Robbie up at school in the afternoon and take him to Sandra's office, leaving him with Sandra if she were in or with the receptionist if she were not; and that he would return her car to the same garage before making his way to the Sixth District for the evening shift.

Temple arranged by telephone to have his car towed and repaired; he cooked eggs and bacon, read the morning paper and put into his wallet the twenty-dollar bill Sandra had left on the kitchen counter.

This was the advice Lovico gave him:

"You should put your son out of his reach." Lovico was speaking slowly and looking up at the ceiling, letting his big slightly bulged eyes flit back and forth. "Hmm," he said, "yes. You see, Officer Temple, I interviewed him yesterday. I had no need of Sister Mary Joseph's assistance to see into his soul. A perfect vacuum." He looked at Temple and added calmly: "Many people today are incapable of seeing evil when they look it in the face. I am not one of those people."

Lovico creaked around in his chair. He took a full five minutes to read over the notes he had been making on a yellow legal pad while Temple talked. "I am thinking. I am adjusting," he informed Temple. "We have a new situation. We must put your son's safety first. When we have taken the boy out of harm's way we can proceed with the problem of justice for Officer Ruthenbeck. You see, I believe every word you have told me" — he picked up his legal pad and put it down with a definitive motion — "on the incident, on the knife, and on the hat."

A few minutes later, having said nothing in the interval, having watched the ceiling the whole time, Lovico told Temple he was changing his plan.

"I will elicit your complete testimony on the knife at the medical examiner's inquest rather than holding some back for the trial." He seemed to be doing Temple the courtesy of thinking aloud. "I will . . . damnation . . .

"Officer Temple, we do not have the right to assume he will leave the boy alone. So here's what we will do. I will elicit *all of this*" — he again lifted and dropped the legal pad — "and from that point forward, from the minute you have identified the knife in public session and under oath, he will have nothing to gain by threatening and intimidating you. I had intended to withhold some of your testimony to pry Officer Banes away from Ruthenbeck or to extort from Ruthenbeck a guilty plea on a lesser offense if necessary. Now I cannot. We can and we will remove his motive for striking at you through the boy — but you must not be overconfident. Actions do not always proceed from motives. There are actions that give satisfaction in themselves. There is still, for example, revenge."

The prosecutor's sagging eyes seemed to tighten as he sent a piercing look at Temple.

"But that," he resumed, "is your problem, not *our* problem. Now as to the fat lady, she may not be so worthless as you suppose. However dissipated and self-abandoned she may seem, she can be cleaned up and she can speak the simple truth. I will assign a man to help you look for her. If we don't find her we won't worry about it; if we do we'll consult Sister Mary Joseph. You are certainly correct that she is an excellent candidate for impeachment on the witness stand. But so are you, Officer Temple — so are you."

Lovico now entered territory heretofore unknown to Temple. He said: "Am I correct? You have been under the impression his purpose is to silence you?"

"Well, sure."

"Suppose," Lovico proceeded, "that he is not so stupid as that. Suppose his brain is a little more nimble and his vision a little broader. He might indeed think it's worth a try — you might be a moral coward under all that useless muscle, mightn't you? So he might say, 'I'll see if Temple can be intimidated.' But I see another possibility, don't you?

"You are not the fat lady. You are not a drunk, a criminal or a junkie. You are a brave and truthful man, if you don't mind my saying so, and let us suppose that Officer Ruthenbeck knows it too. Brave and truthful men can also be impeached. A perfectly good prosecution witness can be destroyed if the defense by introducing credible and sometimes incredible but *tangible evidence* can suggest to the jury that he is biased; that he hates the defendant; that he has a vendetta against him; that he would do anything to destroy the defendant, his career, his good name, his marriage, his life, his fortune.

"Now if the defendant could show that the witness had assaulted him, had sworn to destroy him, that the witness blew up . . .

"Officer Temple, with your permission I will recall yet another incident from your brief but illustrious career as a gladiator. This one I read about, yes, but I also saw it on television.

"We are at Soldier Field, Chicago — the Bears leading the Packers by six points — and the clock is stopped at one minute ten seconds to go. A defensive linebacker hits you like a cannonball at the very moment you catch or almost catch a pass —"

"It was interference," Temple cut in.

"Perhaps. I saw the replay and I am not sure. That's not the point."

"I know what the point is, you can stop. You're wasting your breath."

"Am I? You went ballistic, Officer Temple. You went — mad."

"I wasn't the only one."

"No indeed, but you were the first one. Five seconds later the whole field was swarming with raging maniacs trying to kill one another."

Now Lovico stared at Temple as if in mild reproach, while Temple remembered how quickly he had surrendered his reason. Lovico said:

"Be cool, Officer Temple. If you strike out at this man, he wins."

Chapter 18
Father and Son

Robbie and Jeffrey were supposed to meet at the trophy case in the front corridor of Robbie's school. But boys do not always heed their fathers, any more than fathers always meet their commitments to their sons. When Temple arrived ten minutes late Robbie wasn't there.

Temple had wasted the ten minutes searching for Sandra's car. She told him she always parked at the Great Valley building in Blue 4; if she couldn't get a space in Blue 4 she would telephone. She had not telephoned so Temple took the elevator to the fourth floor and found himself in Red 4. He followed the upward slope expecting it might lead to Blue 4, until he saw he was in Brown 5. He retraced his steps around a curve, still looking for the familiar sporty little vehicle that Sandra had acquired after their separation and still not finding it. Now he was down to Red 3.

He went back up to his starting point and even went back through a door into the elevator vestibule. This was plainly marked Parking 4 in characters a foot high. So with a fury he tried to control he turned as if leaving the elevator for the first time and went out the vestibule door again. He now grasped that there must be two spirals; otherwise cars going up would meet cars going down. Now there was a clever diagram on the wall before him, a big 4 in a circle outlined in black, and each quarter of the circle a different color. The blue quarter was upper right, so he went to his right, whereas he had gone left the first time, thinking it made no difference. Now looking to the left he saw a huge blue stripe around a pillar, and Sandra's car in the same glance. He walked quickly to the car.

When he didn't see Robbie in front of the trophy case Temple wasn't worried. He had given the boy strict and solemn orders not to leave the school building for any reason and to wait at the trophy case. So Temple guessed that Robbie had bent his orders by going to the restroom or to watch the older kids at basketball practice or something like that when his father didn't show up right after school. Temple could hear softly echoing down the empty corridors the gymnasium-style sounds of a basketball team in full scrimmage, with a shout and a coach's whistle now and then. He could also hear the clatter of an old-fashioned type-writer. All these sounds blended to evoke a harmless school-days nostalgia.

When asked how he lost his hat Robbie had said an older boy took it from him and bent his finger back.

Who was the boy? "I don't know."

Was he from your school? "No."

Was he white or black? "White."

Was he alone? "I guess so."

While answering, Robbie had looked directly into his father's eyes. He knew his father didn't like shuffling or looking around; he did not like standing on one leg during an important talk. Robbie's expression showed he knew this talk was important, or at least that his father thought so.

Temple started walking down the corridor.

The typewriter grew a little louder and then ceased. He was walking on a waxed floor between ranks of gray steel lockers, and a window ahead at the end of the hall admitted the afternoon sunlight. Temple looked into each classroom as he passed. All were empty except for the pregnant silence that invests children's places when the children are gone.

He expected to see his son in the gymnasium. Robbie would be sitting in the first row of the empty bleachers with his books beside him watching the older boys, and his father not only saw this image but identified with that deference and hope Robbie must feel watching these experienced boys.

There was a scrimmage and a coach booming forth instructions of which Temple did not approve, but Robbie wasn't there. Temple watched the scrimmage for a couple of minutes and then went back to the trophy case. He went to the main entrance and looked out at the streetside where he often picked Robbie up, and there were some kids there but Robbie wasn't among them. He went to the office where a young male teacher said he had not seen Robbie. What Temple saw, couldn't help seeing, was that the teacher knew who he was even before he asked after his son. This man would now tell his wife or girlfriend: "I saw Jeff Temple in school today."

Determined, not necessarily nervous, Temple went outside and around to the playgrounds. Here was the basketball hoop where Robbie often played in the morning, just by a street that came up at a right angle to the one the school faced. There were a few kids at a swing and slide but none playing basketball. Temple stood in the midst of the playground looking all around and listening to the cries and chatter of the kids. He would have crossed the field to ask them if they knew Robbie Temple but they looked like small children and they had no doubt been warned about strangers and he didn't want to frighten them.

His conscience asserted itself. And even before he found Robbie the remorse of one who has leaned too much on luck took over his feelings. He had counted on his luck for too long — all his life in fact. He was no longer his own master, he was not the master of his mind but a dummy to be kicked and abused. All that remained of his intellect was the knowledge that he was responsible. This knowledge was a conviction that he, the reckless and self-confident man he used to be, had done something wrong or omitted something necessary. This is how life handles those who press their luck, and they deserve it.

He found Robbie in an alley staggering towards him. His jacket was gone and he carried no books. There was a big patch of blood on his shirt, which was a white sweatshirt bearing his school emblem, now obscured. Temple at first felt a crack of relief at the sight of this blood because there was so much of it. He knew instantly it was blood from his son's nose, because he knew how profusely noses can bleed and how little all that blood means in the end. He rushed up to his son and saw him lurch and fall in the gravel before him, in a sideways fall that sent him where his legs could do him no good. There was a whimpering murmur coming from the boy that frightened Temple and also made him wish he was not hearing such an unmanly sound from his son.

He helped Robbie to his feet, squeezed his hands and legs — the boy did not wince but merely continued the inarticulate, almost animal sounds he was making — ran his thick fingers through the boy's hair in all directions and found no blood, nor evoked any wince of pain.

"He's O.K.," Temple thought and continued his hasty examination, saying all the while, "It's O.K., Rob; it's O.K., Rob."

He lifted the shirt and ran his hands up inside, feeling Robbie's ribs and chest, encouraging his son to be brave and watching for any signal of pain. His mind repeated, "He's O.K.," and again he told Robbie everything was all right.

The boy staggered in his arms, fell in his embrace, and Temple lifted him off the gravel again, and he was very light in weight. Blood was trickling from his ears.

Temple embraced him, held him like a baby and laughed with relief, a queer and not very manly sound of his own. He knew the boy was still terrified but couldn't suppress this blessed laughter. Robbie was O.K.! Some kids had punched and roughed him up, that was all.

He embraced Robbie, pressed Robbie's wet and bloody cheek against his own, and took out his handkerchief and started wiping the blood. The blood from the ears, what did it mean?

He said, "Hey, old man, you got your teeth all bloody! Doesn't taste very good, does it?"

Robbie was looking at him with fear in his eyes.

Temple said, "It's O.K., Rob." He repeated this formula, with Robbie watching him in that terrified, concentrated way.

Robbie said, "O.K.," in a loud peculiar voice, and Temple answered:

"Sure, son, you're going to be O.K."

Robbie's eyes shifted and glazed a bit and Temple thought he was going to faint. He dare not embrace the boy too hard for fear of some undetected broken bone or other injury.

Robbie said in a screaming voice: "I can't hear."

Temple thought, "Right! This whole lake of blood doesn't mean a thing."

He got down on his knees before his son and looked at the mystery of those little drops coming out of the boy's ears. He groaned. He said, "He can't hear." He thought: "Good God, what's happened?"

Chapter 19
A Glass of Brandy

Ensconced in his study Sam Lovico fell into contemplation. His text was that unpredictable line from the notebook of John Shipman Jr.: "I will find a swamp and take off my clothes and wade in. I will know the Hurons better."

Seeing the young man go into the reeds he seemed to grope with his own feet for a firm standing place. He knew that a reedy swamp by a lake can have a hard bottom. His bare feet encountered no sharp rocks or pointed sticks to injure or impede him. He went forward into the green sun-glancing blades behind the young black man, getting a strange feeling of vulnerability in the back of his groin for fear that he might cut his feet or slip into deep water.

"A past-prime white lawyer feeling with a young black man who strips himself naked to *feel with* a tribe of Hurons three centuries dead!"

Somewhat less precise was his realization that both he and John Shipman Jr. were crossing tribal boundaries. Actually he didn't think of this, he only felt an unidentified thrill in the adventure.

He poured a brandy and sat in silence letting the amber fluid cycle slowly round the curving glass, deciding whether to listen to a Mozart symphony or a selection of arias. At length he placed the glass on the table untasted and sank deeper into a silence he now realized he had no desire to interrupt.

His act of imagination seemed at once futile and pregnant. What could he possibly know about blacks? He worked with them every day, yes, but what could he really know? But caught in the vision of the wading youth he asked, What could he not know? What reason had he to suppose that one person's soul was closed to another by reason of a tribal difference? He wanted earnestly to believe no reason existed, while retaining a certain humility, a certain doubt that anything so inspiring as this brotherhood of souls could actually be true.

Now he did open the notebook for there was something he wanted to get right. John Shipman Jr. had described a moment of supreme crisis and Lovico wanted to read his language again. He paged back and forth and finally read: ". . . when they are turning him into a piece of meat, when they try to take him away from himself and *thing* him . . ."

At this crisis he creates his soul. ". . . in the extremity of pain, desolation and *fear*" he springs into fire with a lambent flame, if he can.

To Lovico it had always seemed imperative to avert such a crisis. He excused himself by the claim that most people's lives are designed specifically to avert it. He had structured his life to put off such a moment of extreme trial if possible until the very hour of death. He chose instead to live and work in the world of the possible where men do not wade into swamps except perhaps to hunt ducks.

"I have a good reason for being what I am," Lovico said. "I am not sure how useful a hero really is. I am certain however that a smoothly functioning system of civic relations is useful and good."

He returned to the tribal boundary and sought to cross it.

"A man at the moment of crisis, when they are trying to thing him, affirms the openness of every human soul. Perhaps he affirms it by looking into the eyes of his torturer and appealing to his humanity, an act of faith. Perhaps he affirms it by refusing to make the appeal. He might refuse for one of two reasons. He could refuse because he believes the torturer has already thinged himself; or because he, the tortured, has thinged the torturer."

Exclaiming "No! No!" Lovico took a drink of brandy and said, "That is not clear, that is muddled."

He felt no effect from the brandy unless it was a ripple of amusement at the image of a baby's soul leaping out of its burial place on a path and lodging itself happily in the womb of an unsuspecting woman.

"But I believe," he said, "that he must begin by considering the appeal. If so, he begins with faith."

Lovico still did not stir. There was something so much deeper in this idea of the moment of crisis, so much more alluring even than the thought of bringing into the room the actual strains of Mozart that ran through his mind, so much sweeter, that he refused to let the image go.

"Sweeter!" he exclaimed in disbelief.

How did he ever get there? What could be "sweet" about the final crisis of a brave man's life?

He could only surmise that he somehow had linked his image with a memory, of his wife when young saying to him, he knew not why: "Oh Sam, life is sweet."

He wished he could remember why she said it. He could see her face — but then he always saw her face.

Lovico sniffed the brandy and let it swirl in gentle loops in the glass. He felt as if he could be a brother to John Shipman Jr.

He asked whether he should go further in justifying his own life of civic work and it seemed to him a pretty superficial kind of dedication, compared to some others. Or it might be a deep dedication to superficial things. The truth was he felt comfortable and he wondered if that wasn't a bad sign. He couldn't help contrasting this comfort with "the extremity of pain, desolation and fear" John Shipman Jr. must have experienced in that doorway so close to his father's place of business on First Street.

"That dark doorway," Lovico thought. He rose from his chair. He had imagined following the boy into the swamps. Now he imagined following him into the doorway.

At this hour he could drive to First Street in fifteen minutes. He left the house hastily without hat or gloves and he shivered and his ears began to burn as he walked along the desolate sidewalk towards the red and white Shipman's sign with the snaking border. He slowed his pace as he approached the new plywood blind. A few more steps. He looked over his shoulder. Like the entire Sixth Police District this neighborhood — it was not a neighborhood at all — was unsafe at any hour. He came to the doorway, took a final look at the sign, and went into the triangle. He put his back to the old wood-and-glass door and looked into the lighted street from the dark, imagining how much of the view would be blocked by three men, particularly by the mountainous Jeffrey Temple.

Oddly enough his imagination took no notice of the physical scene in which he stood poised, of the sparkle of invisible glass shivered into atoms scattered over the cement slab, of the crunch as he moved from one position to another on his freezing feet. His senses observed all this but his mind had already raced ahead to a stark drama stripped of all physical detail, a drama of rage and defiance inside the mind of John Shipman Jr. In this drama as Lovico saw it the "historian of the black people" was summoned to prove he was worthy of his chosen task, but if he proved worthy he'd never be given a chance to do the task. He did prove worthy, and he would never have a chance.

Lovico thought, "Ghastly, yet beautiful." He shifted and addressed himself: "You are desperate to find something good in this. You are the last person I would suspect of such sentimentality. I thought you were a hardened realist!" He shifted back to the "I" and said: "I am apparently unable to believe in pure worthless destruction."

He knew what he wanted. He wanted to believe that by elevating humanity the young man had opened his soul to him, merely because they were both human.

Lovico said: "Can't you try to confine yourself to the facts?"

He was reluctant to leave the doorway but his teeth began chattering and his shoulders, arms and neck hardened with chill and tension. This hardening was relieved every now and again by an explosive shudder.

He strode along the wind-buffeted street to his car, and as he started the engine he thought of the unfinished glass of brandy.

Lifting it to his lips he paused. He put it down carefully on the leather coaster on his chairside table in the light of his reading lamp. He paced his study thinking:

"*There* is a fully-formed human being. There is a 'man of force.'"

Chapter 20
The Inquest

Now the predictable thing happened — they released the man they had arrested for the rape — let him out — and he immediately raped again. This second attack was more brutal; he beat and disfigured his victim. Reading this in the paper Shipman realized, first, that he had never doubted that this was the man who committed the crime for which his son had been stopped and, second, that he believed it merely because the police said it was so. Now, still believing it, he was revolted that they had set the man free. It brought him close to moral nausea. He did not understand how they could go on doing it.

They beat the innocent and free the guilty. And this is not an aberration but a continuous cycle, whose plain cause is race prejudice. Nothing else can explain their indifference to the safety of black people still living in the neighborhoods haunted by the predators. Stop a black man on suspicion and what do you do? Beat him. Arrest a black man for raping a black woman and what do you do? Let him go. This was the game they called justice, which is actually the source of power and pleasure. What one sees is an elaborate effort to control crime. What one does not see is that the system perpetuates crime; if crime is perpetuated then the game can go on. The players are gratified in their will to power and given something useful and lucrative to do; careers and money.

Shipman had earlier decided to wait for the medical examiner's inquest, for a specific reason. Now thinking of this second victim his emotions almost got control of him. This was a woman, now disfigured, who had been going to work one morning or doing her hair or dressing her kid for school or — all right! — collecting her welfare check, while at the same moment downtown two lawyers and a judge, or some such little combo of smug and confident men, maybe including the cocksure Lovico, were holding a conference in which they decided to let the rapist go for a thousand or five thousand dollars' bail because — why not?

John Shipman took out Lovico's letter again. "Dear Mr. Shipman: I urge you to delay any conclusions you might be inclined to reach until more facts become available . . . I particularly urge you to attend the medical examiner's inquest . . ."

Shipman would attend. The reason was simply that even with Lucas's help he couldn't kill all three cops. If he listened to the testimony he might learn whom he must kill and whom he might spare, since he had to spare somebody. He had visualized the killings a thousand times, in fact he could not stop his brain from seeing these pictures, but now he began to anticipate his feelings — the way he would take it — when he decided who to kill. The killer's brain is never at rest. Killing would be easier than deciding whom to kill. These feelings distorted his thinking. He was playing God but at least he wasn't playing a game. Nevertheless playing this role planted doubt in his mind for the first time — but he had never expected to carry it through free of all reservation and conflict. What difference did it make what happened in his soul?

He wondered why he kept feeling this scorching pity for the woman who had been raped and mutilated. Sometimes he thought more about her than about his son.

If he did what he must do, what he could not refuse to do, what he wanted to do, what did it matter if he had to suppress these shouts: "You are not god!"

"Never said I was, but I am going to kill those cops."

And wasn't he ready to die for justice? Paying that price would almost make it right.

"I got to be god to do this? O.K.! God damn this foolish idea, god damn it!"

He began to curse and pollute his mouth with words of filth and degradation.

"Stop!" he cried. "Be clean, be clear, pull yourself up."

Utterly strange, utterly silly, but when he said words like motherfuck and dickhead he felt physically smaller. The neck through which the words passed seemed to get thinner.

"If I'm going to die for this I —" He searched his —

"O.K., call it 'soul,' what's the difference, soul, soul, soul."

— searched in his soul for a feeling of the dignity of his mission — and didn't find it.

"So this is something only god can do, decide who he's going to kill? — But I don't have a choice. If it rips me, makes me be false, pollutes my mouth with words of filth and fury — I still got to do it!"

Now that the watch at Hawk's apartment was ended Shipman spent most of the time with his wife and her family, who had gathered like a flock from the moment of his first telephone call. He said aloud to Odell Diann difficult words to comfort her, believing that she was so distant, owing to her religious beliefs, that a direct message, as it were, from his region to hers was necessary. She'd be all wrapped up in her pathetic Jesus if he didn't talk to her. As they lay in bed he said, "You were a good mother to him." She turned her face to his and smiled, but he knew her consolation lay in her God, not her husband.

A few days after the funeral he resumed the normal operation of his businesses except that he didn't go into the blind pig. The funeral was not like an event that has an end, but a vast cathedral of the dark, where he wandered blinded listening to cries and weeping from people he couldn't touch.

One night he closed the door of his office, sat at his desk, unfolded a newspaper clipping and spread it out before him. Taking a pack of three-by-five cards from a drawer he copied the name of each of the three police officers from the clipping onto a card, and under each name, leaving a space after each entry, he wrote: "Home address — hours of work — day off — make and model of car — color of car."

He put the three cards in a pocket-sized leather portfolio in which he carried important accounting notations and returned the portfolio to his inside coat pocket. Then he hesitated over a decision that kept pressing him and which he had not planned to make yet. What about Lovico? He took off his reading glasses and seemed to stare at a fixed point in space. His eyes rested and focused on nothing, but his plans circled the decision. The trouble was he had no way of predicting certain things. What was Lovico going to do? It was already obvious Hawk's death meant nothing to him. It was already obvious that his role was to bring the cops safely through the legal maze and to prove that nothing really important had happened.

Shipman leaned forward and to one side, took his wallet from his left hip pocket and removed Lovico's business card. He took a fourth index card from the pack and copied the name Samuel Lovico on it, wrote down the same blank entries, and put this index card in the portfolio with the other three.

At the inquest Lovico proved himself a master player. The drama began and continued smoothly, and was marked by an order and dignity appropriate to its solemn purpose. This was to enlighten the medical examiner who was charged by law with the duty to pronounce the cause of the death of John Shipman Jr. As Lovico arranged matters the first witnesses were medical and the first morning was consumed in taking their testimony. The medical examiner being a doctor himself, although by the look of him one who could not have assembled a private practice, understood the proprietary language of these witnesses. He would occasionally interject a question in order to flourish a term such as *apnea* or *intracranial pressure*. But in the main it was Lovico who asked the questions and Lovico alone who called the witnesses. He too seemed to understand medical terminology but he was scrupulous in requiring each witness to translate his responses into plain

English. And thus it might have appeared that the whole drama was being played for the tall black man who sat alone in the front row.

He sat in the center with empty chairs on either side. A tacit agreement had spread among the people in the audience, before the first witness was called, that the front row should be left to the family, as at a funeral. Since neither Odell Diann nor Winslow came, and no other relative of the dead youth was bold enough to claim a front-row seat, the father sat alone and foremost. Nobody ever looked directly at him but nobody ever quite turned his back to him either. Lovico would stand at his table to Shipman's right front, or walk before it, facing the witness and Shipman both, looking only at the witness, who always looked at him or at the medical examiner, whose desk was directly in front of Shipman. The reporter sat at his little typing machine perched on its spindly legs, with his head cocked and his attentive eyes on the witness's lips. And it was only rarely, when Shipman for example would look at the medical examiner during one of his "clarifying," that is to say superfluous, questions, that a witness would take a casual and quick look at John Shipman. It was as if the rite required that the father be placed just in the center but forbade any open and shameless staring at him.

He was dressed in a blue suit that was darker than his skin; it was made of the finest fabric and cut to the latest variation in the most reserved fashion. The medical examiner wore a suit to help him disappear and Lovico presented himself as well as a man of his means and taste could. If both these servants of the state had been stripped naked and their clothes sold at auction the proceeds would not have paid for one of John Shipman's elegantly simple shoes.

That the feet within these shoes had suffered frostbite and infection and had been mutilated and saved by numerous small amputations — this of course was not obvious. An intelligent visitor from an exotic culture might have concluded after a few minutes' observation that the black man in the blue suit concealed behind his silent eyes the religious force that regulated the whole ceremony.

The testimony was that Hawk had sustained three or four blows to the head. Three were certain, the fourth conjectural. One blow came from a policeman's club, from the side, and was clinically unimportant. It was, however, not a trivial blow. It may have stunned Hawk; if it came first, it may have made him less able to evade or block a traumatic blow to the jaw. The pattern of trauma left the pathologist in doubt as to whether another blow may not have been struck at approximately the same angle and place, more or less squarely on the jaw, but with a few degrees of "twist." (It was impossible to avoid visualizing the twist.) Lastly there was a glancing but heavy blow on the lower side of the head which probably was not delivered either by a human hand or a club but may have been the site of a sharp scraping contact with a low window sill as Hawk fell.

None of the medical witnesses wished to speak with any precision about how quickly he died, or even when his brain may have died. The medic said that the man was not breathing when the ambulance arrived — it was here that the medical examiner threw in the word apnea — and that Officer Temple was administering mouth-to-mouth resuscitation. The more elaborate measures taken by the ambulance crew were unavailing.

Explaining how death occurred the pathologist said the brain had been shaken in its case by the force of the blow or blows to the jaw and that the glancing blow on the window sill added another insult. John Shipman remarked this word insult. It would have been better, and the young man might be alive today, had his skull fractured. But it did not; it was quite intact.

In cases of this kind, the pathologist added, when the surgeon drills holes in the skull to relieve internal pressure the traumatized brain matter will often ooze out like toothpaste from a tube.

He didn't say any such holes had been drilled in Hawk's skull; to the contrary, he found no evidence of surgical intervention. The emergency-room doctor and a staff surgeon from St. Claire's later testified surgery was not indicated. The pathologist explained that in acceleration or deceleration injuries the skull is set into sudden violent motion or else a fast-moving skull is stopped, for example when the head of a passenger in a car hits the dashboard as the car hits a tree. But the brain, which is gelatinous, lags in its response a fraction of a second behind the somewhat separate motion of the skull. Thus at one end of the motion or the other the brain is slammed against the skull. The worst such injuries involve deformation of the brain and gross trauma, often including trauma to the cells of the brain stem. The pathologist said he could not testify to every element of the fatal sequence but it was likely the young man stopped breathing almost immediately, that hemorrhages and contusions began engorging the brain with blood and other serous fluid, mostly blood, and that as the brain swelled in its case the intracranial pressure began to approach arterial pressure. When the pressure in the skull equaled the pressure in the arteries, naturally the flow of blood to the brain stopped. This was the moment when brain death occurred.

John Shipman ate a junkfood lunch from a vending machine. He stood at a window looking down through the dirt to the Courthouse Square, where foreshortened squat creatures with legs flipping back and forth were strutting in a big hurry in all directions across the open cement.

One must be truth and the other an illusion. Either the view we get from an airplane or high building, of insects not worth noticing and little toy motorcars buzzing along threadlike roads, ought to blaze its incontestable meaninglessness into our minds — either this — in which case the only thing to do is forget freedom — or the paper cut on the tongue, the joy in our son or daughter is the truth.

Shipman watched the little squat figures crossing the square. He wanted to be a good man but if he had to choose between goodness and strength there was no doubt which he would choose. It seemed he had already chosen. When he sat in the diner waiting for Lucas's breakfast the decision was already there. But it was a decision with no history. No record existed in his mind or feelings of the struggle that led to it — only the two conclusions: if he had decided to kill the cops, Hawk must be dead; and now, if Hawk was dead, which all this business of the inquest implied, then he would kill the cops.

But this was nothing but mind-work. It had no feeling. The only sensation it brought was as if somebody who knew his life better than he did had said: "This is what you're going to do." It had all been determined when they killed Hawk and now it was a simple matter of his recognizing that Hawk really was dead, and that was what these fools and devils were saying.

When he did his duty he'd be himself alive again perhaps for as long as thirty seconds. If he didn't do it then the killers would have killed not only Hawk but his whole family.

Yet he felt an insistent pull to be a good man. As a boy he had read Booker T. Washington and the spirit of toleration and gentle love that animate Washington's writings appealed to him. He felt Washington had at least one of the right attitudes. "I would gladly let them do it," he thought, meaning the prosecutors and the courts. The trouble was they would not do it. "They are not going to take this off my hands."

"Mr. Shipman. Excuse me, Mr. Shipman."

Here stood the bouncing man with the baggy eyes and loose cheeks and loose lip.

"May I ask you," Lovico said, "if you will come to my office when this afternoon's session adjourns? It is Room 680. Take those elevators," he said and pointed.

"I want to talk to you too," John Shipman said. "I want to know why you didn't ask any of those doctors was such force necessary and right."

"You'll have your answer this afternoon," Lovico said. "Will you come?"

"Yes."

When he returned along the crowded corridors and reached the hearing room Shipman saw that the group parted to admit him and he heard their talk cease as he approached, and resume when he was well into the room. If he was the object of special attention it wasn't the first time and he ignored it. He had likewise ignored, after one courteous sentence of negation, an importunate white lawyer named Murphy who had come to his office one afternoon with a proposal to represent the family. Whether Murphy intended to gouge the city or make a new kind of reputation for himself was a matter of indifference to Shipman. One thing was clear, Murphy intended to orchestrate something that would drag out for years and signify nothing.

The first witness was this Officer Jeffrey Temple and Shipman looked at him from a distance of ten feet with cold hatred. Shipman had never cared for Malcolm X but here before him sat exactly the kind of white man Malcolm would have called a blue-eyed devil. He was blue-eyed for certain, with high-color blue, blond hair darkening to brown, a busted nose, huge square jaw and football neck, shoulders that projected out over the sides of the witness chair, hands ten pounds each, and a well-digger's voice to go with it all — a perfect, born overseer. Here was a man a foot taller than Hawk and weighing a hundred pounds more, with a reach six inches longer, armed with a gun, wearing a badge, and yet this famous athlete needs the help of two of his brother *police officers* to force Hawk into a doorway and beat him. Shipman knew before the question was asked that this was the man who had struck Hawk in the jaw. The only question was whether he had done it once or twice and the answer wasn't long in coming.

But with it came a little sanctimonious parade of honesty, one of those turns in which a man does the thing he shouldn't do, often at great cost to somebody else, and then expects to wipe out his guilt, especially if it can't be undone, merely by admitting he did it. This is called stepping forward like a man, admitting your faults and all that other cheap shit.

Then comes the really humble part, the Christ-kisses-the-leper part, when he drops his voice and acknowledges that yes, yes sir, I gave him mouth-to-mouth. There is certainly no greater act of heroism for a pure white mama's beef like this than to put his mouth up against the actual niggerlips and blow his precious breath into the lungs of a zigaboo.

Temple was on the stand the entire afternoon setting forth what Lovico evidently wanted to be received as the one true account of the incident on First Street. At the end Lovico asked:

"Officer Temple, was John Shipman Jr. armed?"

"No sir, he was not."

"He didn't have a weapon of any kind?"

"No sir."

"No," Shipman thought as the elevator doors rolled apart, "my boy was not armed, except with courage, except with fight." Yet Shipman wasn't in this elevator as it began the ascent to Lovico's office. He was somewhere else, and he had Officer Temple in his gunsight, with the front post centered in the notch of the rear sight with equal daylight on either side and a perfectly aligned horizontal top line; and Temple's heart floated somewhere in the blur beyond the sharply focused sights.

And he thought, "No, my boy was not armed, but I am!"

And when he walked along the corridor he saw again that heroic image of his son knocking a cop through a window and bloodying another one before the third bashed him twice with his ten-pound fists. Shipman turned to the wall — saw the plaster cracks and chips and the dust and the blue — and wept convulsively into the blackness behind his shut eyes. He pressed his fists into his eye sockets and the blackness sparkled with colors, and his forehead and fists came in contact with the wall, but he himself was in contact with his son. He felt the flatness and coolness of the plaster. He was engulfed by the hot convulsions and the terrible wildness inside him against the flat wall. Wild body unhooked from a wild brain. This was proof that control, intention and thinking are but a small and insignificant part of your life — to cry in a public corridor like this and not even know it till it's half over, to bash the wall and make these strange noises, knowing that in some way these are your own horrid cries of a despair you never guessed at — this indeed is proof of depths and powers unknown within the soul. This is proof that the soul reigns, these noises that are neither animal nor mechanical nor electric, and certainly not human.

It must be that he didn't succeed in ignoring the people of various races in the corridor because he was acutely aware that they meant nothing. He went into a men's room to view the damage and was amazed at the effects on his face of this convulsing sorrow. He rinsed his eyelids and cheeks and spat the salty saliva from his mouth. He would be black ice in the presence of Lovico.

He wiped several handfuls of cold water across his face and felt himself settling down into a deeper trench.

Looking at himself over a paper towel concealing half his face he said: "It don't matter if I look like a crybaby. It just don't matter."

Chapter 21
Shipman's Resolve

"I want you to know," Shipman said as Lovico was settling himself into his chair, "that I am grateful to you for asking Temple whether he had used a necessary degree of force."

"I will ask the other two officers the same question tomorrow," said Lovico. "They are the ones to ask, not the medical witnesses. Only an officer at the scene can make a judgment on the use of force."

"And I was interested in his answer," Shipman continued, "his guilty answer."

"He could hardly have said the amount of force was appropriate."

"No." Shipman himself could hear the resonations of this final word. A whole world of consequences seemed to be suggested. The suggestion was unreal to Shipman.

"An officer has the right in certain circumstances to use deadly force," Lovico said, "and so does any other citizen. But deadly force is a difficult concept to control in a legal arena. The problem is even more complex when officers use deadly force without knowing it."

"But of course," said Shipman, "a man like Temple knows it." John Shipman, sitting immobile and observing the frequent twitches and readjustments of the buttocks and legs in which

Lovico was engaged, uttered this sentence with the same calm as he had applied to his "No."

"Well — maybe," Lovico mused. "Temple says he didn't intend to hit so hard."

"But he did hit so hard, and twice," Shipman said as if it were a discussion of a hypothetical case.

"Yes."

"That is murder."

"I'm unable to agree, Mr. Shipman. So far I have seen nothing to suggest, and certainly nothing to prove, that anyone intended your son's death. Officer Temple on the contrary is very remorseful. Remorse is another difficult concept, but I believe this man is genuinely remorseful and very broken up about —" Lovico did not want to repeat the phrase "your son's death."

"And there was no knife," Shipman said.

"Temple didn't see a knife. That brings us to my reason —"

"He would have seen it," Shipman said.

"I agree. In all probability. But the other two officers will testify tomorrow that your son had a knife and was trying to stab and slash them. A knife was found at the scene."

Shipman dismissed this with a simple gesture.

"Mr. Shipman, here is why I wanted to talk with you. But first, do you have any questions about today's testimony?"

"No."

"Am I correct in my surmise that having listened to the medical testimony in the morning and the testimony of Officer Temple in the afternoon you have concluded it was a blow or blows from Officer Temple that were fatal to your son?"

"Of course."

"Yes. For that reason especially I want to inform you that Officer Temple is being very cooperative. It will be his testimony, when I recall him to rebut his partners the day after tomorrow, which will tend to establish that your son was unarmed. I believe Officer Temple is telling the truth and he is paying a very high price."

"Ah — his friends no longer speak to him? He has been kicked out of the Patrolmen's Benevolent Association?"

Lovico said: "A higher price than that."

And Shipman replied: "Then the murderers are at each others' throats, like it says in the Bible, and one of these white police officers is trying to save the baby buns his mama spanked."

"Mr. Shipman, please, for the sake of intellectual clarity, please stop using the word murder."

"Intellectual clarity, Mr. Lovico, is just the reason I use it. I am not playing a game full of technical rules made up by you and your friends. It's you who are playing a game. I am free to call each thing by its real name."

"I presume then that you know everything, that you have god-like powers of knowing beyond doubt that which other men must grope and stumble after. You know, then, exactly what was in the minds of the three officers, you know who struck the first blow, you know precisely which blow was fatal and whether a conscientious police officer in precisely the circumstances of this altercation — all of which are fully known to you — would have struck that blow. Knowing all this you have no need of the 'technical rules' that govern the investigations and trials of us mortals, because, in addition to everything else, you also know who is telling the truth and who is lying — and you know this merely by looking into their eyes.

"Mr. Shipman, in all respect to your emotional condition, what would you put in the place of this so-called game?"

"I would put justice there," Shipman said. "Don't worry about my emotional condition, Mr. Lovico. Don't give it a thought. You can see for yourself, I'm not in an emotional state. Can you see that?

"No, Mr. Lovico, I'm surprised you would turn this into a debate. I do not profess the fullness of knowledge you describe nor do I need it. Three men drive a fourth into an enclosed space and hit his head with what you call deadly force not once, not twice but three and perhaps, says the medical doctor, *four times*. How much knowledge do I need? You say I pretend to know what was in their minds. Well we know what you mean by that. You mean I pretend to know whether they had decided to kill my son. But pardon me, you are a lawyer. That is your profession and your — I don't know what to call it. That is why you can't see what's staring you in the face.

"Whether they had this intention is unimportant, like the knife is unimportant. I am suspecting —"

Lovico observed the incongruous mix of cultivated and plain black street-speech that gave the man's words an oratorical uniqueness. What he heard was "I'm *suspectin.*" Lovico wondered whether the man had been brought up in the North or South and whether he had ever preached.

"I am suspecting," Shipman said, "that you see this murder as some kind of a nasty accident. Boys will be boys and cops will be cops. They got to patrol, therefore some dumb nigger's bound to get stomped. But they didn't intend to kill him. So what's the fuss? All right I'll tell you something that's missing from your legal education. This thing about intention doesn't enter in here. It's got nothing to do with the case. You talk about a legal arena, that's where intention belongs. I'm talking about the arena of First Street the night they beat my boy to death.

"Intention is when one human being decides to kill another. That's how you mean it. I'm being civil, Mr. Lovico, and I'll go on being civil. Am I right? Is that what you mean?"

"Yes," Lovico said quietly.

"Fine. You're civil and I'm civil. The intention to kill one human being that comes into the mind of another human being. But these cops didn't even get to first base. First base is when they look at my boy and say, 'That there's a human being.' So they don't get this textbook intention in their minds, Mr. Lovico, simply because they can't, you see, because when they look at him they don't see a human being. They can't ever say 'We are now going to up and kill this human being.' They look at him and I don't have to tell you what they see."

Lovico said: "Mr. Shipman. Even though I labor under the handicap of a legal education and courtroom experience I am still capable of seeing what you see in this case — that there is a kind of intention short of the fully developed and quite specific intention to bring an end to the life of a certain human being by a certain act. But the law is written to deal with that kind of intention too, or more accurately that kind of culpability short of the specific intent to kill. That is why there are degrees of murder, that is why there is manslaughter, that is why there is endangering safety by conduct regardless of life. But I admit you are right to this extent. I do see in this case, given what I know at this stage of it, an element of the accidental in that something happened which so far as I can see was not intended. There is nothing wrong with my seeing that, Mr. Shipman. That is not neglect of my duty. That is my duty."

"You're talking about something else. You don't want to see what I'm saying."

"I do see it," Lovico insisted, "and the law sees it too. What you are describing is exactly second-degree murder, which is defined in the statute book as taking the life of a human being by actions that are dangerous and display a depraved mind, a mind that takes no regard of human life."

"Second degree," Shipman said quickly. "You let a killer off easy because to the evil of murder he adds the evil of prejudice. And you have already told me," Shipman added as if to support Lovico, "you'll only charge what you can prove to a jury."

"Exactly."

"And now I tell you — you said justice was your duty. You're saying two different things. But I know which one you mean. You mean you'll play the game. Whatever happens in the end, even if it's nothing, you'll call it justice, just because that's how the game ended. The buzzer buzzes and the ref hollers 'Justice!' But as I told you once, I am going to have real justice, Mr. Lovico. I hope you heard me."

Lovico said: "Should you become a threat to the community or any specific person, Mr. Shipman, I will have you jailed."

"Be serious, all right? One, you'd look like a bigot, two, you'd look like a fool, and three, I'd be out in an hour. Besides, your boss would never let you put me in jail. Anyway I am not a threat to anybody's safety. I meant that I would go to a judge myself and demand charges if you refused to do it. You already told me I could."

"I don't believe that is what you meant," Lovico said.

"You must know everything that goes on in my mind, with your godlike powers."

Lovico didn't respond to this. He seemed to be considering a new approach. He said:

"Mr. Shipman, if you'll listen to a scrap of philosophy — No; you said 'nigger.' That word, Mr. Shipman, is not part of my private or public vocabulary, and I will not be spoken to as if it were."

"Fair enough," said Shipman imperturbably. "I never said you said it."

"Most people think," Lovico resumed, "that the justice system is established to protect the weak from the strong, and it is. But it also protects the strong from responsibilities no man should have to take on. Let us suppose there is a strong man who doesn't recognize that to be strong sometimes means only to endure the unendurable —"

"To be passive," Shipman interpreted. "To eat it."

"And let us suppose this man takes justice as he sees it into his own hands. Let us suppose —"

"That he kills the killers like he has a right to."

"All right, taking the extreme case, he kills. Should he kill someone like Officer Temple he would commit a crime — and kill a good and courageous man who is also seeking justice."

Shipman smiled.

"He would also destroy his own life, turn himself into a murderer, bring new grief and agony to his wife, and condemn himself to live out his years in prison. I will not try to give you a picture of life in prison —"

"For a black man," said Shipman, "who kills a white cop."

"I said I won't try. But to endure, I disagree; to endure is not passive. — Mr. Shipman, I can't say any more on this subject without telling you what has happened to Officer Temple's son."

Here for the first time Lovico indulged himself in a piece of dramatic technique, pausing and throwing at Shipman the penetrating stare for which he believed he was well known among his adversaries.

"Officer Temple has a son too," Lovico began, "a boy of eleven or twelve. His name is Robert."

"Then he's luckier than I am."

Lovico looked at the ceiling and his eyes flicked from one point to another. He had by now entirely changed his mode of address to Shipman and his voice was not so steady.

"This son is — of course — precious — to Officer Temple. We all, we who have children, know what the childless never do know. We have given our hostages to fortune and created a more far-reaching and sensitive web of life. —

"Now. Certain persons have been trying to break Officer Temple, and knowing that the man himself cannot be intimidated they have adopted the usual strategy of cowards and have tried to reach him through his family. At first they warned him by sending a bully to his son's school to steal his hat. Temple later found the hat pierced through with a piece of windshield glass from his car, which had been vandalized. I advised Temple to get the boy out of the city until he, the father, had testified under oath on the knife — not just, Did John Shipman Jr. have a knife? but *Where did this knife come from?* You see Temple knows the answer to that question.

"He said he would take the boy, or his wife would, to her father's farm in the Ohio Valley. But we were too late, Mr. Shipman. Someone had already concluded it was necessary to intensify the pressure. On the afternoon of the day Mrs. Temple was to take the boy away a gang of boys dragged him off the playground and into an alley near his school and beat him. One or two held him and punched his face, and another boxed his ears from behind. He is now unable to hear ordinary conversation. He is almost deaf."

"The sins of the father are visited upon the son."

"No, sir. If Officer Temple were cooperating with his partners instead of with me his son would never have been attacked. You may say 'The conspirators are at each others' throats' or 'The sins of the father' or anything else you please. The fact is that Temple has pledged himself to the truth."

"Now, almost deaf," Shipman said, ignoring this last. "What does that mean? Almost deaf forever?"

"For now he is able to hear only loud noises and he cannot distinguish words unless they are shouted at close range. He has an incessant ringing in his ears. They held his head and gave a violent simultaneous clap to both ears, and the air wave burst his eardrums. He will regain his hearing slowly over several weeks, according to his doctor."

"He will regain it."

"So the doctor believes."

"Then we have a kid who's been beaten up and he'll be fine. So why don't we do this, Mr. Lovico? What's wrong with this right here? We give the just punishment to those who beat Temple's boy, and why don't we give the just punishment to those who beat my boy?"

"Mr. Shipman, I quite agree. The just punishment. Please understand that I do not equate the two cases. I have not so much as implied they are comparable. Your son is dead and Temple's son lives. You drive me — you force me to say on Temple's behalf what he would never say himself. He cares about your son too, sir. Your son being dead it would surely be more convenient and safer for him to decide that there is nothing to be gained by opposing these men."

"Except you'll reduce his charge," Shipman interjected.

"I don't know that I will."

"Sure you will. I'm not a lawyer but I know this building. I can read, I can watch TV. You'll charge all three with third degree murder or manslaughter or some piss-ant misdemeanor and you'll charge the other two with obstructing justice. They planted false evidence. And you'll let Temple off the false evidence charge."

"Wait, Mr. Shipman, you're not reasoning clearly. Without Temple's testimony on the knife there would be no charge of obstructing justice. And if he didn't participate in the obstruction he ought not to be charged."

"My reasoning is clear enough to know that Temple will profit by betraying his partners, and clear enough to know that a man who thinks he can probe and measure the human mind with calipers is a fool."

"I do not think that."

"Yes you do. It's your profession."

"I am saying for God's sake that here is a man who loves his son too, who is doing what little lies within his power for your son."

"No, Mr. Lovico," said Shipman standing. "It is in your power, not his. I will wait to see what charges you issue."

John Shipman left the room.

Sam Lovico paused like a man climbing a flight of a hundred steps. He telephoned Lieutenant Kennelly and recommended that bodyguards be assigned to each of the three officers.

Chapter 22
In the Net

Rolling his head around in the falling stream Shipman found all his senses coming alive at once. The water thudded against his skull and spread its warmth over his head, neck, chest and back; and it played its rippling music both inside and outside his ears; it blocked and then, on its own initiative, re-opened the channel of his right ear; and it pelted his face so that he closed his eyes against it. Then he saw darkness overlaid with a shifting pattern of dim red, suggesting perhaps that something lay at the heart of blackness that was not quite black. So all in one moment Shipman gained a sudden knowledge of what consciousness was and what it would be like to give it up. He knew about that. You give it up in flashes, not blinding flashes, not at all, (not in the daylight), but orange and yellow flicks of light leaping out at you like tongues of reptiles. And you give it up in an eardrum-splitting hailstorm of cracks and bangs and ripping sounds, the snapping of an army of bullwhips aimed at your eyes. And you give it up when the invisible missiles blind you, tear out your eyes and smite your face and open your forehead and pierce your heart and — and the missiles open everything that should remain closed, and close everything that should be open to the light.

But the battlefield at night is another world altogether. They came at his line in human waves that were neither wavelike nor human: so it appeared under the swinging amber lamps as they popped overhead and descended slantwise as the wind caught their parachutes and drove them clear across the black background. The hobbling shadowy figures like crippled apes advancing through the beaten zone never seemed to make it through the invisible wall.

One by one they toppled. Some sank as if they'd stepped in holes. Some threw up their arms like mechanical men. Some crouched and rammed their heads into the screen that nobody could see, and their bodies buckled against it. They weren't firing — he never knew why —

Shipman and Jimmy Maynard, as black as he, were crowded in their hole by the presence of a white lieutenant, the forward observer from the artillery battery, who dived in head-first and then spent what seemed like three or four minutes struggling to get right side up. He said: "Sorry" and then shouted to somebody they couldn't see: "Battery four!"

When they started bursting Shipman took the BAR from Jimmy Maynard, who had died somehow, and poured as much hell as he could into the inferno.

Hadn't he proved it? Hadn't he proved it that night among others.

And yet this new thing was different. In a way, he understood perfectly that it was different; nothing like it had ever happened to him before. But his mind never explained the difference. The fact was that in Korea he had never been scared but now death had gotten inside his spine. The water raced down from his bent face in seven or eight bead-strings and splattered at his feet.

"Why should I die? Maybe that Lovico character can get me justice after all. I'll tell him for Christ's sake am I supposed to die to get my rights? So the fuckin cops get two of us? Is that the deal?" While the bead-strings destroyed themselves against the tiles he hollered in his mind: "And that's what you call justice, you blabbermouth fool?" — where justice meant Lovico lecturing about the law from his squeaky chair while an arc of police officers opened fire on Shipman. And who was the blabbermouth fool now?

He leaped to a new idea: kill Lovico.

"I better kill that poky old DA too, right, the three cops and that little fat hair-splitting — 'This is murder, this isn't murder' — that bald-headed bureaucratic phony fuckin — white! — lawyer! Right," he proceeded in a calmer tone, "he's the one with the brains, the cops are his goons, the three cops, they beat my boy — the cops —"

He covered his face and he didn't feel the water any more. His cocknballs shriveled in the thrill of terror. Desperately they sought refuge higher in his body where of course there was no safety; his whole skin crawled with cold, his guts yawned open and he said: "God damn! Can't I live?"

He spat out the all-too-familiar salty fear-fluid that flooded his mouth and for a second his sole aim in life was just to breathe. And he pulled in a series of breaths that reached to his stomach. He said: "Your boy died fighting but you are a piss-willie coward."

He hadn't thought of "piss-willie" since he was ten years old, so the sound took him back, way back to a softer existence when the kids played ball and had free-for-alls in Jonathan Elms Park, and ran wild till dark while a few blocks away their mothers were hollering them home. But they only came when they got hungry and beat. His mother scolded and sometimes spanked him and it seemed horrible at first, then it turned out it wasn't so bad, and she always gave him dinner.

"Yes," he said, "yes sir, a piss-willie afraid to do what my boy did before me. Oh God," he went on mocking, whining, "it be so *dark* over there, it be so cold, it be so *empty*."

He knew he'd fall into a black sleep as soon as he laid his head on the pillow but at three o'clock he'd be awakened by the usual discomfort. He'd climb out of bed struggling against the doom that always seized his mind at that hour, and would shield his eyes against the white light in the bathroom, the blazing light. And the fear would go away. But he wouldn't sleep again, at least not till just before Odell Diann rose at six to prepare for the day's teaching at West High. Once she left the bed it was a certainty he couldn't go back to sleep. So this was the program: a strange slide through the fear of death into oblivion, then the witch-dance of hours till morning.

The mirrors were clear now and he saw a powerful head and set of shoulders, an exhibition of hardened masculine strength if you didn't know his mind — and he noticed the black hand with its long and too-slender fingers. He was comparing this hand to Temple's, as he had seen the white hands of that man earlier. Temple's hands were bigger yet more compact, with bigger bones, thicker sinew and muscle amid the tough bones, and Temple's wrists were larger.

"Look at'm!" he exclaimed, seeing his cocknballs so desperate to get into his body. He knew they'd be back, but: "Look at'm!"

He splashed warm water on his belly and genitals but they didn't notice. He said, "Jesus, pathetic."

When he fell asleep, the conscious loss of consciousness made life seem sweet all over again. He entered the familiar passage to the strange. And before he slept he lived all over again the horror when he found the gook's body.

Leading his fire team down a narrow passage between two barns he had seen a face pop up in a window. He fired his M1 six times at knee height, right through the wood, and listened to a wheezing, wordless sound. One of his men started to chew the wood with the BAR but Shipman stopped him. He went cautiously into the barn and found the gook bleeding. His eyes pleaded. The one thing he should have done (shoot him in the head) he did not do.

When he awoke with the gangrene of the world eating into his soul he discovered his spine was stiff and his left shoulder hurting. Pulling back the blankets was hard and even painful; he took thirty seconds to get out of bed.

At this hour his mind was assailed by a cosmic knowledge and dread that he might have skipped altogether if only he'd been able to sleep through the night, but his prostate trouble wouldn't let him sleep. It had been ten years since he'd slept through the night.

It was only now that the starving people of the Sahel had any reality for him. It was now that everything that had not happened to him in Korea seemed certain to happen somewhere else in peacetime. And it was now that all the blessings of adversity vanished from the condition of his people and the suffering remained. In truth it was only during these hours of baleful night that he conceived of the black people as his. He never denied them, not even at high noon. But when as now it appeared certain that he himself would die, or when it appeared imminent that he would be thrust out into the cold again, this time without food or clothes — and there'd be no safe haven, no U.S. Army ambulance to take him to the rear, because there is no rear — then he saw that they were his people, and he was theirs.

It is impossible to forget combat and Shipman didn't want to forget. He had faced the bullwhips. So few men that he met in this life ever had. At his moment of weakness when the very act of pissing and shaking the last drops out of his urethra told him he stood at the brink, he knew there was strength in him somewhere.

What was physical would perish. He was proud of his handsome hair and for that reason he did not look in the mirror when he left the bathroom. This iron-gray hair — he liked the term "iron-gray" — was exactly what he would endow himself with were the endowing his to do. It was thick, stiff and wavy, and stood up just right. And it had been given; he did not make it. Like the long slender fingers which he sometimes viewed with surprise and a sense of otherness, this little meaningless gift about which he was so ridiculously complacent was no credit to him at all.

"And not the cocknballs either!"

"And I'll be gone in an hour!" he thought a second later.

If then the strength he claimed were as real as the dread, the question was: what to do with the hour?

He returned silently to their bedroom and knew even before he entered that warm mixed odor of their bodies trapped under the blankets that she was weeping. She didn't move and she made no sound but it wasn't necessary that he see the tears or taste the salt. She lay on her side, curled away from him. He at first lay against her back and matched the curve of his naked body to hers; but when she couldn't suppress it any longer and when the tremors of her agony reached him through his own body, and when she drew breath in a series of shudders and sobs, then he turned her to face him, and pressed her face against his neck and began speaking as if he himself were not afflicted except by her affliction.

When he held her in his embrace like this and tried to absorb the shock of her sobs in the enclosing circle of his arms he had to be something else, not the soldier whose life was already forfeit. He had to be a lover whose love was inexhaustible. He was thinking: "I torture her. That's what all this *soldier* business comes down to." This of course was the talk of weakness.

Here came a clear picture of Odell Diann when they told her he had been killed by the cops. He closed his eyes against it but it he wasn't quick enough.

Sometime that night he took his bathrobe from the hook on the closet door.

It was a spacious old house in which everything that was old was perfectly preserved or restored, and everything that was new was up to date and strikingly modern in the midst of a '20s interior. Shipman's den was a converted sunroom with double-insulated windows and red and blue striped curtains. The computer was linked to the computer at his office. The few books he owned were here in a leaded glass walnut case, and they included one that had been presented to his father upon his graduation from high school in 1919. Whether the old drunk had ever read the book John Shipman didn't know. The father gave it to the son, but John Shipman had not read it through until a year ago, when he began to suspect, by the hints being dropped from time to time, that Hawk's ambition was to write a history of the black people in America. It was then John Shipman opened the book. It was Booker T. Washington's *The Story of the Negro: The Rise of the Race from Slavery*. John Shipman began paging through it looking for a passage. He paused over a document written by the founders of the Free African Society, a group that according to

Washington prepared the way for the African Methodist Episcopal Church. The founders wrote in 1787:

". . . it was proposed after a serious communication of sentiments that a society should be formed without regard to religious tenets, provided the persons live an orderly and sober life, in order to support one another in sickness, and for the benefit of their widows and fatherless children."

He started to move on, but circled back to "widows and fatherless children" and stared at it for a minute. Then he found what he was looking for, which was this:

"The encouraging thing about the relations of the races in the United States," Washington wrote, "is that an increasing number of white men and black men are learning that the highest courage is that of the man or the woman who is helping some one else to be more useful or more happy; that, in the last analysis, it is not the courage that hurts some one and destroys something, but the courage that helps some one and builds something up which the world needs most."

"Courage," he thought, "is when you aim the BAR at his crotch and let the kick lift it." And so theoretically you cut him in two. "Vertically," he said aloud.

Elsewhere in the book, and in other writings of Washington that Shipman had read in high school and in the Army, he encountered a spirit that he recoiled from, that was too generous to the former slavemasters. Shipman speculated that Washington had been the more ready to forgive because he was half white himself.

"My wife has white blood in her veins," he thought. "Therefore my son did. Probably I do too. So we're all supposedly human. Ha! And human is the same everywhere."

Yet black people are different from white people, and white people are different from black. This is the organizing principle of society. Nothing is plainer than this difference; nothing is harder than to define just what it is.

It was only once in every decade or twenty years that Shipman even cared. He asked again: What is this difference that's so damned important? All he could find was a number of outward traits that signified nothing inward. He returned to the second passage and reading it again he reflected that his wife was just such a person as Washington praised.

A woman somewhat older than Shipman, tall and brown, Odell Diann Shipman, Del Taylor, entered the room. There rested in her countenance that very quality of completeness in its gentle form that her husband possessed in its fierce form. This completeness meant she was a finished woman. All the faculties and strengths she would ever need to survive a crisis or combat nihilism she now possessed. By limitless suffering she could survive anything.

She said: "Can't sleep, Big Boy?"

"No, Del, it won't quit." Here Shipman's mind played a trick and he thought of the ringing in Robbie Temple's ears, which wouldn't quit.

"So you're reading — what?"

He gave her the book and said: "The part about working to do good."

Odell Diann read the passage and nodded and returned the book.

Her white robe was open at the throat and tied close about her waist. She sat on the couch next to her husband's desk, crossed her legs and began a slow rhythmic swinging of her ankle. Her calf was slender and firm, but her face was a different case. The almond shape of her eyes had begun to relax towards something more nearly circular and a painful-looking rim of red surrounded each attentive eye. She sought her husband's eyes, then released him, and they sat without speaking.

At first their silence was the silence of two who need not speak, but gradually it turned to the silence of two who can not speak. In addition to the ever-dividing knowledge that Hawk was dead he had to endure Odell Diann's religious way of dealing with the death.

To her, God was a mystery. Yet there was hope of penetrating this mystery if one had but faith. "Faith Is Sufficient." One can penetrate this far: He does what is good. She had, accordingly, declared almost in words that there must be good in Hawk's death. She searched for it. Shipman knew all this because he knew her religion and because she had told him part of it.

The good she ultimately discovered after she regained some of her strength was that God had taken one son, the good one, to open the eyes of his parents. To what? To their neglect of their other son, the worthless one. As for justice, a word she never uttered: what her belief meant to her husband was that the God who supposedly breathed the longing for it into his creatures was himself totally indifferent to it.

Shipman looked up and saw that her eyes were large with tears.

He did, however, agree there was a mystery. He could not understand how a religious belief that would lobotomize him could call forth such a noble beauty in her. Her tears and the beauty of her calm face raised him; he went to the couch and sat beside her, and she began to cry again, as he thought, for Hawk. But when he listened carefully to the half-articulated words smothered in her sobs he heard:

"My poor Big John, my poor Big Boy."

She turned and encircled his head, and drew him down to her bosom. He did not resist her except inwardly.

"This is terrible with Jesus," she said. "I can't imagine how it is without him."

He felt her kisses, her tears on the back of his neck, and he succumbed to the irresistible solace of her bosom.

She was saying: "What you want isn't there, Big John. He won't be back. And justice, there isn't any such thing, don't you know that?"

They went up the stairs hand in hand. She rested her head in the hollow of his shoulder and he drew the covers to her neck and tucked the satin edge of the blanket against her throat as he always did. While she slept he revolved her ideas in his mind. There is no justice. He won't be back.

A half hour may have passed. His feeling of care for her spread gently through his soul but could not drive out the contempt for a theology that would accept the killing of one son for the sake of the other. She couldn't believe that. Shipman's mind formed a half-sane picture of a Hebrew God dressed as a plumber carrying a wrench and tool box.

"If justice were uppermost," said Odell Diann, "we never would have survived slavery."

"I thought you were asleep. There you go talking like you survived slavery."

"Not I. We. — I don't know any hymns about justice, but plenty about grace and faith."

John Shipman said: "Everybody wants me to lie down in the road."

"I want you to see what you don't see yet in your grief. Reason unaided tells you this isn't all."

"*Reason unaided* is preacher talk."

"And here's more of the same. Our son is taken. 'Behold, I will plead thy cause and take vengeance for thee.' What if you took your vengeance? Our son would still be gone and the evil would remain."

"The evildoers," said Shipman, "would not remain."

"Then you would never know peace."

"I don't need peace."

"Oh yes you do," she said. "You have no peace now because God has taken our boy."

"God didn't take him."

"Yes he did. But you can find peace if you surrender your will to his. Since there is no earthly justice you might as well do that."

"*Might as well?*"

"Who cares how I said it? Jesus said that everything else is torment and barrenness."

"You're saying be passive," he said. "You treat me like I was a child, holding my head that way, because the mother in you is so strong. But you're the child. The things you believe are the dreams of a child."

She said, "Yes, a child of God. You are nobody's child any longer but God's. If I press your face to my breast I am not trying to mother you. It is my tenderness, which mothers also feel, but I am your wife and a wife may be tender without being accused of trying to mother anybody. There is no man without a father and a mother, and the father and mother had parents too. And none of them created himself I assure you, Big John, not even you."

Shipman said: "You can still do what's just, or do what would be just if there were any justice in this stinking world."

Whether awake or asleep, she didn't answer.

"There may be — omissions —" He meant omissions that compound the evil, omissions that say *I don't care if you kill my son.*

Some time later when he was again uncertain whether she was sleeping he heard her patient voice and felt her hand moving up his chest. She said:

"You could try loving your other son."

But to his father Winslow Shipman was deader than Hawk; he killed himself every day with booze; and Hawk felt alive in John's mind. He reasoned like this: "O.K., her god is a fairy tale, and my justice is another. Let her have hers and I'll take mine. Let the father follow the example of the son." His mind settled on this as the definition of what he was doing.

Chapter 23
Hey Bombcatcher

Temple had just testified that the kid was not armed. Now he wanted to get out but a young woman stopped him and said Lovico wanted him.

The parties were gathering their papers and spectators were emptying the room — Temple looked around cautiously and saw that the black father was gone. He had not let his eyes rest on the man even once, even for a second. He had a hunger to look him full in the face. He looked from this young woman to Lovico, who was poring over a sheaf of papers with the medical examiner. Lovico looked up and signed to Temple to wait. So Temple and the assistant stood there, not speaking, although wishing to speak. Then the assistant proposed they wait in her office, and gathered her papers into her briefcase. Temple accompanied her into the elevator.

The building felt hostile and mean. Temple's soles made a scuffing sound in the corridor and the woman's knocked out a thin echo. They passed the door to the DA's waiting room and continued down the gloom-ridden hall to an unmarked frosted-glass door which the woman unlocked, and which Temple pulled open to admit her first. He had never met this woman and felt uneasy in her presence and she seemed to dislike his gesture of holding the door for her. But she had a key ring in one hand and a briefcase in another. She said a clipped "Thank you" and led him down a row of office cubicles to her own. She unlocked it and bade him enter and he did.

He thought: "I'd hate to work in a box like this" — yet she was a starting lawyer, and a starting lawyer was just what he aspired to be. "I could be a pretty good lawyer — Christ, I've got to be something."

The woman was transferring files from the briefcase to a set of brackets on her desk. Her endless shuffling of all this dry paper impressed him as utterly futile.

Temple heard a familiar voice and turned in his chair to see Ruthenbeck and Banes walking down the row in the company of another young assistant.

Temple got up as if in a nightmare and started towards Ruthenbeck, under a sudden urge to kill him right now. He saw it happening, saw Ruthenbeck's eyes roll up and go dull in their sockets.

The woman cried, "Sit! — Sit down," in a whisper as if she didn't want Ruthenbeck to hear.

Ruthenbeck's eyes met Temple's and Temple seemed to see his own eyes burning at Ruthenbeck as the black father's had burned at him. He thought, or heard himself think: "I will kill you." He was sure the black father had been watching him with a burning hate as he testified.   He felt the young woman's hands on his shoulders and strained to look around her to Ruthenbeck, who smiled at him with a deftly modulated contempt.

Temple dreamed of the impact of his fist in Ruthenbeck's face and enjoyed a paroxysm of physical revenge, beating Ruthenbeck's face but thinking at the same time: "You beat the black kid but you don't touch this damned killer."

The woman pressed her hands flat against his chest. Temple fell back into the chair, looked up at her, and thought: "Don't touch him! Don't say a word."

The woman still had her hands on him. She leaned close and looked into his eyes as if her fate was bound to his, as if they were lovers, and said: "Don't —"

"It's O.K.," Temple said. "I'm O.K." And he thought: "I could beat that fool to a pulp."

He recalled a doctor's testifying that the brain was somewhat loose in its skull, and imagined his blows jerking Ruthenbeck's skull too fast for the brain to keep up.

He thought: "No, no, for Christ's sake."

The woman asked, "Will you sit there?"

"Yes. Don't worry about me."

Ruthenbeck reappeared in the doorway, leaning in from the side, grinning, and said: "Hey Bombcatcher, he did have a knife — turned you into a pussy with it."

Temple lurched to his feet and Ruthenbeck still presented his leering grin.

As he reached his full height Temple lost all sense of reality. The assistant DA pushed him and he didn't know it; he began a crazy Frankenstein walk towards the grin. The woman leaped forward and slammed the door so hard the glass cracked, and stood before Temple panting with fear and fury — and Temple came to himself and grabbed his head with both hands and squeezed mercilessly and tried to control himself. The woman trembled all over and took a step, then another toward Temple and pushed him back toward his chair, then pushed again, and again.

In his bachelor apartment Temple slapped together a dinner that was simple and disgusting. It would be better not to admit it but he hated this place. It wasn't quite clean and it directed to his senses a variety of messages of ineradicable dirt and previous usage. "One thing," he said, "I'll never study law here. I'll find a better place."

Wherever Sandra and Robbie were, that was his home. He looked around the dismal scene. He had never brought a woman here or gone to a woman's place. Indeed he had not touched another woman. He refused to seek biological release after the teenager's fashion and sank into wretchedness when he suspended his refusal, because in that case he reverted to a form of infantilism. Yet when he succeeded in extending his refusal over a long period and had good cause to respect himself for it he would sometimes lose his moral identity in waves of tender, sensitive longing to be what he was not, and to do that which he surely didn't want to do. "Maybe I can't feel good," he said. "Maybe I don't know how to be happy, but I can try to make sense. That should be easy, just to be rational. Lawyer my ass. —

"O.K., I'll never be a lieutenant or captain, they'll never trust me with that level of responsibility. O.K., I see that, and I can handle it. I'm going to think everything through from the beginning."

Temple sat on a rented chair and ate his dinner from a paper plate on a rented table. The room, which belonged to somebody else and nobody, faded from his feelings and ceased to concern him. He had a new idea. He didn't want to read, watch television or listen to music; he wanted to see his son.

The boy was supposed to come back next week for a doctor's appointment if Sandra could arrange one. But Temple wanted to see his son now; tonight. Temple had his car back, and his father-in-law's farm was only three hours away. If he left now he could be there by ten. Lovico had told him that he wouldn't be recalled to the witness stand until the day after tomorrow at nine in the morning. Tomorrow was set aside for the testimony of Ruthenbeck and Banes. He thought about driving to the farm now and returning tomorrow night. Sandra wouldn't like that. She seemed to imply that the farm, which was her girlhood home, was her territory and that he must not go there without permission, whether Robbie was there or not. Arousing her anger pained him by bringing out the ugliness in her that made his love seem hopeless. When anger distorted her face and she spoke as if nothing had any value he felt an overpowering despair. Each time he slipped into this despair, which was nothing but a special view of Sandra, his pain was worse and recovery slower.

"If I were to die tonight," he thought, "I would want to speak with her." He felt strange saying this and wondered where the idea had come from. He ached to take her in his arms; he remembered her warm loveliness in his arms.

Leaving half his dinner he got up from the table, turned off the kitchen light, turned off the two lamps in the living room and walked to the window. He began to draw the curtain back. Looking down and across the street he saw in the line of parked cars under the streetlights a sedan of a solid color, and knew it at once for a police car. He could see a man in plain clothes sitting in the driver's seat but because of the angle he couldn't tell whether there was also a man in the passenger's seat.

Temple closed the curtain, turned the lights back on and picked up the telephone. He called Operations but none of the ranking officers was in. He asked to be transferred to the field lieutenant. He told this man he did not want to be protected. Another strange insight struck him: that preparing to die and preparing to live were the same thing. The lieutenant said he could not call off the bodyguards. Temple would have to speak to the operations boss in the morning. Temple said:

"I'm leaving the city for twenty-four hours."

"We won't follow you out of the city," the lieutenant said, "but when you come back let us know."

Temple said "Yes sir" and hung up the phone.

He packed his shaving kit, a pair of socks and a change of underwear in his travel bag. He went down the stairs like a man dropped from a height. He trotted across the street to tell the guard that he was going out of town. The man said: "I know all about it." Temple walked rapidly to his car. There was something like a crazy motor propelling him forward.

"Get away from this damned city. Get away from this damned bodyguard!" He looked over his shoulder. The police car crept away from the curb and waited. Temple thought: "I'm not going to die but these bastards are going to drive me nuts!"

Chapter 24
<u>Eyes</u>

Temple awoke in a current of belief, that life is good, that merely to be alive is a blessing.

He saw the figure of his son moving indistinctly in the darkness beside him. It was Robbie who had touched him on the shoulder to wake him. Now he knew where he was. Robbie was sitting up in his sleeping bag and pulling on a sweater, and Temple imagined he could see the boy squinting his eyes as the sweater passed over his head. Robbie was kicking his legs free of the bag and putting his shoes on, and he followed Robbie's example. In a moment they stood up. In the beam of Robbie's flashlight the trampled straw and chaff on which they had been sleeping came to life like a memory rediscovered.

Robbie lifted the light and indicated a gap some thirty steps away, across the open hay mow. This was the opening for a narrow cleft between two stacks of hay. Robbie cast the light back from time to time to light his father's way.

The right stack, irregular and nearly exhausted, was the first-cut hay that Temple's father-in-law had been feeding out to his sheep since October. The left stack was high and still square. This was the second-cut, never-wet rowen, a high-protein hay that Granddad would soon begin to sell to dairy farmers who had not laid by sufficient feed in the fall. The sheep had been fed a little of the rowen during late pregnancy and would get a little more, plus some grain, to sustain them while they were giving milk to their lambs, but in the main they were expected to produce and feed their lambs on the first-cut hay. Therefore the stack on the right was depleted with the advent of spring while the wall on the left rose into the dark of the upper barn.

Trailing his fingers along the wall of prickly bales, Temple followed his son's silhouette as it pursued the flitting light along the corridor. So often did Robbie shine the light back on his father's path that Temple believed the boy didn't need a light at all.

At the end of the passage they came to a chest-high gate made of boards strong enough to keep sheep and cattle from invading the hay mow. Robbie climbed it and played his light upon a silent flock of sheep and lambs that had scattered themselves in sphinx-like attitudes over the floor of a three-sided shelter. The fourth side, to Temple's right, opened south into the night. A lamb gave a little call like a note blown on a child's tin bugle. For a minute Robbie's light went out and Temple listened to the low hollow sound suspended in the air by the flock. They were not quite silent.

Robbie sprang from the gate and seemed to land weightlessly among the ewes. One got to her feet and moved away; the others admitted him to their company without complaint; but a lamb darted away and began bleating; and now a general stir moved through the awakening flock. Robbie turned his light off and stood still, and Temple, watching from behind the gate, could almost see his son's calmness and his instinctive ease with the animals. Did he get this from Sandra? The lamb bleated its lamentations but the ewes, including apparently its own mother, now seemed to have determined that nothing very serious was to be read into these pitiful cries. When Robbie's light came back on, the lamb was standing with forefeet planted in the salt box, looking with urgent eyes over its shoulder and bleating still.

A big ewe who had been standing dropped to her knees and lurched to her side, then righted herself with the heavy exertions appropriate to her present condition in life, which was that of expectant mother. She assumed the sphinx attitude of her community, brought up a cud by extending her neck and began to chew with a rotary motion of her jaw. Robbie moved around her and crouched in the corner where Temple could see only his earnestly bent head, his back and the play of his light on the old gray wall-boards. Robbie conducted the examination that had been ordered by his grandfather and then returned to the gate by a slow circuitous route that left the flock tranquil and confident. The stray flitted and skipped back to its mother and settled down, resting its face on her side.

Temple took a spiral notebook from his shirt pocket, placed it up against a beam and wrote: "How can you tell them apart?"

Robbie said: "They go off by themselves when they're almost ready, and she has a mark."

Temple started to write but Robbie said:

"She has a white streak on her muzzle."

"Is she ready?" the father wrote.

"She will be soon."

"Should you tell Granddad?"

"No. Not yet."

Temple couldn't see his son very well during this exchange because the boy kept the light directed at the notebook.

Two hours later Temple awoke and saw the eyes of the black father staring at him. He didn't try to shake off this vision because how do you try to do that? The eyes came closer and acquired a certain light like ice, or a drop of rain reflecting in the center of each one.

Temple and Granddad had drunk beer for an hour last night and now Temple had to go. He felt in the hay for the flashlight that Robbie had placed between their sleeping bags, wrapped in his sweater so it wouldn't be lost. Temple found the boy's sweater — he paused to feel its texture — unrolled it, took the light and went down the cleft between the stacks. He stopped and made himself known at the gate as Robbie would have done, but the flock was gone.

Temple went out the gate, across the spongy floor of the shelter and into the open night. He could hear the regular click of the fence-charger sending out a pulse of electrical energy every second. He heard the tumbling water of the creek where it descended a short rocky dropoff. This sound reached him from across the barnyard and he walked toward it, without benefit of light, following the sound and wondering whether his son at the present stage of his recovery could do the same.

The eyes of the black father were on him and he thought, "I didn't mean to kill him," but he felt a memory of his rage when he had struck. Hadn't he meant the rage?

Temple didn't know whether his memory, which was at work on the killing, was trying to make his guilt more lurid or was fabricating a false innocence. Another step and he might walk right into the creek. He shone his light on the dark and colorless water then raised it to the bluff on the other side and swept it along the lip of the bluff. Scores of pairs of eyes looked down on him from the entire length of the bluff, green, orange and yellow eyes, and eyes varying from green to yellow.

When Robbie wakened him just before dawn the eyes of the black father were there — black eyes in bloodshot whites with the drop of rain at their centers. Temple heard the words "It is still dark" in his mind. He opened his eyes and realized he was at the bottom of the hay mow with his son and he felt the physical force of his conviction that life is good, no matter what.

"All I have to do —" he thought. The rest of it was less articulate but something like: "Deserve this." The meaning wasn't quite apparent. He missed Sandra. He let himself imagine she was there.

Temple grasped Robbie's shoulder and squeezed, and the boy went motionless, knowing it was his father's sign of love. They passed through the cleft as before, opened the gate and entered the shelter. Robbie went to a ewe who lay on her side, her hooves braced against the east wall and a great lump rising in her side. Robbie dropped to his knees. His head almost touched the ground as he leaned forward and shone his light on her gleaming vulva. A rope of gray mucus dangled and marked the trail of her recent movements across the floor. The vulvae were engorged and a black enamel point could be seen at their center. Robbie said,

"There it is," and stood up, gave the flashlight to his father and said, "I'll tell Granddad." He ran out into the barnyard.

Temple stared with amazement at the glistening streak of mucus on the matted floor of straw and manure over which the ewe had evidently dragged herself, and compared this to the antiseptic operating room where Sandra had given birth to Robbie. He squatted and aimed the light at the ewe's rear end which seemed to be the locus of some awful purple calamity, and he looked at the little black point that Robbie had called to his attention. Robbie had said, "There it is!" but had not informed his ignorant father what it was: obviously not a lamb, because the lambs in the flock were white with brown faces. Their noses were black, it was true, but this was not a nose. This appeared to be a hard shovel-shaped — hoof. It was a hoof. Temple would have laughed if he could have seen himself squatting with his head hanging between his knees for a better view of the sheep's rear end.

"There's a whole lamb in there!" he thought. It was amazing, all because he had figured the hoof out by himself. He was exhilarated at taking this step, from a view of this black object as merely an unidentified piece of matter to a sudden comprehension of the lamb's having touched the threshold of an existence outside the womb.

Without his seeing how it happened Temple found himself looking at two black hooves and a black nose nestled between them. "Jesus!" he exclaimed, and he got up and paced to the other side of the shelter and slapped the wall simply because he had to do something. He turned and saw the ewe making an effort to rise. She rolled like a ship in heavy seas and propped herself up with a leg outstretched, then stood and stared at him for a moment, gathered her forces and strained, expanding her middle and contracting her rear. She took a few steps, fell to her knees, then dropped her rear and rolled again onto her side, stretched her legs and panted with open mouth. She made one cry, a sound unlike any Temple knew, yet not a cry of agony — and then she lay still. It was a cry of mixed agony and amazement. She kept her head half raised and her brown eyes alert, waiting for another movement.

Temple approached her slowly, turning his flashlight off so as not to frighten her (that was how he thought) and realized he could see her pretty well without it. She had a thick dirty wool, a brown face and legs of a brown so dark it was nearly black. The black pupils of her brown eyes were long and oriented horizontally. Temple stood beside her. Her mouth was open and her tongue was hanging out. It seemed strange and pleasant to him that she simply didn't care if he stood close by while she lived out her mysterious obligation.

He looked outside and could see the bluff, a dirt bank opposite the creek, and the weathered boards of the feed-bunks where the sheep ate hay in winter. It was still night but a form of night that gives up her secrets. The air seemed colder with the new light.

Between the hooves, which had pushed themselves quite into the open, lay a small and solemn face sheathed in a gray veil. The line of the mouth was curved in a smile, the eyes were closed, the ears were still concealed by the taut ring through which the hooves and face had already passed.

At some point all progress ceased. Robbie, Granddad and Temple stood for several minutes at the edge of the shelter like farmers talking politics at the feed store on a Saturday. All that was lacking was tobacco juice. Temple saw for the first time that Robbie leaned exactly as Granddad leaned against a pillar of the barn with his thumbs hooked into his pockets; his breath escaped in clouds and streams when he laughed; his hands showed red with the cold and his face was ruddy and alive, and his eyes roamed with an appraising attitude over the barnyard and seemed to survey the sheep without half trying, just as Granddad's did. He looked exactly as he would if he were thirty and the farm were his.

A big gray ewe began bellowing from the bluff, addressing her demands to the men, and Granddad bellowed back: "Go to hell!"

The ewe in the shelter was a lamb herself, although full grown or nearly so, and had never given birth before. That was why Granddad had wanted Robbie to watch her in the night. There was no telling how good a mother she would be, which was another reason to be around when she lambed. But she was three-quarters Clun Forest, a breed that make good mothers. "How's she doing?" Granddad shouted, and Robbie went to check. Granddad said in a low voice: "He can hear if you just speak up."

The boy said something from within the shelter but the men couldn't understand for the blatting of the angry ewe on the bluff, so they went inside.

Robbie was standing away from the ewe. She was trying to get up with the lamb hanging half out of her canal. She gave a half roll and a strain and sent out one desperate bah, then subsided and let her head fall to the ground — so now all four limbs and her neck were stretched out on the ground and the fore half of the lamb protruded from her vulva. Granddad drew a little nearer and bent slightly forward to take Robbie's arm — and held the boy in a gentle way as if he were about to start him in a race. The boy and Granddad stood transfixed by the ewe's stillness and did not seem to know what to do. Temple noticed that the lamb's shoulders were yellow.

The ewe rolled, strained and lifted her rear. The lamb dangled, still with that smile upon its sheathed face. The ewe braced her knees and stood erect. She took three staggering steps. The lamb came slipping out, the umbilical cord ripped, and the lamb fell swinging onto the straw, landing on its neck and shoulders and tumbling onto its side. It lay motionless. The lamb was yellow; that is, it was a white lamb soaked in a brown-yellow fluid.

The grandfather and the boy seemed to be frozen in a sculpture of indecision, but after about ten seconds Granddad said:

"Just a second now Robert."

Temple didn't know whether Robbie had heard.

The lamb lifted and dropped its head; it curved its body, and lifted its head again. Thin curtains of steam rose from every part of its body. It lay still. Its eyes were still closed and it was not breathing.

Granddad's thick laborer's fingers opened on Robbie's arm, releasing him, and Robbie dropped to his knees. He took the lamb roughly in his hands and wiped the face and nose with three or four sharp strokes of his palm, and the veil came off in streaks of slime.

The boy shifted the lamb from one hand to the other. It was so slippery it fell from his hands but the boy picked it up and shifted it twice more, tossing its body back and forth like a football, then laid it gently in the straw. Its eyes opened. Its mouth opened and closed. And it began to breathe, sending visible puffs of steam from its nostrils to mingle with the clouds rising from its wet body.

Standing, Robbie wiped his hands on his pants and looked at his grandfather. The old man smiled, every tooth outlined with tobacco stain, and Robbie smiled too.

The lamb lifted its head and seemed to be searching for something, and then collapsed, as if smitten unconscious. After a second it began to kick and wave its legs; it looked up again. By now there were streaks of sunlight crossing the floor of the shelter and touching the yellow color in the straw into life, and resting in one narrow sparkling bar on the coat of the lamb.

These streaks of sunlight adorned the rude figure of Granddad in his faded overalls, his old Sears denim coat and his red and black hunter's hat. A white forelock lay across his brow. He had a sharp nose and irregular jaw, and he was still smiling with pale blue eyes first at Robbie then at the lamb.

Two streaks of vertical light ran the length of Robbie's body. Temple looked at the east wall and it was ablaze. The sunlight flooded in around each board and penetrated every crack and knothole. And looking back at the illuminated figure of his son Temple saw him as if he had grown up in a single night. Here stood a rather tall blond boy with blue eyes, eyes that looked almost joyous, with the beginnings of a build, with shoulders that looked half again as broad as his hips, and with hands that were already the embryo of his grandfather's: sturdy, thick and strong.

Temple saw Sandra's vitality in Robbie's clear blue eyes, the broad curve of her brow in his brow and her mouth replicated and enlarged in his.

As Temple walked up to the house with Granddad for breakfast he kept seeing the image of this newly revealed son of his. He saw the boy drop to his knees and take the slimy lamb in his hands and remove the veil. He admired his rough but deft movements as he passed the slippery little body from hand to hand. He saw the boy's smile, and felt the answering smile spread over his own lips.

Granddad started the coffee and the two men ate bran cakes baked by the housekeeper the previous afternoon, and apples and Swiss cheese. Granddad said the lamb had defecated in its sack and was lucky to be alive. There had been no white cord in the afterbirth, therefore another lamb might be waiting to be born. Temple spontaneously echoed the phrase "waiting to be born." He imagined the smiling face of a lamb curled up in the dark of its mother's womb. He asked what the white cord was and the old man looked surprised. He said: "Damned if I know!" Then he said: "Why don't you and Sandra go back?"

"She doesn't . . ." Temple replied. "She won't."

Granddad grunted and drank his coffee.

When Temple thought of Sandra he didn't merely think. He felt the entry of a form-giving influence. The knowledge of Sandra, his knowing her in all ways, shaped his knowledge of himself.

"She's out of patience," he said. "She wants a steady man. Mr. Steady. Mr. Got It."

Granddad acknowledged this.

"She doesn't love me and even if I did all the right things she wouldn't want to be married to me."

Granddad's chin changed its shape, his lips pressed hard together and he said he thought that was right but love was a temporary thing in anybody's life. "You don't dare base your long-range plans on it," he said. "What does she want you to do?"

"She wants me to be something regular and I don't blame her for wanting it."

"Sandra has ambition," said Sandra's father.

"Yes she does and I won't stand in her way. I call her Sandra of the World."

Granddad's head tilted a little and he smiled a tobacco-juice smile as if he nearly understood. His blue eyes were small lively lights in a face that was the record of seventy years of sun, wind and dust. He repeated the phrase to indicate that it called for explanation.

"She has a new briefcase like a lawyer's," Temple said. "That's O.K. with me. She wears suits and really small, expensive jewelry and a short haircut. You've never seen her in this getup. She's very beautiful but she isn't the girl you raised or I married."

There was more, that Temple did not say: "She wears suits like a man's and goes to work like a man and somehow it makes her more feminine than ever. But she will not have another child. At least not by me."

He said to his father-in-law: "I have said to her, 'Let's have another child.' She'd rather take poison."

"She's right, if you're going to get a divorce."

"Yes. She's right," Temple conceded, "and we are going to get a divorce."

Granddad looked contemplatively out the window and nodded a few times. "But if you could have another boy like that fella out there . . ." he said.

"I want another child," Temple repeated but the words were hard to force out. "Sandra doesn't."

"Here's another child," Granddad said when they returned to the shelter under the barn and beheld a new lamb wobbling under the tongue-strokes of its mother.

Temple was still thinking of Sandra's face — of her lovely face, of this template of ideal womanly beauty.

"That's over," he thought. "I can live without it. It'll be a different life."

He had been thinking about coaching. Sandra would groan and say, "My God, what about your career as a lawyer? You're going back to coaching? I give up!" But it was obvious he could never have an effect on millions or thousands, so why not have an effect on hundreds? What could he do with his life that would be better? If he went into the black schools he would always be the cop who killed a black kid — but he could show them a white man is a human being. "Or I could come to a place like this," he thought, "— if they don't want me."

"Humble, useless, stupid!" This was her voice. "Burying yourself as if you had murdered somebody."

"I will live — with the eyes," said Temple to himself.

The new lamb was still steaming. It placed its head between its mother's forelegs and groped about with its muzzle, but fell upon its hindquarters under the force of a maternal lick. The ewe lowered her brown muzzle and licked its face, making a chuckling-gargling sound and nosing the lamb this way and that. Meanwhile the first lamb had struggled to its feet and taken two precarious steps towards the ewe. It halted, placed its legs more firmly, and continued its advance of desire upon its mother.

The ewe's eyes shifted from the loved one to the beshat first-born. She lowered her head and lifted her eyes, and when the lamb reached her she swung her muzzle upward and sent it flying. She resumed licking and chuckling and murmuring at the second-born, removing the veil, the blood and the slime, and when it regained its feet she nosed its rear just as if it were nursing, even though it hadn't yet discovered the teat.

Granddad pulled an old towel from his overalls and spread his legs over the contaminated one, bent stiffly down and scooped it up in one big hand and began to wipe off the fecal fluids. When he had done as much as he could do with the towel he said to Robbie: "Let's go now, Robert."

The boy caught up one lamb and then the other and held them side by side under the muzzle of the ewe. She let out a blat of protest followed by a long guttural chuckle of maternal reassurance to her loved one. Robbie began backing toward the open side of the shelter, still crouching and holding the lambs under the mother's nose. The mother, after a push from Granddad, followed.

The lambs drooped in Robbie's hands. Their tails hung limp and nearly reached the ground and their ears were in a position of discouragement. They seemed to know this was no way to travel.

The procession went into the barnyard, around the part of the barn where the hay was stored and along a lane between two woven-wire fences. Granddad opened a gate and Robbie backed through, the ewe followed, trotting now and then and sometimes getting ahead of Robbie and turning, on such occasions, as if to get back to the flock. Then Granddad would intervene and bump her back on the path. Robbie would pop the lambs under her nose, and she would willingly take up the routine of chasing her offspring. Temple closed the gate and followed her — followed, that is, the bloody streamer of afterbirth with the white cord waving between her legs. Granddad opened a wooden door and admitted Robbie and the lambs to a long gallery in the upper barn. This had once been a machine shed and now served as a nursery. Granddad had built a row of wooden pens along one wall. Inquisitive eyes gleamed from these slats. The old residents hailed the new arrival, and she in her confusion of fear and happiness blatted back at them.

Granddad swung open a pen gate, Robbie backed in, still crouching with the dangling lambs held low, and the ewe followed. Granddad closed the gate and tied it with baling twine. Robbie carefully placed the favored lamb under the ewe's hindquarters and tickled its bum with his finger. Nothing happened and the boy looked up at his grandfather.

The old man gave no sign, just watched the lamb.

The dirty lamb staggered around in the straw, and settled down as if to sleep. The favored one thrust its nose into its mother's belly, then tried a leg, and then worked its way forward thrusting its muzzle up into the ewe's underside repeatedly till it reached the forelegs. The mother resumed licking and nuzzling and chuckling to it.

Robbie picked up the dirty one and lifted it to ascertain its sex. "It's a ram," he said and placed it by the mother's bag. He took the other lamb, the favored one, and announced it too was a male, and put it beside its brother. The mother looked round at the sopped little rams and changed her position, knocking both to the floor. She dragged her afterbirth in a half-circle and began sniffing through the slats at a lamb in the adjoining pen. But she didn't chuckle and gargle to this stranger. She turned again to her own twins and licked the favored one, and Robbie put the dirty one at her bag again, and then in one effortless motion the shit-soaked refugee took a teat between his eager lips, clamped down and began to suck.

The mother's eyes moved from the lamb she was licking to a point in nearby space. She stared — and she seemed to comprehend something, then she turned her nose to the sucking ram and licked its rear and began chuckling to it, and the little ram's long tail began waving and wiggling.

When both lambs had sucked for two or three minutes and napped for another five Robbie and Granddad trimmed their umbilical cords to an inch of length, and Temple raised an open jar of iodine and immersed each cord. The mother protested not desperately but persistently until Robbie returned the lambs to her. Then she made her purring chuckling noises to them, sniffed the iodine and turned her attention to the afterbirth in the straw.

Granddad, Temple and Robbie walked abreast up the lane to the house. The sun was higher and they walked into their shadows and Temple felt the heat on his shoulders almost as in summer. A brown rivulet ran next to the lane and birds were swarming in a budding maple. The house enlarged against the sky as they approached. Temple looked as always at the window on the upper right that had been Sandra's room when she was a girl.

When Temple returned to his apartment that night he turned on all the lights and went through the place with his gun in his hand. Then he complied with the order to inform Operations he was back in the city.

The sergeant said he would tell the field lieutenant. "I got a message for you, Temple," the sergeant said. "From Sam Lovico. It says, 'We found the fat lady.'"

Chapter 25
A Grove of Honeysuckle

Lovico said: "We have located a witness, a black woman, who will testify at the trial that Officer Ruthenbeck took the knife from her. She had no trouble identifying him from his photograph because, in her own words, he tried to hobble her every time he saw her last summer. She is a confessed junkie and drunk but her memory of the incident is clear. Officer Ruthenbeck approached her in the parking lot of the McDonald's on First Street, called her a drunken gorilla and took the knife. We have placed her in a recovery program. She can describe the knife in precise detail."

Lovico paused and looked at the unyielding face of John Shipman.

"Her testimony," he continued, "together with Officer Temple's, gives us a fair chance of securing convictions against Officers Ruthenbeck and Banes."

"On what charges?" Shipman said. When Shipman asked a question, Lovico observed, it didn't always sound like a question.

"Perjury — for lying under oath at the inquest. Obstructing an officer in the performance of his duty — for planting the knife and inserting false statements in the Use of Force reports submitted to their superiors in the Police Department."

"Perjury," Shipman repeated, "and obstructing."

"Obstructing an officer, interfering with the administration of justice. — Of course you don't consider it justice."

"What else?" said Shipman.

"I am not going to file any other charges," Lovico said.

"None at all. None against Temple," Shipman said. His eyes which directed an assault at Lovico were sleep-deprived eyes. "Not even manslaughter. Not even going too far, whatever your word for that is."

"Our word for 'going too far' is misconduct in public office. Not that either. Not manslaughter and not murder in any degree. May I explain that?"

Shipman made no answer but utter indifference was written on his face.

"The charges of perjury and obstruction to be filed against Ruthenbeck and Banes rest on the premise that Temple is a truthful man. If he is not there is no case against the other two. If he is, there is no case of wrongful death in any form against anybody, none at least that I could hope to prove to a jury and none, I am obliged to tell you, that I myself believe in. Temple testified at the inquest that your son struck first, indeed that he knocked Banes through a window. If that is so then the reaction of the three officers as described by Temple was not inappropriate. There is no case, for example, for second-degree murder. You will not agree, and I understand your not agreeing, but your son's death, Mr. Shipman, was a terrible accident. I cannot view it in any other light."

"Perjury and obstruction break the rules of your game," said Shipman. "Killing my boy does not."

"In the light of the evidence, sir, I do not see, and I certainly could not prove, that any of the officers committed a crime until the planting of the knife. They may have acted imprudently but imprudence is a problem for the Chief of Police, not the criminal courts. I must recognize the probability that if one intends to kill a man one doesn't hit him in the face. And a jury would believe Officer Temple. In that belief all criminal charges dissolve. Nothing remains but the conspiracy to obstruct justice. If Ruthenbeck had done nothing at all he would be in the clear today.

Or if Temple had joined the conspiracy all three would be in the clear. Mr. Shipman, sitting in this chair you could not do other than I have done."

"I would like my son's notebook," Shipman said.

"Ah!" exclaimed Lovico, and got up and opened his briefcase which lay on a heavy oak table. He placed the book in Shipman's hand.

"My son . . ." Shipman began, and stopped.

"He was a promising scholar. Please don't deny me the privilege of making that observation."

"Yes, he was a scholar. He wanted to write — history and . . ."

Lovico turned away and privately gave thanks that he had brought forth grief instead of rage. He decided to launch upon the argument that had taken shape in his mind the night before. He said:

"There is no listening device in this room and we are free to discuss openly what is on your mind, Mr. Shipman, the thing you call justice and I call murder. You may take my word as a man of honor that the room is not bugged. I believe we should talk."

A smile spread slowly across Shipman's tired face but he did not look at the other man.

Not quite sure of Shipman yet determined to lay before him his thoughts of the previous evening Lovico continued: "I know what murder is," Lovico said, "not because I have committed it myself but because I have seen it a thousand times from the vantage point of a prosecutor — and the prosecutor is closer to the murderer, believe me, than the counsel for the defense can ever be. I recognize true murder. It is vile, sir, but it always justifies itself with a pretense of necessity or duty.

"I see in your eyes a resistance to everything I say. You would rather not listen to me. I am grieved because I must entertain the possibility that you discount me because I am white. Mr. Shipman, we are not talking about race but about humanity and what it means to be human. Ask what a murderer does, and then ask whether any man who does those things can be justified. Can a man really commit murder and call it justice?

"A man owns a rifle, presumably a deer rifle. He begins to ponder a certain act. Consciously and subconsciously he considers it for many days or weeks, and his mind is ultimately exhausted with the hundreds of similar scenes it invents and watches, and with the variations that multiply these scenes from time to time.

"He makes no decision because no question is ever presented to him. The act is transformed one day from a play of imagination to a pledge against his honor. If he is the man he thinks he is, he will perform the act; if he doesn't perform the act he is a coward. He must now decide, not whether he is a murderer, but whether he can escape this lofty duty. He finds himself at the sporting goods store buying a telescopic sight. He has still decided nothing. Making a deliberate decision is the last thing he wants to do. Perhaps he never *will* decide. But the scenes in his head suddenly show a radical defect, an element of the contrived and the unreal, whereas they used to be quite convincing. They have lost all realism. And why? The defect is that he has realized he cannot see his iron sights in the dark. A telescopic sight, on the other hand, would gather available light as all telescopes do, and place the crosshairs just in the field of light. If he is to fire at night he must have a telescopic sight. And of course it is absolutely necessary that he act in the dark. This deed of honor, this execution of the higher justice that transcends the law, this noble act of self-sacrifice which is fully justified before the tribunal of mankind, must for some unknown reason be done *in the dark*!

"He buys a telescopic sight, not the best but a good one, let's say good enough. He may use that phrase: This will be good enough. Why spend $200 when I can murder for $100. Now his scenes are more real. In the dark — not because he is too vile and cowardly but only because it is necessary to act at night if he is to accomplish his work. He tells himself that. It is only the smallest of the lies he feeds himself and he consumes these lies like a starved fish and demands new lies every minute, always more lies. I am speaking of an actual murder, Mr. Shipman, which occurred twenty years ago. One or two more details and you will recognize it. The rifle by the way is a thirty-ought-six. I am not a sportsman or a military man; I derive my knowledge of firearms solely from my experience as a prosecutor. The thirty-ought-six as you may know is the M1 rifle, the standard army weapon of World War II."

"And Korea," Shipman interjected ironically. "Everybody forgets Korea."

"Yes. A very potent gun. A heavy bullet propelled at high velocity. He drives his car through the victim's neighborhood, examines the victim's house in daylight and darkness from every side, and chooses a place to wait in ambush. His lair is a grove of honeysuckle about two hundred feet from the house. A pretty easy shot, wouldn't you say, two hundred feet? With a telescopic sight and a big man — in fact a former football player — as the target?

"Now sir this is not a quiz but surely you know which murder I am narrating. A black man of your own generation. It is not the murder of Martin Luther King. That killer hid in a toilet as all sneak killers do. They hide in toilets; isn't that fine? But our killer hid in a honeysuckle grove. It is another murder similar to the King assassination in every important particular, just as cowardly and sneaky.

"From a prone or sitting position in the honeysuckle bushes the killer had a clear view of the carport at the victim's house. The carport was lighted from above. The windows and side door were lighted. So when the victim arrived he would pass through the lighted carport and outline himself against the light of the door and windows. It is the murder of Medgar Evers, field secretary of the National Association for the Advancement of Colored People, in Jackson, Mississippi, June, 1963."

This drew no response. Shipman was slumped in his chair and his brows were raised a little, his eyes open and staring.

"Of course I do not know the most interesting part, and I suppose nobody does, not even the murderer. What was he thinking as he lay in the honeysuckle grove during those hours from nightfall till midnight when Evers came home? In what terms did he address his conscience during those minutes. Everybody says our conscience speaks to us until we silence it, but far more often than that we speak to our conscience. What vocabulary of justification did he invent in his dialogue with his conscience? Did he say, 'I am doing this for my race?' Did he say, 'I am doing this for justice?'

Imagine how the word is profaned on the tongue of such a man, a murderer.

"The night was hot and muggy and he must have sweated. Did he wipe his eyes with a handkerchief? Did the touch of his hand against his eyes remind him of his mother's touch? After he'd fired and his bullet had gone clean through Evers, entering of course *from the back*, did he hear Evers' children scream Daddy! Daddy! After that did he still think of himself as the champion of his race? Because I assure you Mr. Shipman the children called out to their father, it's in the reports. Daddy! Daddy! These may well be the last syllables Medgar Evers heard, and you know how precious they are.

"It has always seemed especially instructive to me that the police found a flattened place in the honeysuckle — where a man had lain — meaning that a murderer retains the shape and weight of a human being even at the moment he changes himself into something other than human. So you can look at these murderers who put bombs in restaurants and hotels, who strike the unarmed and unsuspecting from behind, and they appear to be human. But it is only an outward appearance. The killer who lay in wait for Medgar Evers was not a man. One who would do what he did, even if only to prove his manhood, is no man.

"It must have occurred to you already that you can't fight a duel with these three officers to kill them with some false semblance of honor. Banes would run, Ruthenbeck would shoot you in the back and Temple would refuse to fire. Are you going to hire an assassin then? Is your family honor to be vindicated by a secret transaction with the scum of the earth? Or, supposing justice to be an exact balancing of scales, are you going to kill Temple's son?

"You may think that the state monopolizes force and denies justice. Many people think that. You are therefore in a dilemma. Accept the murder of your son or kill the killers. But I say to you —"

"Stop," said Shipman looking up. He said nothing more and at length Lovico asked:

"Yes?"

"I like that elegant language, the state monopolizes force and denies justice. I wish I had said it first."

Now they did look into each other's eyes as Shipman continued:

"And it puts me in a box but you seem to be saying there's some way out. What is it?"

"It is here," said Lovico, "in these charges," and he raised a sheaf of papers.

"In perjury and obstructing justice? When you say that, I'm tempted to kill you too. Comparing me to some bigot that killed Medgar Evers."

"I made no such comparison. It is for you to decide whether such a comparison is fair."

"If you insult me," said Shipman without any observable malice, "you'll pay for it."

"Mr. Shipman I am trying to present a real-life definition of a murderer, nothing more."

"Then you don't understand the word in spite of all your education," said Shipman still with the tone and force of an utterly exhausted man. "Like you said something about the most interesting part. I forget what you said."

"That we'll never know what he was thinking as he lay concealed."

"But you haven't been talking about anything else. No, the most interesting part is when the killer goes up and looks at the body."

Lovico went cold. After a second he rose abruptly from his leather chair. "Do you still have the business card I gave you?"

Shipman said he did.

"May I have it?"

Shipman presented it.

"I am writing my home address on this card," Lovico said. "You will not kill me, Mr. Shipman. You may hate me but you will not kill me. I want you to come to my house whenever you feel the urgent need to talk to someone who understands the trap you are in, because I do understand it. Your son has been taken from you and the law mocks you by doing nothing in retaliation, yet it ties your hands. Think again, though. You seem to believe that taking vengeance is a way out. I say use your imagination and ask how you would feel killing men who are not murderers. Could you live with what you had done?"

"I am using my imagination and whether I can live isn't the question I turn it loose on." Shipman rose too and looked down on Lovico. He reached into his inside pocket and for a moment Lovico expected to see him draw a gun. Shipman opened his leather portfolio and took out three folded sheets of notebook paper.

He handed them to Lovico and looked at him as if he expected him to read the pages. Lovico read "Finding the Path." He read of the ambition of a young student to write the history of the black people in America. With a solemn face and no attempt at words Lovico handed the pages back.

Shipman said: "That man you were talking about was not subhuman because he killed somebody. He was subhuman because he killed Medgar Evers. And the men who killed my son — see — killed —" Shipman held up the pages and moved them, and then let his hand fall. "You made the wrong comparison," Shipman said.

"Sir," said Lovico, "I wish to God your son had lived to make his great effort."

"And do you think I would willingly do what that reptile did?"

"No," Lovico said immediately.

"But if a man had no alternative —"

"A man cannot become a murderer except by an act of his free will," said Lovico.

"Oh — is that true?" said Shipman. "When the only *way out* is this joke of a charge of perjury?"

"Perjury and obstructing justice. And you could stand fast," Lovico added, "and endure it."

"I have another name for that. — If," said Shipman after a moment's hesitation, "a man insisted, if a man did the only thing he could do, you would see that he paid. I know that a killer has to pay. Everybody knows that."

"But he could never pay enough. Think, Mr. Shipman. Again I say use your imagination and see yourself standing surrounded by your family. You can make this decision only once and it shapes your whole future and theirs. You would spread suffering all around and call it justice."

Slowly John Shipman returned the pages to his pocket and extended his hand and Lovico gratefully clasped him by the hand. A surge of some passionate feeling passed through Lovico.

Shipman said: "A man is never a murderer except by his own free will. That's what you say."

"I am certain of it."

"False," said Shipman releasing the other's hand. "You don't know. You can't know."

Next day listening to the testimony of Banes and Ruthenbeck Shipman saw his task growing simpler. He put Banes down as a brutal moron who was nothing more than Ruthenbeck's dog. He saw that if he were omnipotent he could kill them all, but since he was less than that he would have to choose. Banes went to the end of the line.

That night at eleven as he prepared to leave his office he burned the card he had written with "Banes" at the top and "make of car, address and hours of work" below. He held the burning card. Staring into the flame he took his leather portfolio from his inside pocket, and opened it and flattened it on the table with the side of his hand, and moved his eyes from the dying flame to the open portfolio. He dropped the card into the ashtray before him. It seemed he had to decide before the feeble little flame went out.

There were now two Lovico cards in his hand, the business card and the one with the blanks for "make of car" and so forth. Shipman returned the printed card to the portfolio and advanced the other into the guttering flame and held it till it flared up in a gentle yellow tongue. He cocked it so the tongue licked upward to consume the whole card and name of Samuel Lovico. He let it fall into the ashtray with the ashes of Banes's card. He shrugged into his coat, buttoned and belted it, and darkened the office.

He walked for nearly a mile under the blue-white lights of Western Avenue then turned down a dark street leading after a few minutes to Jonathan Elms Park. This, the playground of his boyhood, had been condemned for a freeway in the era of urban renewal, or "Negro removal," so the baseball screens, the swings, slides, jungle gyms and all the rest had been leveled and then of course they never built the freeway. All that stood in the wasteland was the portico of the old picnic area, like a Roman ruin catching the weak light from the nearby street.

It was a mild night and Shipman almost felt spring in the air. But it was much too early; the heart of the winter lay ahead. He walked the length of the portico, every column and arch validating the fantastic notion that he had once played hide-and-go-seek amid their shadows.

There was a dark police car parked in the drive and Shipman approached it. The driver's window rolled down and a voice said:

"Big John."

"My man Sandy."

"How much tam you need? Got me a call, boyfriend-girlfriend."

"One minute," Shipman said and opened the top of his raincoat. He took out the leather folder and bending down asked Sanderfare if he could shine a light. A red beam illuminated two index cards, and Shipman handed them to Sanderfare.

"Can you fill in the blanks?" John Shipman said.

Sanderfare studied each card in succession.

"Yes on this one," he said pausing, "and yes on this one." He put the cards in his shirt pocket and buttoned the flap. Looking at Shipman from beneath the shiny visor of his cap he said: "Gotta boogie, watch your feet," and he was gone.

Walking back to his office Shipman opened his coat to let the breeze in. He thought of the two cards burned and the other two delivered. He took Lovico's business card from the portfolio and burned it.

Chapter 26
Odell Diann

Odell Diann said to her husband: "Now what am I supposed to do with this heap of money?"

"I don't know — buy shoes?"

"Shoes, Big Boy. How many shoes can I buy with thirty thousand dollars?"

"Socks too."

"Twenty-eight years of marriage and squeezin pennies the whole time — household pennies I mean. Prowlin money, let her rip, but money for the *house* and furniture no *sir*. Every stick in this house I bought with my own money. This mattress and blanket and that special thick pillow that cost twice as much as an ordinary pillow to hold up your busted neck that you stuck in the wrong place playing basketball when you were forty trying to be twenty — wallpaper, rugs, everything but your computer I paid for out of a teacher's salary."

"Thanks to the NEA," said Shipman.

"Don't tell me about those me-firsters. Plow in, plow in. We're plowin in, Baby. Get your fingers offn that money, Woman, that's going back to the business where it came from. Now I catch you like a thief in the night throwing thirty thousand dollars in my bank account while my back's turned. I want to know are you in trouble with the IRS?"

"Del Honey, me? A thief in the night? I cleaned out my petty cash and found this loose change and said, I wonder if Del could use it? Are you mad? Should I plow it back in?"

"You try it," she said. Actually there wasn't much life in his voice and she couldn't see that he took much pleasure in giving his gift.

"Are you quitting business?" she asked.

"You mean get out? Hell no. What would I do with the rest of my life?"

Odell Diann was lying on her side with her head supported in comfort by her pillow. She felt young. She knew this was the effect of the money. An amount so large seemed to promise change but she hadn't had time to ask whether she wanted change or what it might be. Her first question was whether the money could help Winslow. She believed only Winslow could divert her husband from thinking about the wrong things, but he could do this only by earning his father's respect. And John was factually right about Winslow; he was always drunk.

She contemplated John's profile, seeing it as a proof of God's existence. These striking features could not be an accident because chance doesn't write a clear message. (Between chance and God's will she recognized no intervening ground.)

She passed her eye along the lines of this masculine profile and discerned God's intention to create a certain kind of being, a strong, potent, struggling man. Here was the proof and the success of his creation. She inferred that God was not vague, celestial or abstract. These attributes were the inventions of men of a weak and diluted faith. Nor was he like a man. God as a man was Jesus. That was why Jesus existed, to embody God. But *God the Creator* passed understanding without quite passing out of reach. He, not Jesus, was the god of hurricanes and street violence but also of a cosmic if not an indulgent love. His signature was the cosmos. Yet he descended to earth in the love of parents for their children. This was all her faith understood and she was content with it, as far as knowledge can make anybody content.

Odell Diann imagined a world split into atoms by the power of selfishness and lust, a world set on destroying families and churches, where small children were abandoned by their parents to wander at will in the squalid streets. Politicians plundered the cities and no one respected the existing law, which upheld everything that was tortuous and abnormal, nor cared to write a new and purer law. In just such a world the first Christians had lived, preparing every day for the cataclysm that should bring it all to a fiery end that none should escape and few survive. These few were the despised, huddling and secretive believers in the most implausible of all the gods then worshipped. After two thousand years He was just as implausible. So the intellect would declare. But the disintegration of values and the sweeping away of another generation of youth in the city, save a few, made Him shine, so it appeared to Odell Diann, with the same light that must have spread around Him in slavery days. Incredible how the God of the slaves was still the God we need. He entered the heart as strong as before, provided only that the heart were opened to Him by a free act of the human will and by the grace of God.

"The heart must be opened," she thought.

When she prayed to Jesus as the supplicant had prayed, "I believe, help thou my unbelief," she asked for the grace without which her life would be a scene of naked chaos. *Having grace* she could live in this city and bear to see all that happened here, not just the murder of her son, so long as she strove to prevent the subverting of another generation. *Lacking grace* she could never keep on striving against the chaos and the sweeping away of the children. Once she withdrew she would suffocate in indifference. "I strive or I die." And yet she could easily imagine her final withdrawal from the fight, and imagine herself trying to make the most of the remaining years. But her imagination proceeded so fast and vividly that she saw in the same glance the pitiful absurdity of anything she might do in pursuit of "making the most of life." For instance taking a young lover and paying him to anticipate her wildest whims. But she suspected she'd have very few whims, and she disbelieved in the continent of sensuality; she thought it was a narrow patch of dirt. She saw the exhaustion of sensuality quite near by, and the surfeit of material possessions already behind her.

But! How sweet it would be to sleep until eight or nine in the morning, to go only to places that were clean and beautifully decorated instead of to that worn-out school building where a child's comprehension of a simple algebraic proposition was counted a victory. How pleasant it would be to spend the winters down South and the summers at a cottage on some lake, or to open a nice little shop downtown and let everything else take care of itself.

She awoke with the feeling of something smooth and new having entered her life but as her feet touched the floor she realized it was the money. "What's going on?" she asked. And the ache, the half-sleeping tenant, the grief unseen. She washed, dressed, breakfasted and organized her papers in her "West Dragons" canvas bag. She went to her sewing room which was an old pantry off the kitchen, closed the door and spread her Bible on the table top that was formed when the sewing machine was folded away. There was an east window and it cast a glare on the page. She read Lamentations.

"Is it nothing to you, all ye that pass by? behold, and see if there be any sorrow like unto my sorrow, which is done unto me, wherewith the Lord hath afflicted me in the day of his fierce anger.

"From above hath he sent fire into my bones, and it prevaileth against them; he hath spread a net for my feet . . ."

She read two chapters entire. Since childhood she had been unable to fathom God's anger. These verses in particular made her shiver yet she could give thanks that she didn't feel that way any more. The day of his fierce anger had surely passed.

Closing the book she slid a strip of carpet from under the table and knelt. The sunlight shone in upon her. She closed her eyes and felt the heat on her face.

"Jesus," she said, "he is not coming up. He is still in the pit. He's lost one son but thinks he has lost two."

She knelt with her hands at her sides and her face lifted. She was a thin willowy woman and the sun seemed to surround her body and make it less substantial. It glazed the color of her face. She wore her hair curled tight and cut short. Her black hair, her brown skin and gold necklace glistened each with its own style of light. Her gently closed eyes would sometimes crease, and so would her brow, as one thought succeeded another.

"Jesus I need your help, if in your mercy you want to save this man from poisoning his mind by thinking the wrong things all the time. You see how it lowers and threatens to destroy him. If your Father would give grace to this poor father and if you would teach him to open his heart . . ."

She came upon the paradox of grace. Here stood a man otherwise condemned, who could neither see the need nor accept the gift of grace. Yet grace was all he needed and it was freely offered to him. For a few moments the complication of it diverted her. The will of God is the only force in the world. The man God loves is saved by it. But God's love in the form of grace is lost on the man who spurns it. Evidently it cannot penetrate a cold and resentful heart. She thought of the seed cast upon stony ground, then of a heart deliberately hardened; and of what God does to the man who hardens his heart. But she stopped short and exclaimed:

"This is my John!" Yet it was plain that his being "her John" would not save him if he chose not to be saved. So how far does God's love extend?

Fleetingly she acknowledged, "Hawk was my boy, beaten to death." She saw him falling amid the legs and the swinging boots of the policemen. This was a repeating signal like a light that catches the mariner's eyes through the night watch. The image defined the terms under which she must live.

"Bring Winslow back to life," she said. "Please, Jesus."

Her body swayed and she seemed to feel herself in the midst of the congregation and seemed to hear the music. She couldn't make a joyful noise but she wanted to hear one.

"He thinks Winslow is too weak to be a black man," she resumed. "His mind is closed and locked on the belief Winslow was overcome by this city — not strong enough. 'Winslow is deader than Hawk.' He said that and thinks his family is destroyed, that he's got nothing to live for." Here lay a buried thought: that she herself meant so little.

She paused again, "Grace Is Sufficient" playing in her mind, and swayed lightly, her face passing in and out of the shaft of sunlight entering through the pristine windows. The alternation of light and relief-from-light upon her eyelids distracted her and she opened her eyes, shielding them from the glare with a raised hand, palm outward blocking the sun. She looked around at the pantry shelves holding skeins of manycolored yarn, at the button boxes and the stacks and shreds of material new and old, at the machine folded in upon itself and hanging upside down beneath its table just before her eyes, and she could not help seeing a tweed sportcoat perched on a hook. It was one of Hawk's she had promised to mend. Upon this sight she closed her eyes and said: "Help him to start thinking of the right things, of love, forgiveness and peace."

She stopped praying. Her body curved slowly forward and she covered her face with her hands and said aloud in a muffled voice, "Don't hate, my John."

Then, detained by some impulse in this dark world where the pressure of her hands against face and forehead brought a pleasing sensation, she happened to listen, as it were — at the same time catching the scent of the soap on her hands — and listening she again heard her husband say "I *am* going on." She had told him he must go on. Now he seemed to be saying again: "I am going on." But there was a crack of menace in his voice.

She thought of the money as an opening to freedom.

"I been free for years," she thought. "John been making money for years. So what's this striving anyway? Call it striving and it plays like a battle of the angels, but what is all this fight, work, persevere? A better life or just money?"

She was now in a driving mood, maneuvering her old hog onto the freeway ramp, casting a look over her shoulder and slipping into the stream of traffic in the right lane.

"I see kids sliding to hell — I ask for the strength to contend against it — He give me strength — 'He give the strength to carry on' — so here I go carrying on, all blowed up with how mighty a fortress am I, while a whole other batch of kids going down the sewer. From the West Side Gardens, I'll take the worst example, five per cent stand up and ninety-five percent crawl and flop. And I feel good because I try! Look at this whole Babylon and say Honey it don't matter, you doin your best. It matters!"

She drove with a hand on either side of the wheel, thumbs up, giving the car so many little contradictory commands that it managed to describe a straight line in spite of her. Cruising, never taking her eyes off the traffic and the unpredictable crazy drivers all around, she contrived to extricate from her handbag a single perfect cigarette. She punched the lighter, passed the cigarette before her eyes without changing her focus, and placed the weed in her lips. Her mission in the social biology of freeway travel was to impede traffic in the slow lane, and her two-ton Buick Electra 225 was the correct vehicle for the mission. When drivers rode her rear, when trucks hissed their brakes and important men in Volvos lost valuable minutes, when her irrational mode of navigation drew uncivil gestures from motorists who had finally broken out of the dead zone behind her, she noticed nothing.

She inhaled and expelled smoke. She pressed a button and the right rear window dropped an inch.

"Hawk is dead," she thought. "You teach a few of these children to reason mathematically," she continued after a minute, "to speak moneymaking English, to understand values . . ." She trailed off, "Hawk is dead" coming back instead. "What is that man up to? What if I bought a thousand pairs of shoes for poor kids? — Don't be stupid, there's too many handouts already and too little charity."

She glided over one of her bitterest complaints, that too many white teachers dropped their standards for black students. She was in no frame of mind for a tirade.

"Never forgive yourself," she had told Hawk and Winslow from babyhood. "Let God do the forgiving." One of the rewards of having kids was that a parent was obliged to say things like that. "If you say it they believe it — if it's true," she affirmed.

Over the next ten minutes she grew bored thinking about the money, but it pursued her into the schoolyard. There she met Lucy Williams, one of her brightest mathematics students and eldest stepdaughter of Lucas Jones, her husband's security guard at the First Street barbecue.

"Lucy, dear," Odell Diann asked, "is that a new coat?"

"Yes, Mrs. Shipman. New coat. New earmuffs." The girl spun around and had to conquer a splendid smile before she could say:

"New boots." She spread her hands and cocked her head in a rag doll pose. "New gloves. New dress inside the new coat!"

"Why Lucy, that's wonderful, dear," Odell Diann said.

"Uncle Lucas gave us new outfits. We all went out in his car last night, Mama and Holly and Billy and me, and got everything Mama said we needed."

Odell Diann patted the girl on the shoulder and walked beside her across the asphalt yard and hugged her with her free arm and thought that money was suddenly flying everywhere.

At the end of the day this encounter with Lucy repeated itself in her mind, with the girl smiling brilliantly, spreading her fingers apart and dropping her head to one side. Odell Diann started the Buick and sat in the cold until the engine ran smoothly, then backed carefully out of her place in the faculty and staff lot, looking repeatedly in all three mirrors and over both her shoulders, twisting her body on those slim hips that had never seemed quite good enough for childbearing.

When she pressed the activator that lifted the garage door and drove in, taking the space beside her husband's, she formed a mental picture of the silver Lincoln that he would drive into this same garage a few hours hence. She could see him driving in. Both this picture and her consciousness that she was sitting in her car seemed remote and strange. She herself did. She shut off the engine and pressed the switch again and heard the door rumbling down behind her. Now she realized she did not remember driving home from school.

Her watch told her it was four in the afternoon. But it seemed only a minute ago that she had opened her Bible, and now a single sentence isolated itself: "He hath spread a net for my feet."

She went directly to the sewing room, without removing her coat or even her gloves, and opened the Bible by its ribbon to the morning's page. There she read the dire sentence. With the toe of her boot she slid out the strip of carpet and knelt.

"Jesus son of God Almighty, Jesus son of Mary, Jesus who walked on the waves, tell me I'm crazy. Tell me I'm a woman possessed by a crazy idea, possessed by a mad devil and thinking his thoughts like a distracted maniac, so tell me *now*, because you are merciful, and I will abide by it. I will walk in my illusions thank-

ful till the end of my life and never cease to praise you. I do not
know what my praise means, whether it pleases anybody, but here
I am, a creature, I didn't make myself, and I doubt my creator made
me just to scorn me and laugh at my praise — so I say *praise God.*
Thanks be to God Almighty for sending Jesus down to mingle with
us and get down to our level. Now Jesus I pray that this mad idea
is a devil's doing. Rather a devil in my brain than this be true.
Jesus, let it be that I am prompted by a devil and I can beg you to
drive him out, or I will suffer with him as long as I must. But don't
let it be true, please. You can undo what's been done. Even if it's
true now make it false in a minute. I pray and beg, make it false. I
close my eyes, I shut down my mind, I kneel and I wash your feet
with my hair — or I would, but you gave me curly hair! — Jesus,
black folks have to be strong and the strength can come only from
you. Don't take away my strength.

"If it's true then it's a warning from you — I have not begun to
suffer. Oh but I have! Falling! Abyss! Pit! — Descend, drop and
tumble — Collide! — down, down. Think you hit bottom in a bil-
lowing wave and all you get is this tenant in the skin leaping into
your throat, into your chest, in your mind, to remind you your boy
is no more, he's snatched away. I don't mean snatched, forgive me,
please dear God, but to me it feels like snatched. I can't help it, I'm
his mother. My boy in the morning and my life swings on him, next
thing I know, gone!

"But Jesus why would anybody *spread a net* for this man's
feet? He is a man making his way by hard work in a world he never
made. He does not worship, it's true, but the word has never been
properly preached to him and he grew up in a godless home, still
he walks upright among men. I will lead him back to the love of
his other son, by love, by tears, by smiles and little plans and tricks,
by my deep-hearted love, I vow it. You will see this man love his
son or I will die trying. Touch his heart with one drop of your
blood. Coil up this net.

"I don't think I could stand it if it were true, if you made it true.
I think I know where this would lead. I would lose the knowledge
of your love. I just don't see how I could understand any more
blows. Don't, God, for Christ's sake, push me back where I was

when my boy died. I am out of the pit, I dread the pit. Why should you throw me back in? And when will I ever find the bottom? I am a sinner, sure. God, is that a reason?

"Jesus, my boy Hawk is gone. I am just asking: isn't that enough? I will meet him in Heaven! But my loneliness is here and now. If this is true, this devil's mad idea, do you think I can stand it? I will twist up like a bug on its back and wave my legs.

"Jesus, did you give me this idea as a warning so that when he does it I can have exquisite educated suffering all in one blow? The whole understanding of it, all worked out ahead of time, and it all come raining down at once? Lose your husband, fall in the pit of chaos, lose your strength, lose your faith in My Father's goodness, defy and spit and snarl like a crazy demon, and be cast into the chaos all at once, in one single blaze of terrible punishment because you thought losing your boy was enough, Who are *you* to decide!

"Jesus, I believe, I believe. I do not look for a sign, I don't need any sign. I should ask you to strengthen my faith for this test, but God you know what's in my mind. Why test me again? Didn't my boy die in the fullness of youth? All I pray for — forgive me for Jesus' sake — is please, don't let it be true!"

Odell Diann waited up for her husband even though he telephoned to say he was working late. When the headlights of his car sent a pattern of lights and shadows wheeling across the wall she rose from the couch where she had lain for many hours. She turned on a lamp. A dull distant thud signified the closing of the garage door. She did not hear his approaching footsteps but she heard his key turn the lock.

He said, "Hey, Honey, you been sleeping down here?"

"No. I have not been sleeping."

He caught her tone, and stood still.

"If you kill those policemen," she said, "I don't care how white or how guilty they are, you'll kill me."

Chapter 27
Little Teeth

"Hey what're you, runnin?"

Temple's heel pivoted in the cinders.

"Atta boy, don't be afraid."

Temple stared, and thought: "What small teeth he has," rows of straight little biters, each one outlined in dark shadow.

"How's the kid? I heard some cowardly bullies ran him into a pole, slapped him upside his breakable head, boxed his itty-bitty ears and what-all. Eh? He O.K.? No *grave and permanent* injury? Jeez I hope not, Temple, how'd you explain *that* to im later, like, I mean, you say it's a cruel world my boy, what can I say, I just fuckin threw you to the wolfs. Jeez I wish you'd just hold out your hand with Shake Partner. All these Third Relief peacekeepers'd be fuckin inspired, you know, give us all a lift for the night's sewer-swim. Hey kids!"

He raised his voice and surveyed the lot where the Third Relief was beginning to arrive but nobody wanted to get mixed up in it.

"You know Temple when you get that *pale with rage* expression an all I fear for my life, I really do, a proven certified fist killer like you seething with fury and hey, take a crack at it. Why not? Go on, here it is, my little glass jaw" (touching it with his fingertip). "No? Yeah I guess you're right, pop me and I die and all of a sudden we got a double murderer in our midst and Christ think of the legal fees.

"All right that's a problem right there, ain't it, I mean you and money's getting to be a real problem, eh, cause I mean obviously you're through as a cop, you know it? and through period for all I know, washing outta football and then that short tragic coaching career pushing black kids around a field. Hey teach them po black boys to play a stupid game and then the business career, your wife told me all about it the other night, you know, jeez what a woman! My god Temple if I'd known you had something like that at home — anyhow I saw that story, 'Winner in Football Loses in Business' or whatever, did you see it? Huh? Huh?

"Face it, that's why you're tryin to ruin me, Temple, is because you're a motherfuckin shambles your own self, do you think I don't know it? Hey I don't *care,* you think I care? Nawww, I just recognize a master, the master's touch, everything he touches turns to All-American shit, god what a gift. This time you didn't catch the bomb, you threw one, and po little Sambo — Jesus are there any of the oppressed minority around here? Holy shit this could cost me my fuckin *life!* What I was sayin, po little Sambo paid with his miserable life, eh Temple?

"Go on, for Christ sake, turn your back, walk away, *testify,* who cares? You testify, I testify, and you know what? It don't matter a damn either way. The niggerlovers'll believe you and everybody else believes me and Banes, so fuckin what! You po little eyes be squirtin — Jesus slow down — and you think, My how noble I is cause I be weepin an snufflin over Mr. Shitman Junior, but don't you see you be tellin yoself one big lie? Here's why you're all bent outta shape Temple —"

Temple suddenly halted and Ruthenbeck jumped but persevered, coming close and looking up into Temple's face from a foot away.

"You're confused, you know why? Cause you hated the little shit as much as anybody else, you just didn't know it. We give you a chance to smack im, and wham you take it! You take the chance! Lemme whap im boys! Thank you Beck, thank you Banes, thank you Lieutenant for putting me on the Tac Squad, gimme another crack at im, that uppity pipsqueak.

"Now all of a sudden the truth is sacred. The truth saves you from what you did. You make me sick Temple cause you is a pussy. Take down them pants I wanna see *have* you got one or not, what have you got, go on, drop'm. By god won't nobody drop drawers for me, I is a fuckin failure at this f. i. stuff.

"Oh god I done hurt his feelins, I done drove him away. Hey Temple! Don't go away mad!"

Chapter 28
Great Valley

Temple was driving a radar cruiser. His aching teeth seemed to have been pushed deeper into their beds by constant clenching. Taking both hands off the wheel he stroked both jaws. His neck was hard as a sack of rocks and he stroked it too, first on the sides and back, then in front where he felt the strange, tender windpipe. It felt like a part of an animal. "So I'm an animal and I care about all this?"

He guided the cruiser between concrete pylons into the Great Valley Building. He jerked a ticket to stop the bell; the gate rose and he began ascending the spiral. The engine of the big car scarcely noticed the incline.

When he reached the fourth level he patrolled Blue till he found Sandra's car. He stopped and backed the cruiser amid the whine of its gears to an empty slot giving a view both of the door leading out from the elevator vestibule and of the indentation between two larger cars where Sandra's rocket lay concealed. Temple shut off his engine. He couldn't see the rocket but he could see the pavement she would traverse to reach it. He turned down the volume on his body radio and on the radio embedded in the dash, so that he could hear the dispatcher but just barely. It was 5:30 and he was fifteen minutes of rush hour driving away from his District; longer if he had to wait in line to get out of the building. If they caught him out of the District they'd come down hard. He could barely sit. The muscles in his neck had hardened again and he stroked them and swung his jaw from side to side.

Cars passed before him one by one, of people going home. It didn't emerge in English but it had a force that he felt through his body: these were people who had homes, and wives or husbands, and children in the homes.

The pillar with the blue stripe supported the low gray ceiling a few yards in front of him near the elevator door, and a row of cars on either side made jagged edges to the aisle down which he kept his watch.

A new group of people dressed in the middle-class uniform came out of the elevator vestibule and dispersed at the four-color diagram. One of these, a trim, quick young woman with light blonde hair, carrying a briefcase, dressed in a calf-length tweed coat that Temple had never seen — one of these people was Sandra Temple.

"Sandra," he called and got out of his car or started to get out.

She turned as if by electric shock, saw him, and began walking as fast as she could toward the indentation.

Never in his life had he experienced anything quite like this. She was running away from him! He called again but she went even faster.

Turning her back, running away, hopping away with that abrupt gait imparted by high heels — he watched this unbelievable sight and slid back into the cruiser and slammed the door. She turned at the sound and she looked positively afraid. This decided him. He started the engine. She had disappeared into the indentation and he knew she was going to lock herself in her car and drive away. He made the huge cruiser leap, and skidded it to a halt behind her car. He turned on his blinkers and got out, and the slam of his door boomed in the huge cement chamber.

The knowledge that people were watching crawled along his back and up his neck. He tapped on her window with his knuckles. Her engine was running and she was looking straight ahead. He knocked again and she paid no attention. She gunned her engine and shifted to reverse. Her back-up lights lit up the side of the cruiser. He knocked on the glass with a dull knock that didn't penetrate or resound. He knocked again till his knuckles hurt.

The rocket jerked back and lurched on its springs, stopping a few inches from the cruiser. Her back-up lights shone on the blue metal and the white city seal. But Temple knew she would never damage her beloved rocket. She never went haywire.

He knocked again on the glass. All of a sudden he felt patient. Sandra stared ahead, detesting, ignoring.

He said, "I want to talk."

Her window droned down one inch and she turned to him, showing that distorted face that made him believe there was nothing good in the world.

"You have no right to trap me," she said.

"I know."

"Move it. I will not talk to you. Move it."

To him it sounded like a snarl, it was so different from her real voice. Here was the playful, witty, yielding woman he called "The Face," for her beauty, her eyes, her happiness. Here was the woman whose face and voice had made hope compatible with peace.

"Move it," she said.

"Will you talk with me?"

She breathed — that was her only answer — and looked straight ahead.

Temple stood erect. All he could see now was her shoulder and her hand on the wheel, and no wedding ring. He went back to the cruiser and backed it up ten feet, opening the way for Sandra to back out, and he waited. Her car didn't move.

He went to the passenger door of the rocket and found it locked. He gave a soft double knock on the glass — and she reached over and unlocked the door. Temple got in. He said:

"Robbie wants to go to his own school."

"No. He's staying with Dad. He's going to school down there."

"He doesn't want that. He's not afraid to come home."

"No."

"He asked me to ask you."

"Is that all you wanted?"

He didn't answer — and they sat there for a few minutes, and the shell zone in Temple's mind was original and unique. It had no counterpart in the physical world — neither desert nor junkyard nor scream of dying animal — it was not like any of these. It was only itself, a concavity he had never seen and couldn't see now —

He cried out: "Jesus, don't you love me?"

"No," she cried instantly.

"Do you love somebody else then?"

"No. That's so awful that you should say — no, no. Dad told me you said you wanted to go down to Wellston or someplace down there and coach. Did you really say that?"

"Yes."

"Good God, now you're a coach again? Not a cop, not a lawyer — Jeffrey, are you falling apart?"

"No. I want to do something that's worth doing."

"That's what you said when you became a cop."

"I know it."

"And now —"

"Now I can't go on being a cop. I'm going to get Ruthenbeck kicked off the force and then quit and go down there in the hills and get a coaching job, I don't care if it's grade school, I'm going to coach kids, I'm going to —"

"I can't stand it. Go on, go on, say it."

"Say what?"

"Jeff, are we —"

If they had a train of thought it had skipped its track. For Temple the "original" scene of a void returned to oppress his mind, to disconnect him from all physical realities, his own breathing, his own heartbeat.

As if this mental horror led directly to love he said again: "Let me move back in."

"Oh God no!"

"Yes."

He groped for words. It was easy for her, all she had to do was say no. He had to plead their cause with the detachment of a lawyer and the passion of a lover.

"Sandra, for Robbie's sake."

"Don't you dare talk about Robbie."

"What, am I too dirty or something?"

"Don't make me say it, or you'll be sorry."

"All right I won't make you say it. It's my fault, obviously. I know that. Do you want him to be one of these kids without a home?"

"He has me, and he has Dad and he has a home."

"And he has me!"

She turned to him and said: "I think it's inappropriate of you to use Robbie as a weapon against me."

"I'm not using him as a weapon."

"To use him as a thing to get me back. Why should you want me? You don't want anything else."

She squinted and pressed her hands against the sides of her head and began to rock back and forth, so that her head almost touched the steering wheel.

"Don't want anything?" Jeffrey exclaimed. "What in hell do you mean by that?" It would be foolish to try to force her to explain herself, to see how crazy this was. He said to himself, "I'm killing her, I'm torturing her." He couldn't stand to watch her rocking back and forth. But no matter what happened he always circled back to the primary idea, and said in one way or another: "Do you love me?"

Sandra said: "I can't make myself love you. It's not the money."

She kept putting out these jerky sentences, telling him two or three times it wasn't the money, and that she had been promoted to a higher paying job. Temple listened to this jumbled speech and understood that she believed he had somehow made it impossible for her to love him. He said:

"Are you saying it's my fault?"

"No, no, just that it's impossible."

"We loved each other for ten years and now it's impossible to love each other again?"

"Yes, that's what I'm saying. You destroyed it — through no fault of your own."

"You loved me," he said letting himself slide, "when I was a big hero at Ohio State. You loved me when I was making big money on the Packers." He boiled with shame even as he said this.

"It is not the money," she declared as if correcting a minor error.

"You just can't help yourself," he said, "and I can't help myself. 'Through no fault of my own.' You can't make yourself love me. So it's nobody's fault."

"Exactly." She sat erect looking straight ahead.

"It's just some kind of accident. It's out of our hands. We loved each other, we couldn't stand to be apart for even one night, we had Robbie, and I begged you, I said for Christ sakes Robbie is so wonderful, and you're so beautiful —"

"Oh, must you go on about this?"

"Why can't we have another child? But it's all out of our hands, you can't make yourself love me."

"No I cannot."

"Because you're helpless, it's not in your power."

"That's part of it. — I'm miserable, I'm awful, I feel awful — but *I don't want to love you.* I'm bringing Robbie up for a couple of days," she added without missing a beat, "and I wonder if you'd help me. He's got a doctor's appointment, and another hearing test, and a dentist's appointment. Will you help?"

This sudden shift to the mundane lifted him into the illusion that they were married again, making the kinds of arrangements married people make. She told him exactly when to pick Robbie up, to get there early but wait in his car ("Do not come to the door, just wait in your car") and he agreed to it all and felt normal, almost happy for a fleeting moment, a gliding disappearing sensation of being her husband, the balancing sensation all through him that she was once again his wife.

As he touched the cruiser forward foot by foot, creeping in line behind the rocket, holding two dollar-bills in his hand, looking at the back of her head, reading her license plate over and over, he thought:

"I can live alone. It won't kill me. I can still go down there and coach. Maybe see the old man every once in a while. I've still got

Robbie." And with sudden elation he thought of Robbie brushing the veil from the face of the lamb and throwing the slimy little body to start its breathing. He knew he had to press something into the void, had to create hope out of his own mind. Nobody gives it to you, you make it.

To die was inconceivable. "I can't just fall apart," he thought. It was impossible that he, Jeff Temple, should just disintegrate.

Instead of a plan of the future he saw an image of the past, of Sandra's unutterable beauty arching beneath him. He heard her soft moans of happiness. He projected this into a hope. Seeing those loving, clear eyes looking gratefully into his own eyes, he said:

"I'll try again. I'll speak to her again."

And it was only extreme caution, which is to say hope, that kept him from running up to her car and knocking on the glass.

Chapter 29
Forward

Thinking physical stimulation would perhaps shut down his mind, he went to the shower as soon as he rolled out of bed. All he got for his trouble was a new question: "If Hawk were alive, would I let them kill him?"

He stood for some time with the water drumming on his shoulders, and when he thrust his head under the stream he was still in the same world, which was all internal. He didn't need a shower and what did it matter if he was clean? He stood there — his mind churned on — it was as if he approached from behind and slipped his arms under hers to take her streaming breasts in his hands. She turned and they embraced. From their chests to thighs they were quite single, the sensation of his skin touching hers having dissolved as soon as it came. There was just time to feel the curve and hollow of her body when these ceased to exist except as elements, powers, in his own body, which ceased to be his own.

Being outside her body as well as inside, his mind knew an ellipse of unity with her. He surrounded her body, which surrounded his. As compared to the ellipse orgasm was a poor show, and he couldn't define or desire it. It was hard to utter the word "love" but the ellipse made utterance unnecessary, as it made it impossible.

When he could feel again that he was stroking her side, then he could feel the water, and he turned his face up and let the vision pass, as life would soon pass.

He liked to walk up and down the hall with a towel wrapped around his waist before starting to dry himself. He found a note under the black onyx bowl on his dresser. It consisted of one word: "Forgive."

A drop fell and blurred the ink. Had Shipman discovered his coins and keys scattered out of the bowl his expression would have been the same. He looked on this word as the mewling doctrine of a bizarre Jewish cult. That the cult had spread over the world and, especially, consoled the slaves didn't impress him. It remained alien, Eastern, white and queer. This particular aspect of it, the doctrine of forgiveness, while he willingly forgave some people some of the time, struck him as a pathetic sentimentality, as if the victims wanted to induce a feeling in themselves, for the sake of the feeling itself, first, and then to open the way for a "normal" life in the victimized status. He folded the paper three times, tore it twice and threw it in the wastebasket.

The second note, which he found under his plate, was another pluck on an old string. It said: "It is a crime to deprive a boy of his father."

To which Shipman retorted: "Boy my ass. He's twenty-eight years old."

At that very moment he added a new line to the day's plan: he would visit this twenty-eight-year-old "boy" named Winslow. "If his eyes are O.K., that's one thing. If his eyes are oily, god damn him forever!"

He placed a pan of water on the flame and watched the beads forming, and the subsequent turbulence of the water, the rupturing of the surface and finally the gusts of steam rising. He lowered two eggs into the pan and observed that neither cracked. He pressed the timer button on his watch (it was set to beep at three minutes forty-five seconds), poured a glass of orange juice and put two slices of whole-wheat bread in the toaster. The eggs and the toast were done at the same time, and Shipman buttered his toast, broke his eggs and began a meditative and rather satisfying meal. Odell Diann's second note lay before him. He threw it into the trash with the egg shells, made coffee, and went to the front door to get the paper. While his coffee brewed he perused the inanities of the press.

A telephone call came from a man in Cleveland who was interested in the franchise offering. Shipman's subtle encouragement of the man's interest was flawless by Shipman's own standards. For instance he was sure he had talked just black enough and not too black for this man. But when he entered the garage he failed even to see the big leather portfolio containing the architects' sketches, although it hung directly in his line of vision. This and all other business matters were behind him. Insofar as they could be resolved they were resolved. Since his whole life was over it followed that business was over, yet he had jawed this man from Cleveland.

He started the Lincoln, activated the garage-door opener and backed into the alley. It was a fact, yet it seemed to have no particular meaning, that the cars, garden tractors and lawn mowers on this alley were better housed than four-fifths of the people in Africa. Shipman's Lincoln glided down the alley with a silver cloud of vapor swirling in its wake. This was soon lost in the crisp air.

He drove to the airport, where he put his car in long-term parking and went to the Hertz counter in the terminal. He gave a minute's amused thought to that "long-term parking." He presented his Hertz card and rented a car, as he had presented his Avis card to rent one for Lucas yesterday. While he was signing the contract he felt a signal in his bowels. It occurred to him that after he was shot the feces might be ejected into his pants — he had seen this in Korea — but as soon as this came to him he realized it made no difference. He went to the men's room, therefore, simply because it would have been uncomfortable not to. He laughed to think: "Makes no difference if I shit my pants?" Another idea claimed his attention in the course of this, presumably his next to last act of involuntary contraction. He thought that the name he had just signed, John Shipman, was a name he had learned, and learned to write (his mother had taught him before he went to school) a very long time ago. His life did not seem short.

Driving back to his native city he thought about Odell Diann. It seemed he was in the shower imagining what he had imagined before, and the complexity of his mental life had a strange and friendly poetic effect. It seemed to him that this was "life itself," this state of distance and intimacy. He reached her through two planes of imagination and she was just as intensely his, just as forward and open, as he could want her to be. Here was a fantasy that was not false but a picture of reality. She had borne their sons. She was faithful and good, and so forward in love as to cleanse him of every taint and resolve every doubt. Here too was a kind of theology, by which she completed his identity in sensual acts that obliterated his senses and carried him outside himself. And it was here in the so-called outside, when he was in ecstasy, that he was most certain of being himself because he had no role to play. This was what he must leave, not just the various roles but this authentic life.

When he crested the last rise and beheld the city spreading across its valley ten miles ahead he changed his plan in one particular: he would try again to dissuade Lucas. He must make it clear to Lucas that he didn't have to do it. "I have to; he doesn't."

The two men were eating lunch in Shipman's office. A girl in white slacks and a "Shipman's" shirt had just brought Lucas a second helping of barbecue with hot sauce and a fresh can of beer. Shipman was drinking coffee after sending his lunch back untouched. All that remained was to show Shipman's car to Lucas. They would act independently but had agreed it would be prudent if each could recognize the other's car in case they found themselves improvising.

In his mental life Shipman no longer found a need to improvise. To be an entrepreneur speaking moneymaking English, to issue forth into the business world dressed in a competition suit and up-stratum necktie, to impose on a roomful of bankers, to sell himself and his "concept," were all unnecessary now and it all had the taste and smell of bullshit. He settled back into a simpler self. He might have been roaming the streets of his boyhood, when he and

Lucas thought the older boys going to Roosevelt and Dunbar high schools were gods upon the earth.

"There was nothing wrong with that," he thought, meaning the role of entrepreneur. "I had a gift." In the free exercise of his talent he had discovered a more complicated self. He chuckled aloud, thinking of the money, which was pointless except to show that he had won.

Shipman began to make his case. He said: "I can get one alone."

"One plus one makes two," Lucas replied looking up from his plate with his usual under-the-eyebrows glance. Lucas watched Shipman as if to see if he was wavering.

Shipman regarded his friend with a calm detachment. Lucas was exactly Shipman's age but looked older, not because of arthritis only. But he also looked unstoppable, with his lowered head and the bend of his body.

"The D.A. says — accident," Shipman proposed as if for consideration.

And Lucas responded: "Right, Big John, but this kind a accident only happen to black boys."

"Your guy got a guard," said Shipman.

"Sho."

"When you show your gun, Dunbar done shinin."

"Sho, *you too*."

"The big puppy don't seem to have a guard."

"Don't seem. Look out, Big John."

"You'd have a better chance if you used a rifle," Shipman suggested. "We could delay a few days, I could find you a good rifle with a telescope sight."

"Better chance of gettin away, you mean."

"Yes."

"But my guy got to know."

"He'll know; he only has to know for a second. Put your first one in a leg then finish him."

"While he squirmin on the sidewalk."

Shipman said after a pause, smiling: "He'll understand."

"He got to know," Lucas said stubbornly, "and I got to know he know. I ain't gonna think about this again, John."

Shipman, who had been tilting in his chair, now came slowly forward until the front legs struck the floor, and said: "You kill him, his guard kills you."

Lucas seemed to hover and brood over his plate, his almost-white, short-cropped hair and his brown skin, his deeply scored forehead and heavy lips giving an air of prophetic solemnity to every gesture, word and pause. But now he looked at Shipman and the semblance of a smile crept into his features and animated his eyes. He said: "But you gettin away! You shoot your man, pop! and catch a plane to Reno. First class seat! You rent a room in the casino and send for your money." Lucas straightened up as much as he could, which made his shoulders rise around his head. He laughed, with his pain-charged eyes on Shipman.

"I'm thinking — your wife," Shipman persisted as if he hadn't been paying attention. "Your stepchildren. Those kids love you. They were deserted once, now they'll be deserted again."

"Your wife," was all Lucas said.

"But he was my son."

There was a twinge in Lucas's face and he looked away.

Shipman thought: "I hurt him," this man who least of all men deserved such an injury. And yet he, Shipman, didn't feel his friend's pain. He said "Sorry" but it seemed unimportant.

They sat in silence for a long time, during which Shipman thought about his son. There had been a young man who could rise above every obstacle — but more than this, there had been the son he loved past reason or explanation. It was pointless to try to tell his wife how he felt about Hawk. To begin was to discover the futility of it. If he began, "This is how I feel about Hawk," the first problem arose: the word feel had nothing to do with it. Having this boy as his son had made him a different man. "And I shall be changed from this creature that I am."

Shipman began: "What if . . ."

"What if what?" said Lucas a few seconds later, looking patiently at his friend.

"What if they were black."

"If they was black, our boy be alive and you know it. Before ever Hawk was born," he said, "I knew I could live, and I could tolerate. In the old days I used to feel sorry for the dumb ones cause I figured somebody jokin em, they feelin so full of bein white, when you look at it, white is all they got. And what's it amount to? So I said I'll live an I won't bother. I lived all right. I said somethin else. They kill my family, I kill back. One devil touch me, he be sorry. They killed Hawk an I goin to kill back cause he was my boy too. You know he come to me, from the time he was a baby."

"I know that. I know you're the same man now. There's an hour left, you're the same man."

"Big John, you the same. Death don't start yet."

"Yeah, that's why we gotta decide."

"I done decided."

"I mean, if they were black."

"I don't have to decide what I don't have to decide and neither do you."

"I do," Shipman said.

"Well that's you. I can do my part alone."

Shipman sat silent, erect, with his eyes cast down at Lucas, while Lucas's face all but touched the table — his gaze bent up to meet Shipman's.

"Del doesn't understand," Shipman said. "Here they kill my boy, and the D.A. is an honest man, and he calls it an accident. That's the part I keep coming back to, Lucas. He's an honest man."

"So — they's a big slit, and this honest man say it come out of the sky — then you know it's a fix. Fixed so good the honest man don't see it."

"I don't have a choice."

"No you don't."

"If I do nothing —" Shipman began.

"You got this on you the rest of your life."

"Yes," Shipman said. "I can choose which kind of death I want."

"That's right, John. Live like a dog or die like a man."

Lucas extended his right arm and examined his hand. There was a sharp bend at the last joint of his index finger. He would have to turn his wrist at an angle to get the finger through the trigger guard.

Shipman again leaned back in the chair with his hands on the wooden arms, and he raised his face and thought: "It'd be worse to live." Each time this crossed his mind it seemed new. He said aloud: "If I survive I'm going to the D.A. 'Here's my gun, and here I am.' They can punish me. I won't run and I won't care." He thought justice should be free. Since it is not, he would pay the price.

Lucas said: "All right. I ain't goin to no D.A."

"No," Shipman agreed. "Fine."

Again they lapsed into silence and again Shipman saw how strange it was, that living should be worse than dying. But at length he said:

"We spread suffering all around us. We leave our families — we cut our women with knives —"

"Sho but it's fixed," Lucas insisted. "It's all built an all we do is move in. This way we alive till we die."

Yet Shipman could not push away or evade the picture of Odell Diann, nor silence her words: "You'll kill me." This picture, of his tall brown woman when they told her, and the power of his son's life in his intellect: all this was Shipman now; there was nothing else to him and there was nothing less. His son's life.

He looked at his watch and for a second it appeared to be on somebody else's wrist. He recognized the instrument but not the wrist. He pictured himself going up a dark walk to Lovico's door, but he knew it would never happen.

With that same hooked index finger Lucas drew back his cuff and consulted his watch, a gold bracelet circling a dark wrist. "Anyway," he said, "they's white. I knowed this'd happen or somethin like it. Didn't you, Big John?"

Shipman felt a deep quiet, but no peace. He said: "I'll show you my car."

For Lucas getting into a car was no easy job. He bent himself slowly and with as much difficulty as if he'd been trying to stand straight. It occurred to Shipman: "Can't stand, can't bend!" Now he had to countermand his disease. He groaned but he did it, and Shipman slammed the door on him. Shipman went to his own car and entered, and buzzed his window down. Lucas rolled his car slowly forward and paused beside Shipman. They both smiled. And they held the smile, till Lucas rolled on, and Shipman steered into the street and followed in his wake. Lucas turned one way and Shipman another.

Beyond the point of no return, instead of a new and open country Shipman found the same world as before.

"You are the same man to the last minute. — Then death is not so terrible. 'Death don't start yet.'" He saw his woman, like a marble statue of a nude goddess. He mounted the stairway to the apartment where Winslow had lived when he last knew Winslow's address. "If he's gone, so much the better. Why do I want to see him anyway?"

"I am the same man. Everything is just the same."

He was thinking of those minutes in the diner and how, when he reached the street and opened the door of the Lincoln, he knew he did not belong in a little apartment on wheels, with velour seats, a controlled temperature and polished instruments. "Walk, walk, walk naked and barefooted, walk on your stumps, let your cocknballs shrivel in the freezing wind, hold your arms away from your body — don't hug yourself! Stand erect. Walk. Go on!"

"We spread suffering all around." He halted on the stair and said: "Eat it!" The two were equally unimaginable: that he should afflict Odell Diann and that he should eat his son's death.

He rapped on the door, stared at the old brass "G" that was two feet from his eyes, and rapped again.

There was a master sergeant in his battalion in Korea who at the time seemed like an old man, who told his troops there were two ways to deal with the cold. The smart way is to find a means of keeping warm. The dumb way is to fight the cold. "Be cold!" Shipman whispered without knowing what he meant. He knocked a third time.

The sight that met his eyes was the sight he expected to see. You could see everything but little flakes of dried puke in his whiskers. You could see last night's wallow just as clearly as if it had been performed before your eyes. You could see he had lain in bed till noon. You could see him decide it was useless to shave and wash and eat breakfast. You could see him wander from room to room for a few minutes for the sole purpose of lying to himself: "I don't drink as soon as I get up." You could see him take the first little drink to hold him until he went out in the afternoon to beg drinks from the bartenders at his father's taverns.

"Pop! What the hell!"

The father said nothing.

The son had oily eyes. He smiled uncertainly but did not invite his father in. In this refusal Shipman saw the only trace of the young man Winslow had once been. So slight a trace as this found Shipman's heart and made Winslow's crime more terrible.

"Goodbye, Winslow," Shipman said.

"Hey man, what's this? You going to kill me? Ha ha ha!"

Shipman turned.

Winslow demanded: "What's this?"

Winslow's laughter rang through the stairwell as Shipman descended.

He covered the distance to his car but his mind wasn't with him. "The peace of the condemned man," if there is such a peace, eluded him. He noticed in himself a certain exhilarating careless-ness that was not quite recklessness. Sitting in the car, parked on a heavy-traveled street where there was also a considerable pedestrian traffic, he took out the .357 Magnum and swung its cylinder free. Cupping his right hand behind the chambers he flipped the gun up so the barrel was aimed into his right eye. He felt the heavy bullets slide free in their chambers and drop their weight in his hand. He looked down the bore but it was somewhat dark. He did ascertain it was not obstructed, which was all that was necessary — this was an old army habit — but he so admired the craftsmanship of the Smith & Wesson that he wanted a better view. He took the white handkerchief from his suitcoat pocket and placed a corner behind the breach. Now the bore lit up. The lands and grooves of the rifling twisted in a glistening spiral towards his eye. He said half aloud, "Clear bore," and he said, "I have killed lots of men, bags full, scores," but of course there's a difference between killing in a firefight and this other kind.

He seated the six cartridges in their chambers in a single deft motion, swung and snapped the cylinder shut and put the revolver in the holster inside his suitcoat. It was surprisingly heavy on his chest, and reassuring. The weight was the weight of a thing that could do the job. He folded and replaced the handkerchief in his breast pocket, with a corner up. He was not wearing his leather overcoat but he was not cold.

"It is also a crime," he said starting the engine, "*it is also a crime* to deprive a father of his son."

He turned the center mirror to his face and looked at himself, especially his living eyes, but took little notice. He straightened his necktie and adjusted the knot till it was tighter and smaller. He was amused at Lucas's dictum that we remain the same men until the last. And he retraced the syllogism that if this is so, death must not be as frightening as people believe. Addressing the man in the mirror he said: "The question isn't whether you can make money on a Shipman franchise. You can. The question is whether you are going to kill the man who killed your son. You are!" He realigned the mirror and drove into the stream, heading for the freeway. He soon left the black neighborhoods behind.

He realized the first benefit ever to be derived by a black man from residential segregation. All three of the apartments — Ruthenbeck's, Temple's and Temple's wife's — were located inside a driving radius of seven or eight minutes. Lucas and Shipman were working within a twelve-minute time frame. Each must act within the time frame or not at all. Each could come to the aid of the other if he had any time left.

Observing a hillside of fine homes Shipman thought: "They envy us. They don't know it but they do."

To him the privileged class of whites were like spectators at a football game. Their assigned role was to watch and exclaim over the struggle and to maintain the pretense that being above it was better than being in it. They would applaud and even admire the winners and hold the losers in fear and contempt.

"I'd rather puke!" he thought. (Not everything he said was perfectly rational.) Next — that is to say the next idea to which he gave full articulation was: "There are too many losers." His voice was hard, not audible. He was thinking of the oily-eyed puker who had drawn the life out of his elder son, the elder brother that Hawk used to worship. "Goodbye, Winslow," he repeated, "goodbye Winslow." His verdict was: "Not strong enough to be a black man." In Winslow the weak had triumphed over the strong. Oily Eyes, who could do nothing, had smothered every effort of the vital boy Winslow used to be.

"Shit!" he said and repeated it several times. He did not want what he called "another fucking tragedy." He cursed, deploying a whole army of obscenities and scatology. It made him feel worse, so he stopped. He swung onto an exit ramp and now he was in Jeffrey Temple's neighborhood.

Having driven this route a dozen times and crossed the area in every direction he knew the relation of each street and major building to the whole. The Mobil station he was now passing marked the street leading to Temple's wife's place. He said: "There's the Mobil station." The voice was unrecognizable. He saw the next landmark, a supermarket at a big intersection overhung by a triple set of traffic lights. Even here he seemed out of contact with his own knowledge. Should he want to reach Ruthenbeck's place he had only to turn left and drive ten blocks. But his sense of it was that he knew a man who knew this fact.

Each cross-street and landmark represented a step, like a step in a staircase. Ascending, he was stricken as if from behind by a new idea. Suppose Odell Diann had meant, not his own son, but Temple's. "It is a crime to deprive a boy of his father." Did she know Temple had a son? Had a newspaper story or television report ever mentioned it? He believed not. But she could have meant that he intended to take that boy's father from him.

"Quiet!" he shouted. Then he reverted to the sentence that cleared away every opposing idea. He said slowly: "They shall not kill my son."

He turned and he was in Temple's street. He said slowly and quietly his sentence of last resort: "You may not kill my son."

His hands were steady on the wheel. He touched his revolver through his suitcoat, and he thought of Lucas holding out his bent trigger-finger and looking at it with a queer smile.

He was two minutes early. He detoured around a block and re-emerged into Temple's street just as the twelve-minute period began.

He cruised the street in both directions and didn't see Temple's car in any of the places where he had seen it before. He entered the narrow drive between buildings and went from one end of the parking lot to the other and still didn't find it. He turned around by a trash dumpster, drove at a safe speed out of the drive, and, casting one more look up and down the street, set off for Temple's wife's apartment.

This consumed more than half his time, and it seemed a long drive because he passed through the curtains of death in the air. He noticed something unexpected but was too busy to pause and see what it was. It was this, that the presence of death arching over him lifted him into the very height of the arch, a place he hadn't been since Korea. It was a mad place where he breathed a form of ecstatic joy. In this way it recalled his youth and he experienced the limitlessness of youth.

Turning into Temple's wife's street he had to deal with a tactical problem. Her building was the first one in the next block, on the left, and the street was one-way, narrow and descending. If he stopped he would obstruct traffic and draw attention to himself, perhaps creating new problems. If he made a pass down the street he would consume two minutes or more circling the block before he could make another pass. The buildings were set back, but there were solid lines of cars parked on either side. The effect was constricting and in some degree blinding. He couldn't deal with all this automatically like a robot following his program. Now he had to throw himself mentally into the game. The street was like a game board. He must find the green Ford but he feared Temple wasn't here. "I'll go to the damn police station and kill him there," Shipman said.

So he had a backup plan. Good. If you don't find him here go to the cop shop. He reduced speed and went carefully down the defile of cars. Shipman saw the old green Ford parked ahead on the left. He was approaching it from the rear, and he passed slowly. He saw Temple sitting in the driver's seat alone. Whether Temple recognized him he didn't know.

Shipman accelerated, turned his car around at the first intersection and drove back, going the wrong way on the one-way street and stopping in the middle of the street a car-length short of the green Ford. He rammed the gear-shift lever into Park, opened the door and stood in the street. He was not aware of anyone else but Temple, or of any traffic on the street.

He could see Temple imperfectly through a rectangle of reflected light on his windshield, but as he walked around the front of his car and approached Temple's the reflection shifted and revealed his target.

Shipman drew his gun from inside his suitcoat and he could see Temple move his body to the left, reaching for his own gun. Shipman took aim, thinking for a fleeting instant that Hawk had not been armed, and fired.

In one deafening action the revolver recoiled upward through a circle of flame, the windshield shattered in a radiant pattern around a central hole, and Shipman's stunned and ringing ears just barely detected, as if from far away, the sound of a human being in pain.

Shipman stood and fired again, another hole opened, and the pattern of rays and shards rearranged itself. His eyes retained a quick-fading imprint of yellow light, in a small circle of fire. His ears rang with a lingering sound, and this admitted Temple's partially-deaf son to his mind.

In three steps, gun still in hand, Shipman was beside the car. He yanked open the door and screamed, "Come out of there!" and grabbed Temple's jacket and dragged at the bleeding body and it tumbled out. He pulled so hard that the jacket gathered and lifted under Temple's arms and he could see two wounds in the back as the body settled.

Temple lay on his side and on a shoulder with his feet still in the car, and Shipman noticed a little red nick on Temple's cheek where perhaps he had cut himself shaving, or a piece of glass had hit him. The other cheek lay flat against the sidewalk.

Shipman looked for a gun and found one on the car seat.

He looked at the man's close-cut blond hair (not at the wounds in the chest and back), at his face in strange profile, at the wrist and hand turned back by the pavement. Looking at this huge hand that had killed Hawk he saw only that the wrist was turned sharply back in a very unmasculine way, and that the fingers were spread and slightly curled. Shipman felt a dismal foreboding.

There was now some blood on the sidewalk and Shipman was surprised at how red it was. But he kept looking at the hand forced against the sidewalk by the weight of the body, and at the little red nick in the right cheek. He could not look into the man's eyes, although this was what he wanted to do — and again he experienced the cold dismal feeling that something lay before him. He returned his gun to its place of concealment and turned toward his car.

Now he was aware that there was a car on his right, which had come down the street and encountered his own — so his car and this new arrival were face to face. His brain registered this fact and nothing more — except that he knew he would have to back down the slope to the intersection, and he didn't like driving in reverse because his neck didn't turn as easily or as far as it once had. He didn't give any thought to the problem of backing the car; it was merely a source of vague unpleasantness.

For a moment he identified this with the foreboding, and thought: "Is that all!"

Then he saw the boy running towards him — a white boy of twelve or thirteen. Almost before he realized who the boy was he felt a thin edge enter his mind, a foreboding still, a petrifying knowledge that he couldn't quite understand.

He evaded the boy just in time, and realized he had leapt out of the way as if he were terrified of this thin child — but there was such a look on the boy's face that something was communicated to Shipman in that instant, and the entering edge grew thicker. He got into his car. He couldn't see Temple's body, only the open door of the old Ford. Yet now, even more immediately than when he had touched it, the body was before him. It was, as it were, in his hands.

He heard a cry, a howl. The boy was crying: "Dad. Dad."

Shipman turned and began backing away down the street. Somebody was getting out of the car facing his — he turned away — it was an extremely fat, bearded white man dressed in paint-spattered white coveralls and a green visor cap. Shipman reached the intersection and braked to an abrupt stop, turned his car around and looked up the hill. He now had a direct view of the car door hanging open, and the boy and the man in coveralls crouching over the body. In the ringing of his ears, which still vibrated from the reports of the Magnum, he could hear, or perhaps only imagine, the boy's crying out: "Dad."

Shipman drove away and there were screams or shouts in his car, ringing and droning in his ears, and an unbelievable horror in his mind.

Now he saw the body and the fatal hand, and the boy's uncomprehending but frightened face as he had first seen it. Now, even as he correctly followed the route to Ruthenbeck's place, he heard the boy calling his father, as the son of Medgar Evers had called his.

Shipman knew that he was screaming and understood that to scream afforded no relief. His mouth and throat ached. Soon he could make no sound at all.

"I did it!" he cried, and no sound came.

"They killed my boy," he said, and felt that by saying this he blasphemed against his son.

"Don't bring Hawk into this," he thought involuntarily and this was horror of a new kind, of a kind he could never endure.

"Death! Death! Death!" he screamed, quite soundlessly, and the ringing in his ears intertwined with the keening of sirens as he approached Ruthenbeck's street.

He was driving too fast and almost cracked up turning the corner. He saw the street straighten itself before him, as he shot down between the rows and bore down on a little crowd of five or ten white people. They scattered, except for a few who were transfixed by what they were looking at, and would have been run down had Shipman not halted his car.

Again he rammed his gear lever into Park, pushed his door open and stood in the street. He could see nothing, but it was obvious where he had to go. He drew his gun and walked toward the place where the crowd had been. The two or three insatiable ones turned at the sound of a shout from across the street and, seeing Shipman, got out of his way.

Passing between parked cars he reached the sidewalk and stepped over Lucas's body, scarcely glancing at the face.

He saw Ruthenbeck who was squatting at the side of a downed policeman, holding a microphone that he had removed from the shoulder strap of the policeman's jacket. The wire was stretched from the jacket to Ruthenbeck's hand. The hand was covered with blood.

Ruthenbeck had just dropped a Code 99 and so he believed they must be coming to help him. He too had heard the shout, something like: "He's got a gun." Ruthenbeck's own gun was in his other bloody hand.

Seeing Shipman he rose to his feet. He saw a very tall black man dressed in a dark blue business suit with a white handkerchief in the breast pocket, pointing a Magnum at his heart and coming on with a rough but steady walk. The black face told Ruthenbeck everything he needed to know.

Ruthenbeck fired. The sirens were close and piercing. He fired again. The black man still came. Ruthenbeck sensed without quite seeing the arrival of a police car to his right and behind him, and saw the blinking red lights of another careening into the street behind the black man.

"I'm going to be saved!" This message shot through his mind. He fired a third shot.

Then a little yellow light he had never seen and a blow such as he had never felt changed his conviction. He thought he must be down. Somehow he'd been knocked down and now he strained to look up. Despair darkened his mind but that truthful, pale light flashed in his eyes again.

Seeing Ruthenbeck pitch backward, seeing the sag of superfluous flesh under his jaw, Shipman knew it was done. There seemed to be an odd smell in the air and there was certainly a repugnant taste in his mouth. His chest ached from a blow he had scarcely felt.

He watched the body for motion and saw none. But there was a motion of the earth, a slow ominous wheeling, and under the influence of this Shipman lost the will to curse himself.

Holding his arm as steady as he could he cocked the revolver and aimed at Ruthenbeck's body — and the sights trailed over the rubbery abdomen that had been exposed in the fall.

Shipman had no intention of shooting a dead man. He wondered when the police would fire, and had his answer before he knew it.

Chapter 30
The Mirror

"It's too soon. Stay away. Turn back! I want to see the mirror. She wants to see the mirror. Course you do Sis but it's too soon. You ain't yourself. I am, though. I'm nobody else and nobody's me. I am myself *such as I am*. She ought not to go in, I say. Uncle says it's time though. Who, which uncle? Uncle Bama Old-Bones Taylor. My goodness Sis, Uncle been dead forty years. You hearin voices? Oh I don't hear voices but I know what he say. *Take yo key Del, tumble de lock, ope de do*. That ain't Uncle, Girl, it's you. One bullet rattlin roun in your brain is what it is. I didn't die, neither did I live. I say it thataway. I agree, oh how I do agree, so then give it a year Honey. Tell me what difference a year'll make. Well maybe you'll be free of the fever. But I have no fever. Everybody gets headaches and in a year I could be dead.

"I said, 'Mrs. Wilkerson don't clean this room. I am keepin it locked.' Pretty soon we're taking about a museum, Sis, not a room. Yes and I've decided. I am going to see if he left a note, a letter, a message of any kind. I'm going to look-see if he touched the mirror."

And so she turned the key, her solemn enlarged eyes watching it turn, her ears sensitive to the little grinding skerring sound it made, and she entered upon the unaltered scene of her husband's last night on earth. It was here he must have gone after she said, "If you kill those policemen . . ." He certainly had not

come to their bed for several hours. The mirror that she had slant-
ed against the screen of his computer was not there.

"So," she whispered in awe, "you picked it up. This vain
man — knew he was good-looking. Impossible to pick it up and
not look at his handsome self. So Big John did you look in those
dear eyes and gasp! *Do I exist inside this killer?* Here it is, face
down. He looked in his eyes God Almighty and did it anyway!

"Did you know Reverend Beecham came to ask was I losing
my faith. And I said, 'Lord no, God took everything else, He
wouldn't take that.' He reads from the Book of Job, 'Naked came
I out of my mother's womb and naked shall I return thither.' But I
say 'What is my strength that I should hope? and what is mine end
that I should prolong my life?' I know the Book better than he
does. I surely know I won't crawl back into Mama's belly when I
die the death. That's not where you go. The Reverend Mr.
Beecham knows where you go! Mr. Beecham knows it all.

"He says, 'Behold, He taketh away, who can hinder Him?' and
I answer back, 'For he breaketh me with a tempest —' and
Reverend jumps in before I can finish — 'and multiplieth my
wounds without cause.' Then he said: 'Search not for the cause,
Sister, nor try to reason with God. God makes no compacts. Do
you fear the loss of your faith?' and that's when I said, 'No,' but I
slipped in: 'For there is hope of a tree, if it be cut down, that it will
sprout again, and that the tender branch thereof will not cease . . .
But man dieth and wasteth away; yea man giveth up the ghost and
where is he?'

"That slowed the Reverend way down. I told him what I read
in Hawk's notebook: 'Man is the steadfast creator. At the pinnacle
of pain and in the dark pit of distress, when they are turning him
into a piece of meat, when they try to take him away from himself,
he creates his soul.'

"And ever so gently says the Reverend that this is false doctrine, it is the modern myth, that man creates his own soul. 'Had
your son lived through more experience and opened his heart to the
people and daily life of this world, the life of a single city block —
had the boy lived but a few years more and read Scripture with a

humble spirit he could not have embraced such a gorgeously seductive error. He would not want you to be charmed by it now.'

"Thus saith the Reverend Mr. Beecham to save the soul of Sister Del. But this soul — this soul — I almost said is gone! A little rattle in the throat. It don't mean nothin. But when I say the horror without walls, Big John, it ain't quite that bad. I can swap Bible poetry with the Rev and it's easy, easy. But alone, in the sewing room, if I would say out loud: *I have a son Winslow* my breath fails, my throat closes.

"Faith! Lordy it's supposed to be so precious. Without it I'm a chip in the cataract. So true. But I don't fear losing it at all. If it should go, let it go! Once it's gone nobody misses it. But some things when they go — mercy!

"I wake up and find the blankets strewn around and I say, I must be alive even when I don't know it. What does it prove? Alive and don't know why. What does that prove? To be honest I did find the horror without walls, Big John. You find it when everything is the same as everything else, and nothing makes any difference. Everything still exists and nothing matters. It is when I can see no reason to care that I care so much I could die of it. And you could foresee it all couldn't you.

"Uncle Bama Old-Bones Taylor say *Hush, Gal* because it is so hard, Big John, such a struggle to speak. But I think without speaking. I couldn't bear the evil and the error. The deed speaks for itself so loud. If I could I'd spew out this bullet as the whale spewed Jonah. Bible stories!

"My boy Hawk, 'I had a son Hawk,' that I could never say — he wrote: 'Don't you wonder how they created this most valuable essence out of their crazy illusions? It is not the faith so much as the power that creates it. The power of mankind, the flame of humanity.' How it burns!

"When you were thinking about your life did you think about that boy? I know: do nothing and you're changed into a half-man, one who can get along without justice. So let's see — he does nothing and kills nobody. He protests in his heart and starts a foolish lawsuit, and goes right on living and spending heaps of money. 'Your city shall be heaps.' He thinks everybody sees him as the man who wouldn't do anything, an impotent man and a repeat of his father. If he talks about brotherhood he's talking cowardice. If he breathes tongues of fire he's just hating himself. Denied the right to struggle, denied the right to speak with meaning. Everything he says and does empty, selfish and vain. He couldn't live that way so I have to live this way. That's what it comes to.

"My throat, my tongue cannot speak. Defying the evil of indifference — See these two boys."

"When de spirit strong."

"That's right, Uncle Bama. If I could say that I have sons; if I could be a sister to his mother, a mother not to one only but two —"

"You take up de mirrah, Del Honey."

"I take up the mirror and I write on the back."

"In de dus, Honey."

"I write in the dust."

"You know Del I cain't read, remember?"

"I have written: *Robert Temple*, for that is the boy's name. And then *Winslow Shipman*, for that is the boy's name."

"So call out."

"I call: Father of Mankind!"

"Strenthen they knees."

"Let them stand."

"Lighten they eyes."

"That they may see."

"Hold em in yo han!"

"Let them not tremble or be afraid. Give them light in the flame of humanity."